KNIGHT MOVES

By

STEPHEN D. CORK

© Copyrighted. All rights reserved. No part of this book may be reproduced or transmitted in any form or by any means. That includes individual pages or segments of any nature, via mechanical or electronic. No photocopying or recording by any system without the written consent of the author, except by a reviewer who may quote brief passages in review.

Published by: Mangroove Press LLC
4025 Cattlemen Road
PMB 142
Sarasota, FL 34233

This novel is fiction. All characters and names are fictitious and figments of the authors imagination. No incident or depiction relates to any actual event. Any resemblance to actual events or persons is purely coincidental.

ISBN-10: 0-9790701-0-4
ISBN-13: 978-0-9790701-0-5

Cover design by Frank Hopper of Sarasota, FL.
Author photograph by Summer Bentley of Southern Exposure Photographs in Sarasota, FL.
Special Editing by Professor Robert Lechner, University of South Florida

Dedication

This book is dedicated to my wife. Without Peggy's love, assistance, support and encouragement, this novel would not have been possible. She's been a saint.

Prologue

Emergency helicopters circled the flaming wreckage within fifteen minutes of the crash on I-395, west of Washington, D.C. A state trooper had already reached the site and was marking a landing-zone.

The first Huey helicopter landed, and six EMT's jumped off and raced to the nearest wreckage to treat injured motorists. Firemen with 'jaws of life' equipment leapt off a second Huey and teamed with the EMT's. A doctor and physician's assistant scrambled from the third helicopter and began to triage victims for air evacuation. Five minutes later, a larger Blackhawk helicopter landed and a fire/rescue HAZMAT team deployed.

Within thirty minutes, wreckers and other emergency equipment were assembled at a pre-designated highway entrance. All vehicles were equipped with tire chains and high-powered fog lights to deal with the near blizzard conditions. Led by a highway patrol cruiser, they sped to the accident scene.

The Virginia Response Team was well drilled. They'd learned their lessons. After monthly exercises, they were experienced and fast. The injured were evacuated and the traffic lanes were cleared within two hours.

Federal grants funded the team. A rash of Interstate highway accidents had prompted the grants. On California's I-5, scores had died in one pile-up alone. Reports to Congress indicated that many would have lived had emergency response been faster and better organized. Separate financial reports to Congress estimated that the annual loss to commercial trucking from Interstate highway accidents ranged in the hundreds of billions of dollars.

Given this information, Congress acted with unusual promptness. Highway accident response teams were the result. Virginia's was the first.

If there was any good news about the accident on I-395, it was that none of the motorists treated on site died from their injuries. The skilled technicians and their quick response saved several lives. However, seven people were killed in the primary pile up; their deaths attributed to an explosion and a fire from an overturned fuel truck.

Witnesses blamed the accident on the driver of the fuel truck who lost control of his vehicle in the snowstorm. The state medical examiner determined that the cause of death for all seven people was a product of the accident. No autopsies were required.

No one reported the erratic driving of an oversized pick-up just prior to the accident, nor did any witnesses come forward concerning three men who arrived on the scene before the state trooper. The three appeared almost as an apparition, jumping from an SUV parked in the median. Their actions went unnoticed in the chaos, and the men faded back into the white night. Reports of the accident made headline news the following day.

An announcement mourning the death of the chairman of the Joint Chiefs of Staff shared the headlines. It was reported that he died in his sleep at his quarters on Fort McNair. He was beloved and respected; one of a handful of military officers on active duty decorated with the Medal of Honor. The President ordered flags to be flown at half-staff for thirty days in honor of Admiral Sam Collins.

Chapter One

The Board is Set

The whupp, whupp of the helicopter blades and the wind buffeting the aircraft sent a chill up Jenny's spine. She loved the sense of danger when soaring at bird-level, the countryside zipping along close below.

She couldn't help but think, *…a lowly Military Policeman like me doesn't get to ride in one of these babies very often... Hot damn...! ...Even without this ride...be impossible to wipe this silly grin off my face...*

The brown and green patchwork of Korean rice paddies passed beneath the helicopter as her mind swirled.

Colonel Pitman, her brigade commander, had made an unannounced appearance at her farewell to Korea party.

Pitman was a hard-nosed, six-foot-six string bean of a Texas Aggie. He had a tough job, and he didn't have much time for socializing. But, he enjoyed a good laugh and was prone to practical jokes. Jenny thought he was at the party to pull one on her – he was supposed to be in Seoul.

After his arrival at the festivities, Pitman asked for everyone's attention. Once they had settled down, he spoke to Jenny, "Captain O'Shane, I came to say goodbye, and to thank you for your fine efforts in the Brigade." He paused to take a breath.

…OK... she thought, *...be polite...thank him for the usual memory plaque...laugh at his joke...it'll be over soon…*

Pitman continued, "I wanted to be the first to tell you about some news I received today from the Department of the Army."

He waited for a beat, enjoying her quizzical expression. "The Army's promotion list to major was officially released this morning, O'Shane. Guess what? You're on it! Congratulations!"

Weak kneed and in a state of shock, Jenny plopped into the nearest seat and mumbled, "Uhh, is this a joke, Sir? This is two years early!"

He laughed as he rumpled her short, red hair. "It's not a joke. Good things come, etc. It's unusual, but well deserved." He pinned the oak leaf on her collar.

"Thanks, Colonel," she said. "This is totally awesome! But, don't I have to wait for my name to come up on the list before I wear the rank?"

He answered, "You're number one on this list, and that means you get promoted today. Good for you. Now smile."

Jenny stood as tall as her five-foot-two frame allowed as they shook hands for the pictures. *...Hate these photo ops... look like a midget next to this guy...*

Blinded by the flashing lights, she didn't notice the arrival of the brigade adjutant. He appeared at the colonel's side holding two small boxes and some paperwork. Colonel Pitman was tickled that he had been able to pull off the promotion gambit. A mischievous grin made it clear that he had something else up his sleeve.

"By the way, O'Shane," he said. "Remember those awards for gallantry in action we spoke about a couple of months ago?"

"Sir, I recall saying that I thought approval was unlikely..."

He interrupted, "Well, you were wrong. They were approved." With a slight pause for effect, laughing as her mouth dropped open, he directed the adjutant, "John, read the orders."

In accordance with normal military tradition, the adjutant called out, "Attention to orders!" Everyone came to attention. The adjutant then read. “For wounds received during combat action on July 16th, 2003, Major Jennifer O’Shane is hereby awarded the Purple Heart.”

Pausing to shuffle papers and to let Colonel Pitman pin the medal on Jenny’s shirt, he began reading again. “Major Jennifer O’Shane is also hereby awarded the Silver Star for her heroic actions on the evening of July 16th 2003, at Nak Thoo, South Korea. On that date, Major O’Shane, armed with only a pistol, attacked a group of terrorists who were armed with automatic rifles and machine guns.

“With little regard for her own safety, she placed herself at great risk, jeopardizing her personal welfare in order to save the lives of soldiers in her command. Even after being wounded, she continued firing her weapon to distract and draw fire from the enemy force while her soldiers were exposed. After the firefight, she ensured the wounds of her soldiers were attended to before allowing her own to be treated.

“Her actions also resulted in the interception of North Korean terrorists whose mission was the assassination of the President of South Korea. The conduct of Major O’Shane is above and beyond the normal call of duty. She brings great credit upon herself, the Military Police Corps, the United States Army, and the United States of America.”

Colonel Pitman smiled as he pinned this medal to her uniform, saying, “Great job, Jenny. Don’t look so surprised. On behalf of a grateful nation, you have my sincerest congratulations. You are a hero, and I’m proud of you and proud to serve with a soldier like you.” He gave her a big hug. She started to tear up. He put his arm around her shoulders and added, “Now stop that. You’ll get us all started.”

He turned to the adjutant, “John, get us some Kleenex.” Jenny couldn’t help but laugh through her tears as Pitman blew his own nose. “OK,” he said. “Everybody look sharp. We have a surprise visitor due any minute.”

Almost on cue, someone called out, “Attention!” And, in walked Lieutenant General Anh Rhee, the Commander for the South Korean II Corps. His headquarters was adjacent to Pitman’s.

Power seemed to emanate from General Rhee in palpable waves. He was a well-built, wide-shouldered man, impeccable in a tailored, starched uniform. He sported a shaved head -- not common in the cold climate of Korea. It was rumored that this impressive man was being groomed for high-level positions in the South Korean government.

Without pause, he approached Colonel Pitman, “Colonel, it’s good seeing you again,” he said in flawless English as he shook Pitman’s hand.

“General Rhee, thank you for taking time to be here.”

“I always enjoy being with my American friends.” Turning to Jenny, he said, “You must be Major O’Shane, hero of the Nak Thoo crossroads. Thank you for what you’ve done for my country. The South Korean government has asked that I provide you a token of our appreciation.” As he said these words, another South Korean officer approached, handing a medal to Rhee.

The general continued, “Major, it is with great pleasure that I award you the South Korean Bronze Star Medal for your valor. On behalf of all South Koreans, you have my sincere thanks and congratulations.”

Humbled by all the attention, she blushed and muttered, “Thank you, Sir. I’m honored.”

He responded, “It’s well deserved. I’m also told that you were the person responsible for exposing the drug cartel a few months ago. Your actions impose a debt of honor on my country. In gratitude, should you ever find yourself in need of our assistance in any matter, I’ve been instructed by my government to ask that you call my personal phone number."

...Fat chance... she thought.

General Rhee nodded as he handed Jenny his business card. He gave her an understanding smile as if he'd heard her thoughts. Without further comment, he bid Colonel Pitman farewell and left the ceremonies.

Colonel Pitman began laughing again, "O'Shane, you look like a deer caught in headlights!" The room erupted in laughter.

"Very funny, Sir," she said. "You'd feel the same way! Couldn't you have at least given me some warning?" Glancing around the room, she saw that everyone was looking at her, grinning. She couldn't help but blush an even brighter shade of red. "Please! Would you all go get another drink or something?"

That caused more laughter and a general chorus of, "Forget it," and "Too bad," and "Like hell!" Everyone jostled to shake her hand.

Disconcerted, Jenny tried to shift some of the attention by asking, "Colonel, I thought you were scheduled to be in Seoul today? I didn't expect to see you here."

"I couldn't resist seeing the look on your face. It was priceless! Ha!" That caused another outburst of laughter.

The party went on for another hour before Jenny had to leave to make her flight back to the U.S. Colonel Pitman offered his command helicopter for the ride to Seoul. He'd told her as she climbed onboard, "Major, you made a lot of good friends in high places here in Korea, including yours truly. Keep me posted on what's going on. I expect to hear from you."

She gave him another hug and said, "You're a great boss, Sir. It's been my pleasure. I'll keep in touch. Thanks for everything..."

Two hours later Jenny was still in shock. With what had gone on during her one-year assignment in South

Korea, she had more than once expected she would be asked to leave the Army, her career aborted. Instead, she had three new medals pinned on her uniform, and she was now a major, promoted ahead of her peers. Incredible!!

As Jenny reflected on those facts, a kaleidoscope of other, less recent memories flooded her mind, making her almost dizzy. She'd been out of the hospital for three months, but it seemed like everything had happened yesterday. Her side still twinged from the gunshot wound.

Chapter Two

Black Bishop Moves

Jenny's euphoria would have been short-lived had she met Enrique Histaves that day. An aura of evil enveloped the man, a colonel in the Argentinean Secret Police. Without conscience, Histaves was orchestrating events in Washington, D.C. that would threaten Jenny's very existence…

"You have an urgent message on your desk," Kandi told Colonel Histaves when he returned from lunch. "The person said you'd know the name. He said he was a Congressional friend of yours. I didn't get it all. Sorry."

Kandi then returned to polishing her nails. Holding his temper in check, Histaves reminded himself why he tolerated someone so incompetent in his outer office. Feeling a pleasant and familiar stirring, he smiled at the thought. *...She loves it rough and cruel...*

However, sexual pleasure wasn't the main reason for Kandi. Maintaining security had first priority. Histaves' job in the secret police required him to remain unobtrusive. It was often important that few knew of his whereabouts. Kandi was perfect for his needs: intellectually challenged, almost oblivious to his whereabouts, ***and*** a willing mistress.

His current mission was unparalleled in its audacity. It was to steal top-secret prototype weapons and technology – a dangerous and expensive venture. But, success promised huge wealth and assured Histaves of a lifetime of luxury.

Pulling the strings and personally funding the mission was Senor Flaveo Fernando, Argentina's Secretary of Defense. Nicknamed El Toro (The Bull), Flaveo Fernando was the most ruthless man in Argentina.

His empire stretched across the entire country; his tentacles reached every level of government. Over the years, those in Argentina who opposed him or questioned his direction often disappeared or were involved in accidents.

Graft, bribery, blackmail, and murder were his calling cards. Through Histaves, the man called El Toro was using each of his cards in his gambit within the U.S.

El Toro had been selective in picking his man to lead the operation. Histaves was a willing conspirator.

He was embittered by a military promotion system that he viewed as rife with corruption from the influential and wealthy. And, he'd felt cheated by government bureaucrats of his fair share of riches won in a similar scheme he'd managed in Germany in the 1980's. Histaves was eager to make his mark and viewed El Toro's private enterprise as his ticket.

Helping Histaves was El Toro's son, *Teniente* (Lieutenant) Esteban Fernando. Lieutenant Fernando, of aristocratic birth, was a bright and resourceful deputy.

Having El Toro's son at Histaves' elbow would appear awkward at first glance. However, even though the lieutenant feared his father, he was petrified of Histaves. He'd watched as Histaves had tortured and then murdered two scientists to obtain information about stolen weapons systems.

Fernando witnessed the gleam of sadistic pleasure in Histaves' eyes as he mutilated the men. The vision would haunt Fernando's dreams. It was what Histaves had intended. The cowed lieutenant was not a problem.

Histaves enjoyed humbling the highborn, fearful lieutenant by giving him menial tasks. Crating the stolen weapons and test equipment for shipment back to Argentina was a perfect job for this purpose. Histaves knew that Fernando would chaff at the assignment.

This knowledge enhanced Histaves' perverse pleasure when he'd instructed the lieutenant to supervise the warehouse operations. Reflecting on how enjoyable it was to toy with Fernando, Histaves dialed the number Kandi had given him to call his Congressional friend.

After only two rings, he heard, "Hello Rico," – a name Histaves reserved for a select few. With no further preamble the caller said, "We need to meet. Something's come up. It's important."

In almost a whisper, the voice continued, "I can't talk. Meet me at the Smithsonian Aerospace Museum at 3:30 this afternoon at the aircraft carrier. I've got to go." With that he disconnected.

Exasperated, Histaves banged the phone back into the receiver. …*Madre de Dios…working with these amateurs is going to put us all in jail…that idiot isn't supposed to contact me at the embassy…* He dialed another phone number.

There was a prompt answer, "*Hola*?" Histaves recognized the voice of Lieutenant Fernando.

"Please put your phone to secure," Histaves instructed.

Pausing until a beep indicated that the security system was activated, he informed Fernando of his upcoming meeting. "Be there to insure I am not followed."

Happy for a diversion from the warehouse drudgery, the lieutenant was more than willing. "Of course, *Coronel*, I will be there. It will probably slow down our packing schedule, but…"

Preparing the equipment for transport was taking longer than planned. They'd canceled one military transport aircraft from Argentina already. The next was due in ten days.

"*Teniente*," Histaves interrupted. "You assured me we would be on schedule for the shipment. If I cancel this military transport…if that plane arrives and we are not ready…"

"*Coronel*, we will make our schedule." Histaves detected a slight tremble in the voice of his deputy.

He thought, ...*Good...as it should be...* "Okay, Esteban," Histaves said. "Be sure you are, and be at my meeting. And, don't bring one of those American thugs you hired as your back up. Use one of our agents."

"*Si, Senor*. It will be as you ask. But, *Senor*, the Americans have proven useful so far in our operation. They are good."

Histaves answered in a curt tone, "Yes, I know Esteban. But I don't want them to see me, or to see the person I'm meeting. It could compromise us. Just do as I say."

"Of course, *Coronel*. The surveillance will be easy."

"Don't get over-confident, Esteban," Histaves cautioned. "And, don't be so quick to trust the Americans. Keep them at arm's length. I'm still not sure about your recruiting."

The Colonel heard a sharp intake of breath and interrupted before the lieutenant could protest. "Relax, *Teniente*. I know it's too late. They just seem over qualified…ex-Rangers and Seals, and an ex-Air Force Air Commando."

"*Si, Senor*. But, I visited their last duty stations, and our contact in the office of military personnel showed me their service records. They needed a job and we pay them well. They're the real deal. I think..."

"Okay, okay," Histaves cut Fernando off again. "I agree. We're probably lucky to have them. Remember though, I've been through these types of things a number of times…just keep an eye on them. No cowboy efforts on this. I'll assume you will be at the Smithsonian. *Adios*."

Agitated and uneasy, even with Fernando's reassurances, Histaves felt a need to get out of the office. He looked at his watch. ...*An hour to go...plenty of time to walk over to museum...* He put on his overcoat and headed out, ignoring Kandi's inquiry as to his plans.

As Histaves crossed the Mall, past the Vietnam Memorial, he reflected on the past events that led to his current venture…

Chapter Three

Knight Cross

Jenny was also reflecting on the past as she bumped along in the helicopter on her way to Seoul. Her mind was focused on her year in Korea and was revisiting one of her most vivid memories – an episode with someone she had thought was a friend. It had all started on a cold February night…

She recalled leaving her office late that night. She had paused in a building moon-shadow to enjoy the night sky, a beautiful, pitch-black. The stars sparkled, and the crescent of a half-moon was on the eastern horizon.

Fatigue washed over her as she leaned against the building. Inhaling a lungful of the crisp winter air, her thought was, *…you've got to stop working these hours…* She knew there wasn't much chance of that. Her first sergeant had made that clear.

"Ma'am," he'd said, "you need to be on the road again tomorrow." He was pointing to a map on the wall where all twelve of the unit's guard posts were identified with colored pins. "I know this makes three days in a row, but I've gotten several complaints about first platoon's three posts at the fuel and ammo dump. You need to tighten them up."

Jenny groaned, "Great, First Sergeant. When do I get to this stuff?" she asked, poking at a pile of paperwork.

He laughed and said, "Cap'n, that's why they pay you the big bucks." Turning to leave, he added, "And, that's why God made so many hours of night time – so officers can get their work done." She threw her hat at his retreating back as he left her office.

That had been an hour ago. Now, as she began to push off the dark-shadowed building toward her quarters, a voice broke her reverie. *...Who the hell's out at this hour...?* Jenny wondered. She saw Captain Bob Cross standing at a pay phone kiosk.

At six-foot-five, Cross was recognizable even in the dim light. A hulking giant of a man, he'd played varsity football in college and would have turned pro if he hadn't hurt a knee in his junior year.

Jenny and Cross had gone to the officer's club together several times. He'd kidded her about her Tinker Bell stature, and she'd given him an equal tit-for-tat, calling him King Kong. He was married and off-limits for anything serious.

Jenny could hear his deep, bass voice as it carried across the short distance. "Yes, I want the Jane delivered so I can be there," he said. "Bring it all at the same time. My customers are clamoring." She also heard something about Camp Bonifas, March 12th, and 2300 hours.

...Holy shit...drug deal...has to be... she thought.

After he hung up, Cross looked around with a furtive glance. She felt as if he was looking right at her as she hugged the wall. She breathed a sigh of relief as he turned and walked away.

She made her way home in a shocked daze. She didn't sleep at all that night. She knew she had to report Cross. But, her evidence was sketchy at best – a one-sided phone call.

Additionally, because Cross was an officer with an excellent reputation, accusing him of being involved in a drug deal would be a tough sell. Their commander, Lieutenant Colonel John Botler, demonstrated just how tough it would be the next day.

Botler was a good boss. He was an amicable, easy-going guy, but protective of his soldiers. If he didn't think they were getting fair treatment, he'd fight like an alley cat to make things right.

He was completely disbelieving when she'd explained the phone call. "No way, O'Shane," he'd exclaimed. "Cross is a top-notch officer. It's way out of character for that guy."

He shook his head and continued, "You had to have misunderstood. It was late and you were tired. Maybe it's PMS time. I don't know, but it's so unlike what I know about Cross that I'm not going to embarrass myself by bringing it up to him. He's a super soldier and a great commander."

He then looked her in the eye, "I'm serious O'Shane. I want you to let this go. You make this official, and we'll all look like fools." In the following days Jenny wished she'd heeded Botler's orders.

Instead, she tried to find corroborating evidence on her own. That was not the smartest thing she'd done. Botler went ballistic when he learned she was conducting a personal investigation.

"You're doing what!" he'd yelled when he found out she'd requested phone records from the Korean phone company.

She responded, "Uhhh…Sir…I can explain…" She tried to tell him her plan.

"I don't care. That's as stupid a stunt as I've heard. I told you to drop it. I've got a mind to fire you right now!" He was apoplectic.

Worse yet, Cross somehow discovered she was on to him. He'd surprised Jenny, catching her one afternoon as she walked between the headquarters buildings.

"O'Shane, what do you think you're doing? Are you trying to destroy me, you meddling bitch?" he asked. His face was mottled and contorted, and his fists clenched. Pushing himself into her, he shoved her into the side of the building. She had no room to move. He was a powerful man.

"Cross, don't be stupid," she warned. "This isn't going to solve anything." She put her hands up to try to shove him away.

With one hand, he grabbed her wrists and held them over her head. He forced his other hand under the front of her uniform.

His huge hand squeezed one breast, then the other. It felt like hot pincers on her chest. There was nothing sexual about it – he was trying to hurt her.

He hissed in her ear, "You think these cute tits will protect you?"

She tried to wriggle free saying, "Goddamn it, Cross. You're hurting me. That's enough. Stop it, or I'll scream!"

He punched her in the stomach, knocking her breathless. She tried to yell. All that came out was a croak.

Still holding Jenny's hands over her head, Cross reached down and unbuckled her belt and began to yank open her pants, pushing them down. "I'll show you what we do to nosey broads where I come from."

"Cross," Jenny rasped, "please stop. Don't do this." She squirmed and twisted to no avail in his solid grasp.

He hit her in the stomach again. She sagged, helpless in his hands.

He bent her at the waist and stepped behind her, holding her up with one hand. She heard his zipper.

Her mind raged, *...My God...raped in the middle of the headquarters compound...Jesus...!*

And then, a voice... "That's enough, Cross. Stop."

Cross was pulled away. She sank to her knees, gasping, thinking she'd found a redeemer.

Instead, she was stunned when she heard the voice snarl at her, "This never happened, O'Shane. Forget about it." To Cross he said, "Come on Cross, she's not worth it."

Walking away, Cross sneered, "I'm not done with you, O'Shane."

She staggered to her feet and fastened her pants. Tears of fear and frustration coursed down her cheeks. Given the situation, she was certain no one would believe her version of the attack. *...Bringing charges is pointless...Cross is Teflon...damn it...!*

From then on, she experienced an almost daily confrontation with Cross or his cronies. After about a week of hell, at a point when she was almost prepared to offer her resignation, she found a phone message in her office from Jim Cavanaugh.

...Great...need to talk to someone...hope he's got some ideas...this is turning crazy...

She dialed for the operator. "What number please?" the Korean operator asked.

Giving her the number on the message, Jenny explained, "Operator, this number is in Ft. Hood, Texas in the U.S." Five minutes later, after numerous transfers and exchange operators, she was connected.

She heard in the earpiece, "Headquarters, First Cavalry Division. This is Sergeant Davis speaking. How may I help you?"

"Sergeant Davis, this is Captain O'Shane. Is Sergeant Major Cavanaugh still at work?" Davis almost blew out her ear in response.

"Captain O'Shane, how are you?" he said. "I'm General O'Shane's driver, Ma'am. He talks about you all the time. Cap'n, you should know that the Old Man is really proud of you."

"Thanks, Sergeant Davis. I appreciate it. I hate to be rude, but this is an expensive call. Could I talk to the Sergeant Major? Is he still there?"

"He sure is, Cap'n. It's only sixteen hundred here, Ma'am. We'll be here awhile yet. Your dad's still here too, Ma'am. Would you rather speak with him?"

Without hesitation, she answered, "No, not yet. Thanks. Let's try Sergeant Major Cavanaugh first."

Jim Cavanaugh, a long-time family friend, was one of the elite U.S. Army soldiers with the rank of 'Command Sergeant Major (CSM)', which is the top enlisted rank in the Army. CSM's serve as the senior enlisted advisor to unit commanders. Cavanaugh was also Jenny's godfather.

...Hate to bother him... want him to think...can handle own problems...but this is a personal train wreck approaching...need to talk to someone...

"Hi, Jenny," she heard Cavanaugh's familiar voice. "How are you?"

She answered with the usual pleasantries, trying to be casual. Then she asked, "You called me last night. What's up?"

Cavanaugh responded, "No real reason, Jenny. Just wanted to hear your voice and check in." He must have detected something in her tone of voice because in short order he asked, "What's the matter, Jenny? What's going on?" With no more prompting, she blurted out the story, her words tumbling over one another.

He didn't interrupt, and once she finished there was a pause. She didn't think she'd get much sympathy, and she was right.

Cavanaugh said, "Jennifer, I have to say, Botler's right. You shouldn't have launched a personal investigation without permission. You *are* lucky he didn't fire you. You're too smart not to think through the consequences. Use that bright mind of yours."

She gritted her teeth, biting back a defensive retort. She reminded herself, *...Asked for his input...he's right...*

Sensing he'd made his point, Cavanaugh softened a bit, and changed gears, "On the other hand, Botler needs to learn to trust you more. You have great instincts. Be patient. He's a good commander, and he'll figure you out before long."

He added after another pause, "Listen, I've got an idea on the Cross thing. Call an Agent Warren Stanley over at the Criminal Investigative Division (CID)." Cavanaugh read her a phone number. "Tell him I said to call. In the meantime, keep clear of Cross. He sounds desperate."

Not waiting for an answer, he added, "One more thing. Do us both a favor. Next time call me *before* you decide to disobey an order from your boss."

"Yes, I will. Sorry to…"

"No sweat, Jenny," he interrupted. "That's what godfathers are for. Love you. Let me get the boss on the line. He'll raise hell if you don't at least say hello." Before she could say anything, Jenny heard the buzz of a phone connection put on hold.

She soon heard her dad, "Hello, Jenny. How's my girl? To what do I owe this pleasure?" They had a brief, enjoyable father/daughter conversation. He ended with, "I'm really proud of you, Hon. Love you."

She wished him a good night, and they disconnected. She cried herself to sleep once again for what had become a series of long nights.

The next morning she thought over her conversation with Cavanaugh. She knew of the Army CID. They had the mission of investigating criminal activity within the U.S. Army. Tangential to the MP organization but under a separate chain of command, they had a reputation in Korea of being straight arrow.

...Well, I don't have much to lose at this point... She called Mr. Stanley.

Chapter Four

Screened Bishop

…Wind, snow and piercing cold were Lieutenant Enrique Histaves' constant companions almost twenty years before Jenny's encounter with Cross. Histaves was stationed at an outpost in a harsh Argentinean mountain region near Chile. He'd volunteered for the job during the height of a border dispute, hoping to make a name for himself in an expected war.

Diplomacy had resolved the Chile/Argentinean issues less than a year after Histaves' assignment in 1984. Over the remainder of the next four years, Histaves saw contemporaries in his unit transferred and promoted.

Embittered by watching his peers advance, Histaves convinced himself that their promotions were the product of privilege and influence.

Histaves' unbalanced mind overlooked the investigations and the reprimands he'd received for soldier abuse. In one case, he was investigated on the charge of murder.

Authorities were unable to find sufficient evidence to link Histaves to the naked, frozen body of a subordinate. The investigation noted Histaves as the prime suspect, but no charges were filed. Histaves knew the truth and recalled the freezing night without remorse…

"Get up, Joaquin," he'd told the sleeping sergeant. "Hurry up and dress. We've been ordered to move some trucks away from an avalanche area."

The sergeant followed Histaves out of the barracks into the snowstorm. "Where are the trucks, *Senor*?" Joaquin had asked. Histaves kept walking. Soon, Joaquin said, "*Teniente*, I don't remember trucks parked in this area. Where are we going?"

Histaves whirled on the sergeant and pulled out a pistol. “Just shut your mouth and do as you’re told. Next time maybe you won’t be so quick to question my orders as you did today during our drill.”

The sergeant knew Histaves’ reputation and became frightened. He saw that they were now in a construction area near their outpost. It was a stone quarry. “*Senor*, I apologize. I didn’t mean to offend you.”

“Too late. Take off your clothes and put them in this,” Histaves ordered, throwing a canvas bag on the ground in front of Joaquin. The sergeant began to undress.

“It’s freezing out here.”

“Do what you’re told,” Histaves responded, cocking the pistol.

Soon Joaquin was standing nude in the falling snow. Shivering and shaking, he asked, “Please, can I get dressed now? I won’t ever make that mistake again.”

“Shut up. I’ll tell you when to get dressed.”

The sub-freezing temperatures had a stuporing effect. Joaquin fell to the ground and folded into a fetal position, moaning, “Please, please…”

“I said, shut up,” Histaves shouted. He began to hit the sergeant with a steel rod he’d found leaning against a tool shed. Hearing Joaquin moan again drove Histaves into a frenzy. He beat the sergeant until there were no more sounds.

“There,” he screamed. “See what you made me do? When I tell you to be quiet, that’s what I mean.”

Histaves felt justified in his actions. *...The man just wouldn’t follow orders...now have to clean up this mess...! ...His fault...* He hit the body again.

He thought, *...the hell with it...someone else can clean up...* He rolled the body into a crevice between cut stones. The bag and rod went on top. *...Snow will soon cover...*

The fact that he'd beaten the man to a bloody pulp didn't faze Histaves. In his warped mind, discipline had demanded action and Histaves had responded. On reflection, his only regret was that the body was discovered.

Over the next few years, Histaves wallowed in self-pity. He'd never accepted that *he* was the one at fault for not being promoted, nor would he ever acknowledge that *he* was the recipient of special treatment and that *his* was the family of influence. Often disconnected from reality, Histaves viewed his father's interventions on his behalf in military college and in the Army as insignificant.

With promotion out of reach, the family of Lieutenant Histaves finally influenced his transfer from the border assignment. Their feeling was that a fresh start was in order. They convinced the Army leadership that reassigning Lieutenant Histaves was in everyone's best interest.

Chapter Five

Queen Entry

When Jenny called Mr. Stanley at the CID office, he was curt. Without preamble, he gave her directions. “Come over at nineteen hundred hours. Most everyone will have cleared out by then. There’s a rear entrance. I’ll have a light on over the door.”

Using his directions and a South Korean taxi, Jenny arrived right on time at a nondescript building that was nowhere near the actual Eighth Army Headquarters. The building looked almost abandoned. There were no lights on in the windows. She asked her driver, “Circle the building, please.” As they drove around to the back, she saw the lit doorway.

Taking a deep breath, Jenny paid off the driver and stepped up to the door. She pressed a buzzer next to the threshold. A disembodied voice asked through a speaker, “May I help you?”

Nervous but determined, she answered, “This is Captain O’Shane to see Mr. Stanley.” She heard a latch disengage and the door swung open. She could see down a dim hallway. At the far end two men stood.

The same disembodied voice said, “Step through the doorway please.” She did so, and a soft ‘beep…beep…beep’ began to sound. The two men in the hallway disappeared from sight. The voice asked, “Captain, are you armed?”

“I’m a Military Policeman and I have my issue weapon. I carry it in a shoulder holster when I’m off-base in civilian clothes.”

Again, the voice spoke in the semi-darkness, “Ma’am, you will need to surrender your weapon while you’re visiting here. Please keep your hands to your side, proceed to the wall in front of you, and assume the position."

She was put off, but she needed help. She walked to the end of the hallway, placed her hands on the wall, and leaned forward with her feet apart.

Two men appeared, one on each side of her. There was a tension between them. The one on her right said, "Cap'n, please excuse us, but we're going to have to frisk you. We don't have a female agent on station at this hour. It's not customary for males to search females. If you object we can wait and recall one of our female agents."

"Go ahead and search me. I'm sure you won't find any surprises." That brought a chuckle and she could sense them relax somewhat.

She was frisked and her weapon, badge and ID card were placed on a table in a small, windowless office. As she sat in an offered chair, the same man who had spoken earlier did introductions.

"Cap'n, I'm Mr. Warren Stanley, and my sidekick here is Mr. George Hanks." Both had spit-shined boots, poster-perfect uniforms, and firm handshakes. Their shoulders and biceps seemed to be bursting their shirts. Jenny had little doubt that she was in the presence of a couple of super soldiers.

Mr. Stanley continued, "Sorry for the brusque greeting and treatment when you came in. We had a recent run-in with locals.

"Why don't you explain why Jim Cavanaugh asked me to speak with you? He's a good friend, but we won't break rules or violate procedures even for a friend."

"I understand," she said. "Let me tell you what I have, and you can see if this is worth your time." She then laid out her story.

When she was finished, Mr. Stanley said, "Cap'n, you should have come to see us earlier. At least we would have saved you an ass chewing."

Mr. Hanks interrupted, “Don’t mind him, Cap’n. He’s forgotten what it’s like to be young.

“Ma’am, to be honest, we’ll have to make this official if we follow through. That means you will need to file a formal report. We are required to provide a copy of the report to Botler before we investigate Cross. That’s according to regulations.”

Jenny put up her hand. “No way,” she said. “Botler has warned me off twice. The last time was painful. If I pursue this through an official report, he’ll have my ass no matter how it turns out. And, I don’t see Botler cooperating. Can’t you do this under covert ops?”

Stanley and Hanks looked at each other and shrugged. Stanley said, “Sorry, Cap’n. We don’t even do covert investigations without the immediate commander being involved. Unless you think Botler’s in the middle of this in some way, and you put that in your report?”

Jenny shook her head, “Botler’s not involved. He’s so straitlaced, he makes a Quaker look liberal.”

Hanks said, “Ma’am, I’m sorry. It doesn’t look like we can move forward with what you’ve given us. Our investigations have to be official, by the book. We’d love to bust this guy, but...”

Jenny sighed in disappointment. “Damn,” she said. “This just isn’t right.” She stood and began gathering up her belongings. Stanley and Hanks both shook her hand and apologized again.

As they walked back down the hall towards the exit, Jenny asked, “Just out of curiosity, what’s the run-in with the locals about?”

Mr. Hanks answered, “We have an informant in a nearby Air Force unit who helped us bust a drug operation. The drug dealer sent a couple of thugs over to try to bully us into giving up the name of our informer. We gave the naïve fellows a rather rude reception, but we don’t think that will discourage them for long.”

Jenny stopped in mid-stride as Hanks completed that sentence. Stanley almost ran into her, "What's the matter, Cap'n? Did you forget something?"

She turned and said, "I've got an idea. If you already have a drug investigation going, wouldn't that allow you to expand it a little without an official report?" A look of comprehension spread on both their faces as she explained her thoughts in more detail…

Two days later, she was summoned to Botler's office. The adjutant told her, "It's a meeting with some CID people."

When she entered Botler's office, Stanley and Hanks were sitting in two of the office chairs. Botler was frowning as he introduced them to her. She and the agents pretended they had just met. She began to sweat. *…God, please don't let Botler see through this charade…*

Botler seemed to buy into the story as he explained, "These two gentlemen are from the Eighth Army CID. They're conducting an investigation of a drug operation in the area. They're asking local commanders if we've had recent reports as to drug-related activities." Botler paused, scowling, his eyes boring into Jenny. She kept a poker face, returning his gaze.

She watched his eyes shift as if he'd come to a decision. He continued, "I had no choice but to tell them of the conversations that you and I had. Over my objections, they asked to interview you."

Botler turned to the CID agents and said, "I reiterate for the record, I give this report no credibility. However, at your insistence, I'll allow Captain O'Shane to tell you her story."

To Jenny, he said, "Captain, I'll have no embellishments. Is that clear?" He crossed arms over his thin chest and glowered at her.

"Completely clear, Sir." Jenny answered.

Stanley and Hanks were good. They didn't crack a smile as she repeated her story. Hanks asked the critical question, "Cap'n, you say you overheard the date of March 12th?"

"That's correct."

Hanks looked at Botler and said, "Colonel, that's only a couple of days away. It would be easy to place surveillance on Cross on the 12th, and if nothing happens, no one would be the wiser." Botler began to look trapped.

Stanley jumped in, "Sir, we're pursuing all angles. To be successful, we need everyone to work with us."

Sensing Botler was wavering, Hanks added, "We won't issue any official report without catching Cross red-handed." That assurance seemed to satisfy Botler.

He responded, "OK, go ahead with your surveillance. But, before you make a move on Cross you'd better have a damn good reason!"

Jenny and the agents breathed a silent, collective sigh of relief. Hanks answered, "You got it, Colonel."

There was one more issue, and Stanley brought up the subject. "Sir, we'd also like to request that Captain O'Shane be detailed to us for the next few days. She'd be a big help in maintaining surveillance."

"That's a bad idea," Botler said. "She'll be spotted right away with her red hair."

Hanks responded, "Sir, we'll put her in disguise. Even her own dad won't recognize her when we're done." Botler considered the request for a few minutes.

Jenny held her breath and thought, *...please Boss...Say yes...This is my ticket to a piece of Cross...*

Finally, Botler answered, "Oh, hell. All right. She's so damn stubborn, she'd find some way to get in the middle anyway. You got her for a week. If nothing comes of it, she comes back. She has a job to do here. Now get out of my office." Jenny and the agents came to attention, saluted, and marched out.

The meeting had gone almost as she'd planned. She suppressed a grin as they walked out of the headquarters building together.

Sensing her feelings, Stanley said, "Cap'n you better keep a lid on it until we get out of sight of that colonel. I hope he never figures out what you just did."

Hanks retorted, "Hey Warren, don't spoil her fun. It was clever. You're just jealous you didn't think of it."

Two days later, at 10:45 p.m. on March 12th, Jenny had her arm in the crook of Mr. Stanley's oversized bicep. They were pretending to be a young couple enjoying the night air. She had on a blonde wig and big glasses. With light make-up, she didn't even recognize herself.

Chapter Six

The Bishop Gambit

It was convenient that the Argentinean embassy in Germany had an opening for a military liaison officer in 1988. Histaves was ordered from the Chilean border to the Bonn station.

The title sounded important and fed Histaves' large ego. It seemed a perfect fit given the political ambitions he harbored in his ignorant arrogance. He envisioned the position to be an inroad to rapid advancement.

However, the luster of the job title soon faded. Histaves was the junior military officer and he was tasked with menial, administrative work; and often had to run errands for the more senior staff. Frustrated and restless after only a few months, he began looking for diversions.

One dreary German afternoon, as he was doing his daily sorting of incoming mail, Histaves began reading excerpts of correspondence to break the monotony. A communiqué caught his attention.

It announced that the Argentinean Army had canceled a large order for laser-aimed small arms from Remington Corporation. Instead, the communiqué noted, the Army had placed a similar order with an obscure firm called Krueger that was located outside of Bonn, Germany.

By itself, this information was of no consequence. It became more noteworthy to Histaves as he was performing another of his administrative tasks – interpreting news articles.

He had always had a natural ability with languages and was fluent in four. Therefore, one of his responsibilities in the embassy was scanning foreign newspapers and magazines for articles of interest for the ambassador. He felt that the task was beneath him, and so he usually wasn't attentive.

For some reason, a *New York Times* article caught his eye. The article reported a fire in one of Remington's factories. Advanced laser research material and equipment were destroyed.

The report triggered a memory. He stared at the article for some time. *...What is it...? There's something else...not just the Army communiqué...too obvious...* It came to him, *...of course...my magazine...*

Histaves was a small arms aficionado and made a point of keeping current on happenings in the field. He sorted through recent copies of *Small Arms News*. He found what he was looking for – a headlined article, "Remington Executives Claim Breakthrough…Laser-Designated Weaponry Ready for Marketing…"

Histaves laid the *New York Times* report, the *Small Arms News* article, and the Army communiqué side-by-side *...Caramba...! ...It's industrial espionage...*

Although his suspicion of theft was none of his concern, it piqued his curiosity. He reflected, *...international attorneys will have field day ...Remington took major hit...small arms biggest chunk of weapons industry...*

Given the money involved, he was surprised by the fact that there weren't follow-on news stories. *...Curious...secrets somewhere...too bad...may have been fun to watch...*

Though Histaves had no stake in the game, he felt clever in seeing through the scheme. He daydreamed about how much money he could have made had he played a part. *...A gold mine...maybe one percent...billions in trade...wow...that would be so sweet...oh well...* He filed the information into his mental trash basket and looked for another diversion to occupy his mind.

His hobby of shooting targets at a local gun club was one outlet. *...Stress reliever...love seeing holes in target...pretend assignment officer...*

One wintry afternoon, he was looking through his club roster to find phone numbers of shooting partners. The names of two members who listed their place of employment as Krueger Arms manufacturers almost jumped off the page. He'd seen the names before, but it'd never registered. Memories of his discovery about Remington came to mind. *...Well now...a conversation with them might prove interesting...why not...?*

He stared at the names for a few minutes as a plan began to form. He'd already made their acquaintance; they'd competed against each other at club matches. *...Know them by first names...what the hell...maybe free today...can't hurt to ask...*

He dialed their phone numbers. They were free that afternoon. *...Fantastic...this is going to be fun...!* Calling two other friends, Histaves arranged a match.

An inexplicable thrill of excitement coursed down his back. He'd competed in marksmanship tournaments before, but this was different. He somehow knew that he'd just arranged the shooting match of his life.

In his excitement, Histaves had to struggle to keep his composure, and he lost the match by a wide margin. Of course, winning wasn't his goal that day.

Anxious when they finished, trying to sound casual, he asked, "Would you guys like to join me at the nearby gasthaus? Loser buys the drinks." Free drinks were hard to refuse. They all agreed.

They drove to the gasthaus together, and by the time they reached their destination, everyone was relaxed and talkative. He initiated a discussion concerning small arms technology after drinks were ordered. "Have you seen the specs' on the new laser weapons?" he asked. That comment prompted what he was hoping for.

As if scripted, Pedro (a Spanish military liaison officer) volunteered, "It's interesting that you mention laser weapons. My country's armed forces just ordered a new brand of small arms."

"Where'd you get them?" someone asked.

"A German firm named Krueger," he responded. "We got a real bargain. We canceled a similar order from Remington."

With little pause, Histaves chimed in, "Isn't that something. Argentina just did the same thing for the Argentinean Army. We saved a ton of money."

They all shared a laugh about the Americans losing some good business. "About time…" was the thrust of their comments.

Hans and Stephan (the Krueger employees) expressed their pleasure about the change orders, and Hans explained, "Stephan and I are the engineers who conducted the final testing of that equipment at Krueger."

Everyone grinned in amusement at the coincidence of the circumstances. Histaves was more than amused.

The engineers expressed pride that their firm had completed such high-end development, but they seemed reluctant to detail their own participation in the process. "It really wasn't much," Stephan stated.

Histaves couldn't resist. "What does 'not much' mean?" he asked Stephan.

"Well…we're both on the same weapons development team at Krueger," he answered. "One morning two years ago, a senior manager presented us with designs and prototypes of various laser-designated weapons."

Hans continued, "We were told to test them and prepare the weapons for production. Happy to be involved, we both assumed that another team elsewhere in the firm had done the research. We enjoyed a nice bonus for our part."

Histaves asked another question. "Did your firm do the designs?"

Hans and Stephan looked at each other. After a slight pause, Hans answered, "We now realize it's unlikely. However, in the interest of keeping our jobs, we haven't made it an issue."

Histaves smiled at the response. He was more certain than ever that he knew the truth.

The group pondered what they'd heard for a few minutes over another beer, and then everyone seemed to dismiss the matter as the way the world turned.

Histaves wasn't nearly as sanguine as he'd pretended. He knew that there was something irregular. His intuition, combined with crushing boredom, prompted him to decide then and there to investigate further. *...Krueger factory nearby...two key players available...hmmm...*

He first called some friends in other embassies that he'd met at other social functions. "Have you guys flipped any weapons contracts to Krueger?" Histaves asked. In a couple of cases, the answer was yes. *...Madre de Dios...!*

Histaves then made his biggest commitment. He decided to pursue a relationship. He planned to use Hans as an inroad to find out the details of what had happened. He was certain that Hans was gay, and was attracted to Histaves' Latino good looks. At that point Histaves was still on something of a lark. It would be an exciting diversion.

Chapter Seven

Knight in Jeopardy

While Histaves recalled his excitement at the possibilities of a gay relationship in Germany, Jenny's mind was still reflecting on her year in Korea. She remembered two people: One threatened her life, and the other, her career…

…She and Stanley were walking about one hundred yards behind Cross in a small village on the outskirts of Camp Bonifas. Hanks was in front of them, maintaining communications with Stanley over an earpiece radio.

In a sudden move, Cross ducked into a side road and disappeared from sight. Jenny and Stanley sped up to regain visual contact. Rounding the corner, they walked into a dead end alleyway. In the dim light they could see Cross take something from the driver of a white car parked at the alley's end.

Stanley reported in on his radio, "Suspect in contact with a white Mitsubishi. He's just made a pick up. Let's bust him."

Hanks spun around and started running back toward the alley.

At that moment the occupants of the car spotted Jenny and Stanley. Headlights came on and tires squalled as the car accelerated towards them.

Jenny yelled, "Warren, duck!" She jumped to the side and ended up sprawled in the alleyway on her hands and knees.

Stanley moved a split second slower, and the car's side mirror caught his arm. Jenny heard a loud, pain filled grunt as he spun around and slammed into an adjacent building wall.

Seconds later, the car reached the exit to the alley. As if choreographed, Hanks arrived at the exact same instant. He collided with the front fender of the moving vehicle. The agent was tossed into the roadway like a rag doll. The car raced away.

That left Cross and Jenny facing each other in the alley. He began striding towards her with a determined look on his face, a plastic-wrapped package in his hand.

He didn't recognize her until he got within a few feet. Then, "You! Where the hell did you come from? Do you have any idea what you've done?"

She stood to confront him. She said, "I think I do. You just took a package from that car that's probably drugs. Put it down and let me help you sort this out."

Cross barked out an obscene, hysterical laugh. A look bordering on madness crossed his face.

He said in a high-pitched voice, "You have totally fucked me up, you interfering bitch. I'm not putting anything down. Instead, I'm going to rip your head off." Jenny backed away to give him some space, hoping he'd calm down.

"Bob, I can't let you walk away."

He looked at her in disbelief. "You little squirt. You can't stop me. If you think I hurt you the other day, you just can't imagine what I'm going to do right now."

He strutted toward her, relaxed and almost dismissive, assuming she would back away. He was wrong.

She was a Tae Kwon Do black belt and was trained in kickboxing. She had room to move. They were not in the confined space between the headquarters buildings, nor was she surprised by his attack. This time he was the one unprepared.

The smirk of confidence that had begun to appear on his face was replaced by a look of excruciating pain as she dropkicked him between his legs.

After her kick, Cross was halfway bent over, moaning. He was at a textbook height for Jenny's next blow. She spun three hundred and sixty degrees, building momentum, and kicked him in the side of his head.

It was her best kick, and it was powerful. She'd broken boards with that blow. She was sure he'd go down. He didn't. He was a brute.

He shook his head like a bear trying to ward off flies and began to shuffle toward her. A stream of blood trickled from his ear where her shoe had hit him.

She knew she couldn't let him get close, sensing he would kill her if he could. She kicked again. This time she aimed at the inside of his bad knee.

The crunch of cartilage snapping was loud, almost sickening in the confines of the narrow alley. Cross bent, grasping his knee, bellowing in pain.

Showing no mercy, she kicked once more, as hard as she could. This kick was aimed at his face, under his chin. She heard his teeth click as his jaw slammed shut.

Cross didn't make another sound as he toppled over backwards, landing with a thud. His right leg bent at a grotesque angle.

Certain that Cross was out for the count, Jenny went to help Stanley. He was awake but dazed, bleeding from a heavy gash in his forehead, and a deep cut where the car's side mirror had caught his arm. He asked, "Where's Cross?"

"He's out of it," she told him.

"Use my ear phone and get some help in here. There's an emergency number in my jacket pocket." As he spoke, she saw him look over her shoulder in surprise.

Without warning, a vise gripped her neck from behind. Cross was throttling her with his hands, somehow holding her off the ground. She couldn't breathe.

She kicked at nothing but air. Blackness began to close in around her peripheral vision. She pulled at his fingers to no avail. His big hands were locked into place.

In desperation, she reached behind her and scratched at his face, gouging an eye. He howled an inhuman sound and hurled her across the alley.

Jenny bounced off the alley wall and sprawled on her stomach, stunned. Gasping for air, choking, she heard a rustle of cloth on pavement. She looked over her shoulder.

Cross was crawling towards her. Blood was streaming down his face from his damaged eye.

She tried to scramble out of range. Too late.

Cross' hand closed on her ankle, pulling her back towards him. His breathing was labored, the grunting sound of a mating animal.

Her fingernails clawed the road surface as she grabbed for any purchase. Her hand brushed something. A board, a short two-by-four discarded in the alley.

She seized it with both hands and twisted in Cross' grasp. Swinging with all her might, she hit him on the side of his head.

His grip on her ankle slackened. She hit him again, then again.

He sagged, unconscious.

Unsteady, she got to her feet and found her purse. She took out her handcuffs and cuffed Cross' hands behind his back. Taking no more chances, she used his shoelaces to tie his feet together. Then she went back to Stanley and called for assistance.

At first, during interrogation two days later, she felt some guilt in her pleasure at seeing Cross grimace in pain. Then, she thought, *...Screw that...pay back is hell...*

Cross appeared remorseful, on the verge of tears. "I'm so sorry, Jenny," he'd said. "I feel terrible. I was desperate and didn't know what to do."

...You're lying...you knew what you were doing... you made my life hell...!

She didn't say a word. She let him talk. He hung himself.

As the details unfolded, it turned out that Cross was a chronic gambler and had accumulated debts with big-time South Korean crooks.

"They blackmailed me," he whined. "If I didn't help them, they threatened to expose me and ruin my career. They promised that drug deliveries would pay my debts."

Over the next several days she got details sufficient to unravel a major drug operation. In cooperation with the Korean National Police, several gang leaders were jailed.

For her efforts in exposing the operation, Jenny received a nice letter of appreciation from the Army chain-of-command. She also got an achievement medal from the South Koreans.

And, Botler wrote her a special performance evaluation. His comments included, "Captain O'Shane has a level of initiative that is unmatched in my eighteen-year military career. She is the best of the six commanders in my battalion. Recommend immediate promotion."

She thought at the time, *...fat chance...*

The rest of Jenny's year in Korea seemed assured of smooth sailing given a brightened relationship with Botler. And, it was smooth until a new battalion commander was assigned in late May to replace him...

...Lieutenant Colonel Dan Agburg was his name. He was the most prejudiced man concerning women in the military that Jenny had ever met. He made no secret as to his negative feelings and was particularly vocal about female soldiers in Korea.

In the face of these feelings, Agburg assumed duties as Jenny's boss, commanding six hundred personnel. She was in charge of one of his five subordinate units. Her career went back up for grabs.

He couldn't care less that his views were out of touch with the modern Army. He justified his viewpoint based on what he referred to as, "...the reality of the modern battlefield. Today's range and accuracy of weapons, combined with the speed of maneuvering forces, impose a fluid battlefield..."

This battlefield reality was the crux of his argument, "...MP's will be in the thick of combat operations should the North Koreans invade, and female soldiers will end up in the middle. No doubt, their presence will inhibit the reaction and conduct of male soldiers."

He'd acted in response to his convictions. He assigned most of the females, and all the battalion's rear area missions to Jenny's unit. It was ironic that his actions laid the foundation for her heroics at Nak Thoo.

However, it was alarming that Agburg retained his negative attitude even in the midst of wounded soldiers and in the haze of burnt gunpowder...

...Her company had been assigned the mission of traffic control during a convoy movement across the Nak Thoo crossroads. She was doing a routine check of her unit's activities.

To her amazement, just as she watched MP's deploy into the intersection, and the convoy started moving, she heard the crack of rifle fire and staccato of automatic weapons. She watched as one of the MP's spun and fell to the ground. Another screamed as he also took a hit.

Looking toward the noise of the gunfire, she could see a small pickup truck racing toward the crossroads, flashes of light erupting from weapons fire.

...Infiltrators... she thought. *...South Korean briefers warned...increased incursions from North Korea...on alert...fanatics...heavily armed...*

In the midst of these thoughts, she acted from a warrior instinct. She unholstered her pistol, a 9mm Berretta, loaded a clip of ammunition and began walking toward the approaching truck. "Thomas, radio headquarters, and tell them we are under attack," she yelled to her driver. "Then open fire on that truck."

The pickup screeched to a halt at the edge of the intersection. The driver had mistimed his arrival so that he couldn't move forward without colliding with convoy traffic.

She thought, *...perfect...less than fifty meters...can't miss...* She was an excellent marksman. She knelt and fired. Her first shot hit the agent in the passenger seat; his head exploded in a mist of blood.

Unable to get a clear shot at the driver, she aimed at the shooters in the truck bed. One of them took her next round in the chest. He fell backwards, arms flailing.

The agents had initially ducked when she started firing. When they spotted her kneeling in the open road, they started returning fire with a vengeance.

She aimed another shot, but before she pulled the trigger, something hit her helmet, nearly ripping it off. Then, it felt like a sledgehammer hit her in the side. She couldn't breathe. In the next few seconds, she only concentrated on pulling her trigger as fast as she could, aiming in the general direction of the truck, hoping to maintain a distraction.

Bullets from the North Koreans zipped through the air and ricocheted off the ground next to her. She was a sitting duck!

It was then that her driver, MP's across the intersection, and passengers in another Humvee, all began engaging the pickup. The infiltrators were outgunned. They'd had enough. The truck spun in a U-turn and roared back up the side road.

As fate would have it, Agburg had been in a convoy crossing the intersection during Jenny's firefight with the North Korean infiltrators. He'd sought her out in the aftermath and was pissed beyond reason.

"What in the hell do you think you were doing, O'Shane?" he yelled as she finished putting a battlefield bandage on a wounded soldier. "That kind of 'John Wayne' crap will get you killed! Couldn't you wait for back-up?"

She stood – not yet comprehending why she was dizzy – and lost it. She yelled back, "Colonel, I was doing my job. These are my soldiers, and they were under fire. There *was* no back up."

Without waiting for a retort she added, "If you'll excuse me, I have another soldier that needs attention."

She knelt and gently removed the other soldier's helmet, pressing a field dressing to her head to stanch the bleeding. A Korean civilian ambulance pulled up, and the EMTs took the soldier from Jenny's arms.

She stood again, and almost fell on her face. A searing pain throbbed in her side. She was seeing double.

Thomas noticed her wobble. He said something that she had trouble hearing. Her helmet was askew, and jammed tight against her head from the impact of a bullet that had creased it. Thomas helped her pull it off.

She saw his eyes look down. "Ma'am," he'd said, "You've been hit." He pointed to her side.

There was the spread of blood on her BDU uniform jacket. "Medic!" Thomas yelled as Jenny plopped down on her butt.

"Here, lay back. Let me have a look," Jenny heard the medic say.

He and Thomas unbuttoned her BDU jacket and pulled up her T-shirt. They saw a neat, round hole where a bullet had pierced her side.

"It's a 'through-and-through' Cap'n," the medic said, trying to be reassuring, "Not too serious." Blood seeped out of the hole in a steady stream.

Sharp pain came in waves. "Easy for you to say," she groaned.

Just then, Agburg came up, still fuming. All he could see was what looked like two men undressing Jenny. He jumped to a conclusion typical of his mentality.

He said, "O'Shane, isn't it bad enough that you had to grandstand. Now you're going to undress?"

She rolled to show him the bloody wound and said through clenched jaws, "Colonel, I seem to have a bullet hole in me, for Christ sake! Give me a fucking break!"

Agburg glared. She could see him pale in fury. Turning on his heel, he stomped away, muttering, "Impertinent bitch. You'll pay for this insolence." Jenny didn't much care what he said. She'd passed out.

Chapter Eight

The Bishop Control

In another era and time, Histaves pursued his goal of uncovering the details of the Remington affair.

He had never been in a gay relationship. He liked women. But, he'd figured it shouldn't be hard to fake his feelings if there was personal gain, *...identify players...bribery...power... maybe get a piece of the action...?*

Over four months, he cultivated and courted Hans. They went out to clubs, dinner and movies together, and of course they shared the gun range. Histaves used every opportunity to accidentally touch or otherwise tease the young man in sexually suggestive ways. Pretending reluctance, he inferred that he could be persuaded to have a sexual liaison.

The results were beyond his wildest imagination. In exchange for sex, his young German friend revealed the facts of a conspiracy that involved prominent industry and government leaders.

When Histaves was satisfied that he had the complete story, he approached the local Argentinean Secret Service agent. The agent was impressed. "Where did you get this?" he asked. "This is great."

Leafing through the report, he added, "This is way too hot for me to handle. Give me a few days to get some direction, and I'll call you."

Leaving the man's office, Histaves half expected that he wouldn't hear back. He was wrong. Within twenty-four hours he was summoned to the agent's office. "This is checking out. It appears that you have a knack for these operations."

"Thanks…I think," answered Histaves, waiting for the bad news. "What happens now?"

"Well, for now, you're detailed to my office."

Because of Histaves' experiences with reassignments, his look of distrust was evident. "What does that mean?"

"Relax. It's not bad news. You and I are going to work together to develop recommendations on how to make your discovery advantageous for Argentina.

"First though, I've got a special task for you. Depending on how you perform this task, your assignment to my office may become permanent." The agent then provided Histaves additional direction.

It wasn't long after that discussion that Hans and Stephan were involved in an accident on a German ski slope. Local news lamented the loss of two promising scientists from Krueger Industries. It was reported that they had turned the wrong way while skiing with friends and had fallen off a cliff.

In truth, Histaves had removed a warning sign and then directed the two down a back trail that led to a hidden precipice. His tearful report of the accident was convincing.

The success of this mission cemented Histaves' credentials. Soon thereafter Histaves was inducted into the Argentinean Secret Service. The black marks of his past were forgotten…

…Histaves' mind returned to the present sixteen years later when he arrived at the Aerospace Museum. He nodded at Lieutenant Fernando who was standing at the entrance.

"Am I clear?" Histaves asked.

"*Si, Senor*. No one is following you."

Histaves nodded again and began walking up the museum stairs.

The aircraft carrier model displayed in the Aerospace museum always awed Histaves. The power it represented, even though a model, could only be dreamed about in Argentina. His country's impotence was a constant frustration for Histaves and fed his determination to succeed in his current mission. He glanced around the exhibit, looking for the senator.

Histaves' self-important congressional friend arrived twenty minutes late. He didn't bother to apologize for his tardiness. Instead, he launched into a tirade.

"Rico," he said, "The news is not good. We underestimated Admiral Collins. Information I received today indicates that he has a file documenting his Remington investigation. We think he may have names. It could bring us down. I thought you said you had gotten all the copies. The only reason we cooperated was because you said you would destroy them."

"Senator, please." Histaves responded. "The truth is that, had you not cooperated, I would have exposed you and all the others. Remember, I also have names and circumstances. Now lower your voice and tell me about the files that you think are so important."

"Come on. You know what I'm talking about. We took a lot of time and trouble to locate the originals. And, it cost an extraordinary amount of money. Who would have thought that Collins would retain a personal copy? It also appears he's shown the file to subordinates to begin a follow up investigation. God, this is a disaster!"

"Take it easy. We'll just have to figure out a way to get those files. And, we can also insure his silence."

"Oh, great! You're talking about killing him aren't you?" the senator asked. "My God, aren't there enough dead people? Scientists, the military liaison officer…when does it stop?"

"Senator, get a grip! People are starting to stare." Looking around for Lieutenant Fernando, Histaves thought, *...if this fool doesn't calm down...dead man walking...*

The senator wouldn't be deterred. "If we'd known what you'd planned, we would never have cooperated. Even with your threats of blackmail, we should have taken our chances."

"Oh, please. Let's not get righteous. You knew there would be circumstances of this nature. And, *you* told *me* that Admiral Collins had informed you that he was planning to further investigate the Remington affair."

Histaves paused to take a breath and continued, "If I remember correctly, at the time, you and your group were more interested in protecting your combined ass.

"My patience is wearing thin with your little histrionics - we don't need panic attacks." Histaves' eyes narrowed and a distinct edge came into his voice.

Color drained from the senator's face, and beads of sweat formed on his upper lip as he realized that his life was being threatened.

Seeing the intended fear begin to take hold, Histaves switched gears. "Come. Let's take a walk. We could both use some fresh air."

Histaves took the senator's arm and guided him downstairs and out the front door of the museum. As they crossed the street and headed toward the mall, Histaves asked, "Now tell me. What have you learned? Where are the files?"

The senator took a deep breath of the crisp January air. It was cold, but the sun was out for a change, and it was comfortable walking. Histaves watched the calming effect.

"Okay," the senator started, "From my information, the admiral gave the file to an Army general named Tom O'Shane and directed him to form a task force to lead the investigation. So far, O'Shane has kept the file in his briefcase."

"OK. That's good," replied Histaves. "How long has this 'O'Shane' had it?"

"Since he first reported to the Pentagon. That was in late November. We had the surveillance equipment up and running when he moved into his offices after Thanksgiving."

"Are there any other files or notes that you know of?"

"We overheard O'Shane referring to a personal journal he keeps at home. We're unsure if there is incriminating information in it. If possible, we need to get our hands on that journal."

"Alright. What about other staff involvement?"

"As far as staff is concerned, we believe only one of those would be included in any substantive discussion – a Commander Frisk. Collins assigned him to the task force at the start."

The senator handed Histaves an envelope. "Here's a biography and some details about him. He's an experienced investigator who could be a thorn in our side.

"O'Shane also has three administrative staff that includes a Navy petty officer, an Army sergeant, and a civilian secretary. We don't believe he's shared anything of importance with this office staff."

"Good. It seems you have done your homework," Histaves said. "This should be adequate. We will put this to rest. Go home and relax."

The senator had calmed, and seemed reassured by Histaves' positive demeanor. Histaves shook his hand, and watched as the senator walked toward the Capital Building.

Histaves was satisfied that he had defused the situation for the present. He headed back to Embassy Row. He decided to walk again to give himself more time to think.

He called Fernando within minutes of arrival at the embassy office. "Esteban," he said once they were secure, "I will need you to develop a plan for neutralizing a man named General Tom O'Shane. It also appears as if we need to arrange for the admiral's demise. Come by my office in the morning and we will flesh out the planning."

The lieutenant responded, "*Si, Coronel.* Anything else?"

"There is also a Commander Adam Frisk," Histaves continued. "He is in Redstone Arsenal in Alabama at this time. You will need to find him. I may have more instructions in a few days."

"We can do that," Fernando answered, "It will require some adjustments to our plans, but it should not be difficult. I will see you in the morning." They hung up and Histaves began to relax.

His peace was short lived. Kandi buzzed him on the intercom. "Colonel Histaves," she said in her irritating twang, "there are three men here to see you." Without waiting, Kandi showed the men into his office.

He jumped to his feet when he recognized Flaveo Fernando.

Histaves stuttered, "Minister, I did not know you were coming. I apologize for not meeting you. I'm truly sor…"

The Argentinean Defense Minister held up his hand, "Rico, relax. No one knows I am here, not even the ambassador. I came by private plane and will be leaving the same way in a few hours. I came here because I wanted to introduce you to these two men.

"Their organizations have been helping us financially and are advising us in some important areas. I want you to give them your full cooperation on the project you are working on. Do you understand?"

…What choice do I have…? Was Histaves' thought. But, he answered, "*Si, Senor. Comprendo.*"

"Good, good," said the minister. He then introduced his two companions starting with a very dark-skinned man. "This is Commander Jorge Garcia. He is with an organization in Peru that you may have heard about. It's called the Shining Path.

"We will be providing them some of the early production weapons and ammunition. Jorge will be observing your operation and providing assistance where necessary."

"Of course," responded Histaves. He offered to shake the man's hand saying, "Nice meeting you." The man stared at Histaves without speaking or moving.

Ignoring Garcia's rude behavior, Minister Fernando introduced the other man, "This is Dr. Achmad Mohammad Ami. He is a senior member of the al-Qaida in the U.S. His organization has been very generous.

"You are to turn over to him some of the prototype weapons when he requests. He, too, will remain in the locale. Do you have any questions?"

Histaves shook his head. "*No, Senor*."

"Then I'll leave you to it," replied the minister, "*Adios*, for now. Meet me at the private plane jet way at the Reagan airport in two hours. I'd like to review our plans." With that he walked out the office door and closed it behind him.

As the door closed, Dr. Ami moved to within inches of Histaves' face. Spittle sprayed as he spoke. "Colonel, I am not impressed with this organization or the operation of your Secret Police. You are poorly trained and incompetent.

"From this point on I will be watching everything your do. If it even smells like you are bungling this operation, I will step in and take it over. I have a cell of operatives here in Washington D.C. prepared to activate on a moment's notice. You will be the first one eliminated. Am I clear?"

Histaves was not accustomed to being addressed in this manner. He said, "I thought we were working together?

I've got this project under control. There's no point in being rude or making threats."

As he spoke he moved away from Ami and around his desk. He reached inside a drawer to grab the pistol he kept there. Before he could pull it out, the drawer was slammed on his hand. "Aarggh!" he yelped in pain.

Garcia jammed a silenced pistol in Histaves' open mouth. "You even breathe in the next sixty seconds, and I will kill you now," Garcia hissed in his ear.

Histaves held his breath while Dr. Ami continued with his instructions as if nothing had happened. "You will call me if anything abnormal occurs in your operation. Do we understand one another?" Histaves nodded.

Ami continued, "Good. Here is my phone number. Memorize it and burn the paper. Call me anytime." He placed a piece of paper on Histaves' desk, and walked out of the room. Garcia followed.

Histaves rubbed his sore wrist and stared after the two men, his fury building. *...They're a couple of lunatics...it will be a pleasure to kill them both...incompetent, huh...? We'll see about that...*

Nonetheless, he put the piece of paper into his wallet.

His thoughts turned to a more interesting diversion. *...Still have half an hour before leaving for airport...what's Kandi doing...?* The familiar, pleasant stirring recurred. *...Hmmm...*

"Kandi," he called, "Could you come in here? I have some dictation I want to give you." That was their personal code for what he had in mind. She could barely type on her computer. Dictation was out of the question. She came into the office, closed the door, and locked it.

Chapter Nine

Knight Takes Bishop

The morning after Jenny's firefight in Korea was the most exhilarating of her career. Right at the start of visiting hours, 'C' Company soldiers crowded into her hospital room. Each had to shake her hand, and she got lots of hugs.

"Ma'am, you were totally awesome!" was the consensus comment. She must have blushed twenty times at words like bravery and fearlessness.

...No hero, for Christ's sake...just doing my job...! This is embarrassing...

Exhausted after her room cleared out, Jenny crashed and didn't wake up until Corporal Thomas came in and began what was a terrible afternoon.

Jenny could see on Thomas' face that he wasn't there for a social call. *...What the hell's eating him...? I've never seen him so mad...almost sputtering...*

He said, "Afternoon, Ma'am. Hope you're feeling better." He started to put away some of the clothes and personal things she'd asked for. He was slamming drawers and doors.

...What...? Is he pissed at me...? She had to ask. "Thomas, what's the problem?"

"Cap'n," he said, his lips forming a thin line. "You won't believe this, but Agburg's writing you a letter of reprimand. He's citing you for endangering your soldiers, for conduct unbecoming an officer, and, for disrespect to a superior officer."

"He's doing what?"

"You heard me, Ma'am. I mean…it's not right what he's done. And, he's the one that started yelling in front of everyone. This sucks! Excuse me, but he's an asshole!"

Thomas paused for a beat as Jenny fumed. He then got a sheepish look on his face. "Cap'n, I have a confession to make. This is interfering in your business, and I know you won't like it, but I e-mailed that Sergeant Major friend of yours."

Seeing her eyes begin to flash, Thomas quickly followed with, "Cap'n, Sergeant Major Cavanaugh told me when he visited that I could e-mail him anytime with a question; and if I ever needed anything, to send him a message. Sorry…"

Her mind seethed. *…Calm down Jennifer…Thomas did nothing wrong…just your pride of independence being offended…you're being silly…really sweet of him to care…*

Taking a deep breath, she assured him, "It's alright, Thomas. You did fine. You go on back to work. It'll sort out. Thanks for the heads up."

To herself she muttered, "That lunatic writes me a reprimand, it'll kill my career. I'll have to write an appeal to the brigade commander. What a mess!"

…Returning to her office after convalescing, she found a note to report to battalion headquarters. Thomas drove her over in silence. They both dreaded what was coming.

Arriving at the headquarters building, Thomas pointed towards the parking area. "Cap'n that's the brigade commander's vehicle. We haven't seen Colonel Pitman since the battalion's change of command. Wonder what he's doing here."

"I think we both know," she responded.

Girding herself for the expected fireworks, Jenny headed into the building.

The brigade command sergeant major, Corky Stephens, was just coming out of Agburg's office as

Jenny walked into the headquarters. In his loud, booming voice, with the walls seeming to reverberate, he said, "Captain O'Shane, let me shake your hand, Ma'am. You are a hero, and I'm proud to know and serve in the same unit as you. Well done!"

"Thanks, Sergeant Major." She glanced toward Agburg's door. "Too bad everyone doesn't think so."

"Cap'n, I don't think things are gonna' go the way you expected this morning."

"Sorry, I don't understand."

"Ma'am, I had an interesting phone conversation with Jim Cavanaugh yesterday. He's a friend that I have a lot of respect for. So does the brigade commander. You couldn't do better."

Stephens grinned and added, "I think Colonel Pitman will explain. He's waiting to see you in Agburg's office."

Jenny must have looked as stunned as she felt because Colonel Pitman chuckled out loud when he saw her. "Come on in, O'Shane. I don't bite."

Her cheeks flushed and she said, "Sir, I don't know what to say…"

"You don't have to say anything. I just wanted to tell you personally that I think you did a fantastic job at that crossroads."

Pitman let that sink in and then added, "I read the reports. Your actions saved the lives of those soldiers and I intend to write you a special performance evaluation and recommend you for a valor medal. Congratulations."

"Uhhh, Sir, I don't really think…"

Ignoring her protests, Pitman changed subjects. "O'Shane, tell me what's going on with the battalion's female solders. What's happening?"

She felt unsettled as she detailed the circumstances. It was awkward, and she sensed Pitman was somehow judging her based on her response. She sighed with relief when the meeting ended.

Pitman was as good as his word. In his report he wrote, "…on multiple occasions O'Shane demonstrated selfless service by placing the well-being of her soldiers over her own." In several places in the narrative he recommended, "…promote this officer now!"

...Fat chance... she thought.

Her days in Korea from then on were a whirl. Pitman made immediate changes. "I want you at brigade headquarters," he told Jenny. "I know it's only for two months, but I need someone around who's not afraid of their own shadow."

He also relieved Agburg from battalion command. Not pleasant, but fitting.

Jenny e-mailed Jim Cavanaugh, explaining what had happened. "I can't thank you enough," she said in her message. "It looked like certain disaster. Once more, I owe you big time!"

Two months later, Pitman's helicopter was taking her to Seoul. She was a new major and had thirty days of leave before reporting to her next assignment at MacDill Air Force Base in Tampa, Florida.

Her plans were to spend a week at Fort Hood visiting her dad and Jim Cavanaugh. Then she wanted to go to D.C. to see her older brother, a civilian medical doctor. They always had a lot of fun together. After D.C., she planned to go to MacDill and scope out her new home.

Jenny recalled her discussion with her assignment officer at the Army Military Personnel Center (MILPERCEN).

"You'll be on detail to the Commander of Central Command (CENTCOM)," he'd said.

"Hmm. That sounds different," she'd responded.

He'd explained, "It is different. But, after 9/11, the CENTCOM commander asked for and received special permission to have an Army MP security detachment." He asked, "You're familiar with CENTCOM, right?"

"Yes, Sir. CENTCOM is responsible for all U.S. military activities in the Middle East. But, what's with the additional security?"

"Because MacDill is ripe for a terrorist attack," the major answered. "There are four multi-service commands headquartered on the base that you'll help protect. The Air Police are hard-pressed.

"Doesn't the Air Force take exception to the Army's presence? It seems like they'd have major heartburn."

"That high school rivalry stuff went away since 9/11," he'd answered. "We're partners in a war now, and the Army is helping fill in for our Air Force brethren."

...You hope the rivalries went away... she'd thought in silence.

The assignment officer wished her good luck, and gave her the phone number for her future boss.

Jenny enjoyed talking with her new commander. "Welcome to the 509th Airborne Military Police Battalion,' said Lieutenant Colonel Ed Cox. "I look forward to meeting you. Colonel Pitman had high praise."

She'd responded, "Sir, I think he exaggerates a bit." She then explained her leave plans. "I'd planned to see you the second week in November. Will that be alright?"

"Sounds fine. Get down here as soon as possible. I need to get back to Bragg. I only came down until I could assign an acting commander for the detachment. I thought you'd like that job. What do you think?" She couldn't get the word yes out fast enough.

Her mind was racing. *...This is plum...in charge of two companies of MP's and a dog platoon...Hot damn...!*

She could have walked on the clouds to get to MacDill!

Chapter Ten

Bishop Challenged

The voice purred, but an undertone of menace was evident. “You will be ready, won’t you, Rico?” Minister Fernando asked Histaves as they stood in the main corridor of the Reagan airport. “Rescheduling transport aircraft will be difficult.”

“We’ll be ready,” Histaves was quick to answer. “I see nothing to interfere at this moment.”

“Good…good. The drawings and prototype of the steerable munitions are what we want on the first load.”

“That is our plan, *Senor*.” Histaves answered. He squirmed; irritated at himself because he couldn’t help but sweat whenever he was around El Toro.

“*Excellente*. I’ll be speaking with you soon.” They shook hands, Histaves self-conscious at his sweaty palm.

Fernando headed down the jet way. At that instant, a woman stepped between them, hurrying down the corridor. The edge of luggage she was pulling caught Fernando’s pant leg and tore the material.

…Oh shit… thought Histaves.

The woman said, “I beg your pardon. I’m so sorry. That was my fault. Please allow me to have your trousers repaired for you. I sincerely apologize. *Please* call me when it’s convenient and I’ll pick them up.” She handed Fernando a business card and started to walk away.

“Wait a minute, young lady,” Fernando said. Histaves could see the vein on Fernando’s forehead beginning to throb. For those who knew him, it was a dangerous sign.

With disdain, Fernando threw the card into a trash receptacle. “Don’t you think that this deserves more than a simple apology? You were rude, and your bag ripped an expensive pair of trousers.”

"I said I was sorry," the woman answered. "There's not much more I can do in the middle of an airport."

"Yes, there is," responded Fernando, a flush creeping up his neck. "You could start by acting more respectful. You're not much more than a child, and a female at that. Where are your manners?

"Besides, that bag is way to big for someone so small. Why don't you have a luggage handler carry it? What is your name?"

"My name is Jennifer O'Shane. It's on the card you threw away. I said I was sorry. That's about all your going to get.

"You two were standing in the center of the aisle, and I needed to get through. Again, I'm sorry. I'll get your pants fixed, or buy you a new pair. I apologize for any inconvenience." She turned to leave.

Fernando put a hand on her shoulder as if to stop her. She pushed his hand away. "Don't touch me," she said. She was unafraid, and stood up to the much bigger man without flinching.

Fernando then started to do what would be natural for him in Argentina. He swung a backhand at the woman. She ducked under his swing and punched her extended fingers into his solar plexus.

"Huumph!" Fernando gasped as he collapsed, breathless onto the nearest airport seat.

Histaves stepped between the two and started to push the woman away.

She stomped on his toes with the heel of her shoe. It was excruciating and, for the second time that day, Histaves yelped in pain.

The woman backed away and melted into the crowd. Limping, favoring his bruised foot, there was no way Histaves could follow.

He was embarrassed to be humbled in public by the tiny female. Fernando was even more furious. "I want that woman killed," he said, the vein on his forehead now in prominent display.

Only with a promise to see to the woman's painful demise was Histaves able to get Fernando on his airplane. For a moment, he thought the minister would cause an international incident.

Unfortunately, when Histaves returned from the plane's stairway, the trash receptacle had been emptied by airport maintenance. *...Great...! What was her name...? ...Where's maintenance man...? Going to have to search entire trash collection...*

Histaves soon realized that he was wasting time. He finally decided, *...just as well didn't find her...minimize distractions...Fernando will soon forget...foot feeling better...a little bruising...let it go...home...* His mind returned to more pressing matters…

…Much later that night, his bedside phone woke him. He glanced at the clock. …*Madre de Dios...2:00 am...*

The ring was on his private line. …*Who could be calling at this hour…Fernando*…? Histaves answered, "*Hola*?"

"Rico, is that you?" His congressional friend asked.

"Senator," Histaves answered, "what in God's name are you doing bothering me at this hour? Have you lost your mind?"

"I've just been relayed some vital information that can't wait. You'll want to hear this," said the senator. "It's about that Commander Frisk. He's uncovered some information at Redstone Arsenal and had it sent on a computer disc to O'Shane.

"I think O'Shane will keep the disc with him, at least for a while. I thought you should know. Got to go." With that the senator disconnected.

Histaves was now wide-awake. The senator was correct. Redstone was where the Smith & Wesson prototype weapons had been stolen. If Frisk had somehow uncovered critical information and it became known, Histaves' entire plan could fall apart.

...Frisk needs to be stopped, and we must get that disc... He dressed and went back to his office. He phoned Lieutenant Fernando on the secure line.

"*Teniente*," he began, "we have a slight change of plans. I need you to deal with a Commander Frisk right away. Come by my office in the morning for details."

"Very well, *mi Coronel*." He then asked, "What about the admiral and general?"

"Even with the Americans you hired, we don't have enough manpower to deal with those two and get the shipment ready. I have another plan for those assignments. You need to deal with Frisk."

After hanging up his receiver, Histaves retrieved a small piece of paper from his wallet. *...Well, they wanted to play... let's see what they can do...* As much as it irked him, he clenched his jaw and dialed the phone number Dr. Ami had given him.

Chapter Eleven

White Rook Lost

In January, the Pentagon looked like a prison from the outside. Trees surrounding the building were denuded of leaves. Acres of blacktop covered the grounds – it was stark.

Walking toward VIP parking, Lieutenant General Tom O'Shane tried to shake off the gloom that the wintry sight caused him. Instead, his mood darkened further as he reflected on a meeting he'd hosted that afternoon. It was a disaster.

He thought, *...my involvement in the meeting still strange...but, Vice-Chair specific...*

General Grantley had told him, "I want you there, Tom. It's time you got you feet wet among the power brokers."

"What's the meeting about, Sir? Do I know these guys?"

"You probably don't know them. But, the CEO of Smith & Wesson and a couple of his operations people will be there. They think that the military owes them money."

"I don't know anything about a S & W contract..."

"Exactly. That way, they won't be trying to work an angle on you. Trust me, it'll be for the best. Don't make any promises."

"Sir, I feel like I'm being sent into a tiger cage with no whip or chair. What's going on?" Tom was sure that General Horace Grantley knew more than he was saying. As the Vice Chairman of the Joint Chiefs of Staff, he had his fingers into everything.

"Just let them vent. There's no money and no contract with Smith & Wesson. As you know, Congress takes a dim view of the military paying a vendor without an approved contract."

With a wave of his hand, Grantley changed the subject and asked. "By the way, how's your daughter? Still in Korea?"

"No, Sir. She's working at CENTCOM. Been there a couple of months now. I got to see her before I left Fort Hood."

"Good. I'm sure you're proud of her. She's done well. Come and see me after your meeting."

Tom knew when he was being dismissed. He replied with the requisite, "Yes, Sir." He was thinking, *...Nice of Grantley to ask about Jenny...but he thinks I'm overpaid and under worked...that's why this stupid assignment...*

The meeting went as Tom expected. The CEO was hostile from the moment they shook hands. "Who the hell are you?" he'd asked. "I requested a meeting with senior military brass and I get a brand new lieutenant general. Is this a joke?"

"No, Sir," Tom answered. "This isn't a joke. I'm representing the Vice Chairman."

The CEO blew up, "You don't even know the kind of weapons…You've gotta' be kidding... Prototype weapons and plans are missing. The Smith & Wesson research facility was burned to the ground. And, two of our leading scientists were killed. Millions in research equipment was lost.

"We're talking possible bankruptcy. I've had assurances from you military guys. This stuff was made to your specifications. This is insulting. You'll hear from our attorneys." He stormed out of the conference room, followed by his deputies.

After that encounter, Tom mused, *...Vice-Chair...wanted me to hear that...strange...better alert Admiral Collins that Grantley's on a warpath...needs to* *hear about Smith & Wesson anyway...inform Grantley of results after speaking to Collins...*

As Tom entered I-395 heading toward Springfield and home, he punched autodial on his cell phone. The admiral's aide answered, "Chairman Collins' quarters, Colonel Pitman speaking."

Tom said, "Hi, Allen. This is General O'Shane. Is Admiral Collins in?"

"Yes, Sir. He's here," Pitman responded. "But, he's just sitting down to dinner, and he has guests. Can he call you back?"

Tom knew the answer to that question. "Sure, Allen," he responded. "Ask him to call me at home. I'll be there in thirty minutes."

He'd thought, *...probably some bigwig dinner...guy's connected...* Three different presidents in both political parties had selected Collins for senior positions. Now he was appointed as the Chairman of the Joint Chiefs of Staff.

Admiral Collins was one of the rare military officers extended on active duty past thirty-five years – extensions that occurred only by personal order of the president.

He was a trim looking, gray-haired man with a reputation for being crusty and intolerant with any level of incompetence.

Given that reputation, Tom was a little surprised when he'd reported into his job. The admiral had greeted him in the outer offices, shaking his hand with enthusiasm.

"Hi. You must be Tom O'Shane," he'd said. "I'm Sam Collins. Welcome aboard." The handgrip was firm, and a pair of intelligent eyes focused on Tom. The admiral vibrated with energy and spoke in a stream-of-conscious, nonstop barrage.

Starting toward his office doorway, Collins changed direction in mid-stride. "No. Wait a minute," he'd said.

"First, let me introduce you to Colonel Allen Pitman. I picked him two months ago to be my military aide. I think he knows your daughter. You need anything, he'll get it for you. Right, Allen?"

Not pausing, the admiral pulled Tom into the inner office.

"Coffee?" Admiral Collins asked before Tom had cleared the office doorway. Without waiting for an answer, the admiral poured coffee into two cups already set up on an end table. He asked, "How do you like it?"

Again, leaving no opening for a response, he'd put cream and sugar in one of the cups and handed it to Tom. "Nobody really likes it plain," he'd said. "Here, have a seat. No, don't sit there…that couch is terrible. Use this seat. There now, comfortable?"

Pausing for a breath, he continued his verbal barrage, "How do you like the Pentagon? Guess it'll always be a maze. When were you here last? Two years ago, wasn't it? Not much change. Nothing here changes. Well, anyway, do you know why you're here?"

Tom answered, "I thought…"

"Don't bother answering," Collins interrupted, "You don't know. It's not that drug cartel thing we told the press. It's worse. I know that's got to be hard to believe.

"My apologies for carrying on," the admiral continued after another short breath. "You probably decided I'm a nut by now. I don't blame you. I get like this when I'm really fired up. This is one of those times. Stay seated for a minute, and I'll get something I want you to read."

He jumped up and hurried to the office door, yanking it open. "Catherine," he yelled, "where's that damn folder I asked for?"

Tom heard a female voice answer, "It's on your desk, Sir." Her answer was followed by, "Please stop yelling, Admiral. I'm right here. You're in one of your moods again. Do I have to call your wife?"

Tom heard the admiral answer over light laughter in the outer offices, "Now Catherine, don't get your skirt all a-flutter."

Chuckling, the admiral closed the door, retrieved an envelope from his desk, and gave it to Tom, saying, "Read this when you get back to your office." The envelope was sealed and marked Top Secret. It was covered with black and red lines indicating compartmentalized material.

Puzzled, Tom asked, "Admiral, am I cleared for this? It looks like this is a special classification."

The admiral sat down again. He said, "Don't worry, your new security clearance was approved yesterday."

Collins paused once more. He gave a quick nod of his head as if making a final decision, and then said, "Tom, you need to know right off, this new job isn't a major field command. I know that's what you were hoping for when you first heard the big task force title. I apologize for the subterfuge. You'll understand in a minute.

"The truth is, I need you to supervise an investigation. This is a similar job to what you did in Greenland ten years ago for John Doakes when he was Deputy Ambassador to the United Nations. He recommended you. Now that he's the Secretary of Defense, his word carries a lot of weight."

Collins allowed Tom to absorb that information and then added, "I also asked for you for a couple of other reasons that are just as important to me."

The admiral had held up four fingers and ticked off, "Because you have a reputation of being super smart, you know how to keep your mouth shut, you're experienced in the Pentagon, and I need a good person from another military service so I don't look like I'm trying to provide cover for the Navy."

Admiral Collins paused again, watching Tom's expression. His reaction must have been reflected on his face because the Admiral put up his hand and said, "That's not all. Let me clear the air all the way -- I know I asked you to leave your division command early, and you're probably pissed that the so-called 'task force' isn't a troop command. But, I have other news to help make it less painful."

Collins took another breath, then continued, "Tom, I asked the Secretary of the Army and the Army Chief of Staff to place you in one of their Lieutenant General billets. We had to do a little horse-trading with the other services to make it happen, but a promotion for you was approved yesterday.

"Of course, Congress will need to make it official, but that's a mere formality in your case. The promotion's a little early, I know. However, the Army leadership agreed with me -- you've earned it. And, you'd be promoted in a couple of years anyhow. Congratulations."

Tom was flabbergasted. He'd been a major general only one year. He managed to say, "Thank you, Sir..." before the admiral pressed on.

"Don't get a big head. You're good, very good. But, again I have ulterior motives. First of all, if you're not at least a lieutenant general around here, people won't give you the time of day.

"Secondly, you'll be butting heads with the pricks running the investigative agencies of the Navy, Army and Air Force. They're all lieutenant generals, or equivalent grade level, and most would give you a hard time if you aren't on equal footing."

The admiral paused another beat and then continued. "As a lieutenant general there's only five people who have a final say in your future assignments and promotions. I'm one of them, and my vote is seldom overridden. That will give you the freedom to tell almost all comers to shove it if they become a problem."

The admiral went silent again to allow his explanations to register. His eyes narrowed. "The situation is this…I'm convinced of a conspiracy over fifteen years ago that involved murder, bribery, and blackmail. Our country lost billions of dollars in international arms contracts. I think that military leaders played a key role in the conspiracy, and I intend for the military to uncover the scheme. That's where you come in."

Tom's mind whirled. *…Whoa…! This is incredible…!*

Admiral Collins continued, "Your job will be to supervise an undercover investigation, find out who was responsible, and bring them to justice.

"Even though this isn't the task force organization you probably envisioned, this is just as important. There's a cancer in our country's leadership, and it needs to be excised."

Admiral Collins was silent for a second. He then added, "The reports in that file I gave you were written when I was assigned to NCIS as a junior officer. My findings were circumstantial, but they were more than enough to raise suspicions.

"Two days after I wrote a recommendation to the Director of NCIS to elevate the investigation, I was ordered to shut it down. That reaction didn't ring true.

"My suspicions were confirmed when I discovered that reports I'd written had disappeared from the Pentagon's military archives. Someone's been fiddling the records."

"What the culprits probably didn't count on was that I would keep copies of my letters and reports for my personal files. You have those copies, and I want you to get to the bottom of this…"

Tom's investigative instincts kicked in. When the admiral paused, Tom asked, "Why an undercover, black operation?"

"It's the same reason that I'm not using NCIS, CID, or FBI. I'm not positive who's involved in the conspiracy.

But, I'm convinced that, as soon as those responsible get wind of what I'm doing, they'll hide too deep to find and/or eliminate leads and people who could identify the players. Only a select group of the country's leadership was informed of this operation. By restricting who does what, I intend to reduce the risks of early exposure."

Admiral Collins let Tom ponder what he'd heard and then asked. "Will you help me on this, Tom?"

Tom thought, *...damn...not a major command...! But...if this stuff is true...need to bust these guys...can retire afterwards...wearing three stars...cool...!*

Instead of answering the question, Tom said, "I'd like to bring CSM Jim Cavanaugh with me. He was a CID investigator in an earlier life."

A grin lit up the admiral's face. He had his answer. He responded, "We can arrange that. I've also assigned two people, Commander AD Frisk and Petty Officer Andy Cohen. AD is an experienced NCIS investigator who helped me in Hawaii. He's a tough nut, and you'll like him. Andy is an administrative genius that can cut through the Pentagon's bureaucratic maze.

"Additionally, I've instructed each military service to recommend names to you to work on the team. Personnel files for the nominees are in your new office. Colonel Pitman can show you where that is." The admiral stood and extended his hand. "Again, welcome aboard, Tom..."

...Two months later, heading home in a snowstorm, Tom was frustrated. It irked him that he could only report limited progress to Collins.

He accelerated out of the Pentagon parking area, his back tires slipping as he entered the access road. Falling snow had begun to build up. He muttered to himself, "Wonder what the highway will be like. God, I hope there's not another pile up like last year..." His mind drifted again...

...Glad Cavanaugh had me put Collins' file and disc copy in safe...carried file around too long...Wonder how admiral convinced SECDEF to pursue high-powered investigation...Those reports only circumstantial...must be something else...

In that instant, his mind connected some dots. Out loud, he exclaimed, "How could I be so dense? The Smith & Wesson story is almost identical with the reports about Remington!"

He thought, *...wait a minute...bet Collins already knew about Smith & Wesson...wanted me to host the meeting...hear the story first hand...told Grantley to set it up...this is getting twisted...*

He became anxious to get home and check the computer disc that Frisk had sent him. The Navy investigator had been excited on the phone. "It looks like access codes for the S & W equipment storage areas. I haven't fully deciphered it as yet. I'll get on it as soon as I return from the Virgin Islands. Sorry to run out on you."

"No sweat. Enjoy yourself," Tom had answered. He'd almost told AD to forget about the vacation. But, the guy deserved a few days. Now, Tom regretted his decision. AD was in a St Thomas hospital recovering from a scuba accident. *...Damn...bad luck...*

He began to focus on his driving and started watching for the exit signs. *...Not much farther...visibility bad...snowing harder...*

He watched an oversized pickup swerve through the traffic lanes. *...Crazy asshole...in this weather...*

A fuel tanker had changed lanes twice to avoid the guy. It looked as if the pickup was trying to herd the tanker off the road. Tom slowed down. The tanker driver maneuvered into the right lane to avoid the smaller truck. A bright flash occurred on the berm beside the big truck.

In that instant Tom's mind recorded, *...Holy shit...explosion...looked like improvised explosive device...what the hell...?*

The chain reaction on the highway was predictable. The tanker driver swerved, and the trailer began skidding across two lanes.

A car slid under the trailer wheels. The trailer flipped on its side and careened down the highway.

Sparks flew; fuel spilled, and then an explosion. The fireball was huge. Tom felt the heat through the windshield as he fought to keep out of harm's way.

He had no chance. The car on his right and the one behind him lost control. In split seconds, they crashed into his Camry from two directions.

In lockstep, all three cars skidded toward the ball of fire. They slid to a stop on the fringe of the flames.

Groggy and stunned, he scrambled to get out of his car. The doors were jammed but the side windows were shattered.

He released his seat belt, and pushed the air bag out of his way. He intended to squeeze through the driver's window. The heat was intense.

In the melee, no one noticed a dark blue SUV pull onto the median from the northbound lanes. Almost as an apparition, three men leapt from the truck, each running toward one of the interlocked vehicles.

The men carried what looked like tools. One of them reached into Tom's Camry. Tom had only a second to look over as the man leaned through the window on the passenger side.

He started to thank the man for helping; then, he saw the silenced pistol; then, a bright flash of light; then, nothing...

The men climbed back into their SUV, and it faded away into the white night. The three entangled cars exploded into flames in a renewed burst of heat.

Chapter Twelve

White Bishop Falls

Watching the steward clean up from the dinner party, Admiral Sam Collins savored a glass of brandy. It had been a successful evening in spite of the worrisome snowstorm outside.

As if reading Sam's mind, Colonel Pitman came into the dining room and said, "Admiral, you give nice dinner parties. I think the SECDEF had a good time and mixed well with Senator Englewood. They got along great."

Collins responded. "Thanks, Allen. I appreciate your help. Doakes needs to be close to Englewood. In his new job, Doakes will need to know and get along with the movers and shakers. Englewood carries a big stick as Chairman of the Senate Armed Services Appropriations Committee. He's been on the hill for over thirty years."

"Yes, Sir," Pitman answered. "Plus he had a three-year stint as the National Security Advisor – he doesn't hesitate to remind us. We both know he's an ass." He and Collins shared a chuckle.

After a short pause, as Pitman helped the steward pick up the last of the dishes, he said, "Admiral, not to change subjects, but General O'Shane called earlier. I told him you'd call him back."

Collins groaned, "It's too late, Allen. I'm bushed. Aren't I scheduled to see him in the morning?"

"Yes, Sir," Pitman responded.

Collins relaxed. "Good, then let's wait."

He knew that Pitman had put in an even longer day.

"Why don't you call it a night, Allen? You're welcome to use one of our guest rooms if you don't want to drive all the way home in this snow."

"Thanks anyway, Sir. I need to get home and feed my dogs. They get cantankerous when I let them go overnight."

"Okay, clear on out then," Collins responded, laughing. Allen's Dobermans were the talk of the office. "You have an hour's drive in this yuck. See you tomorrow."

Pitman paid his respects to Mrs. Collins, and then said to Collins, "Sir, there's nothing urgent in your take-home reading that we can't catch up on in the morning," nodding toward a briefcase in the hallway. "You don't need to push too hard." He was referring to Collins' two heart attacks and an open-heart surgery.

"I'm doing fine. You worry too much," Collins retorted. "Now, get out of here."

Pitman knew when there was no point in arguing. He grabbed his own briefcase and overcoat, and headed to his car.

After seeing Pitman out the door, Collins went searching for his wife. *...These senior officers quarters at Fort McNair are too big for us...* he thought.

"Martha," he finally yelled, "where the hell are you?"

He heard a faint response, "I'm upstairs, Sam. Would you please not yell. You're going to have the MP's knocking on the door again!" Collins laughed, remembering when they'd come charging over thinking something was wrong. *...Hell, wasn't being that loud...*

"Okay, Honey," he answered, "I'm going to lock up down here. Be right up."

He went through his normal ritual of checking all the doors, noticing that the steward had gotten the kitchen cleaned up already. *...Guy was great chef...have to ask officer's club to send him back next time...*

Going upstairs, Collins reached the master suite just as Martha was undressing. She'd already taken off her make up, jewelry and dress. He marveled at how well she'd kept herself.

"You still look great after all these years," he said, walking up behind her as she slipped out of her bra. Briefly admiring her nude figure in the dresser mirror, he turned her and gave her a light kiss on the lips. "How about fooling around with an old man?" he asked.

She responded by leaning into him. "That sounds like the best idea tonight," Martha said. Giving him a lingering kiss, she added, "Why don't you get that stuffy suit off and I'll take a quick shower." After a light caress of his crotch, she did an erotic walk into the bath.

He started undressing, singing "Gonna get lucky tonight," in his horrible baritone.

Over the sound of the shower he heard her critique, "You better knock that stuff off, or you'll be sleeping downstairs."

Just as he was taking off his shorts, Collins heard a faint noise. Turning toward the sound, he saw a man in a balaclava holding a silenced pistol.

"Admiral," the man whispered, "I don't want to hurt your wife. If you do as I say, I'll not harm her."

Collins could hear the shower water and his wife's light singing. He said, "We don't have any money or jewels to speak of. My wallet is on the dresser."

"I don't want your money. Move over to the bed," the man ordered.

Naked and unarmed, Collins had no choice. He turned to go to the bed. He felt something pressed against his head. An electric jolt convulsed his body. He fell to the floor, helpless.

The intruder had placed a taser against Collins' head, high in his hair. After he'd fallen, the man picked up Collins' inert form and laid him on the bed. He then inserted a small hypodermic in the side of Collins' eye socket and pushed the plunger.

Collins was roused by the painful prick of the needle and turned his head. He saw a small hypodermic being pulled away from his face…a pistol…the man in black.

At the same instant, he felt an intense pain, a vise gripping his heart. He tried to cry out, but no noise would come. Then, fading…nothing…

Commander Jorge Garcia waited a moment and then checked the admiral's pulse. *...Gone...the poison dart frog solution...perfect...*

Garcia heard the shower water go off. He turned and walked out of the room, pulling on a set of night vision goggles.

He left the house through the back door, silent and undetected. Dodging the MP patrol, Garcia found his way to a padlocked gate on the perimeter of the post. He'd cut the lock on the way in.

Opening the gate, he followed a little used path that led to a tiny harbor where a skiff floated. He climbed in and started an electric motor. Checking a hand-held GPS, Garcia made his way into the snowstorm and open water.

Not more than five hundred meters away, in the Collins' quarters, Martha was drying off. She thought, *...Sam still knows how to turn me on...even after thirty years he's still the best...*

"Hey in there, don't start without me," she called. Draping the towel loosely around herself, she sidled into the bedroom. "Sam, did you fall asleep on me? You dog, get up! Sam? Oh my God! Sam…Oh no!"

With his medical history, the prognosis for Sam Collins had not been good for a long time. His doctor had warned that he needed to slow down. Collins had refused. "There's just not enough time," he would always quip, and then keep going full steam.

Given all the appearances of another heart attack, and having lived with the possibility for many years, Martha asked that there not be an autopsy. She couldn't bear the thought. His death was attributed to natural causes and he was buried with full military honors. The president gave a eulogy at the ceremony.

Dignitaries from around the world came to the funeral to pay their respects. It was a beautiful farewell to a great patriot.

Chapter Thirteen

Knight Retreat

On her flight back to Tampa after her dad's funeral, grief consumed Jenny's every thought. The death of the Chairman of the Joint Chiefs registered only on the edge of her awareness.

"Can I get you anything?" the steward asked.

Jenny looked away and shook her head. "Thanks anyway."

The drone of plane engines was normally a sleep potion for her. Not today. Even though exhausted, she couldn't force herself to relax.

Each time she started to nod off, another image of her dad would materialize in her mind: his promotion to general officer, his brigade change of command, and the tears at her mom's funeral. She felt her eyes welling up – the images so sharp.

With a quick shake to clear her head, she recalled the words of her older brother, Tom Jr., "You need time, Sis. Going back to work won't make the pain go away, and it's just going to hurt everyone's feelings. For God's sake, you're authorized seven days. Use it!"

She was sure he was right, but she just couldn't stand another day in D.C. *...Family and friends at every turn...hugs...food...four days...enough already...!*

She felt she needed more space. Even though Cox had said, "Take what time you need..." It was a new job, and she thought she should get back.

Her plan was clear in her mind. *...Soon as we land... cab to apartment...shower... go over to the office...get up to speed...* She also thought she'd try to fit in a visit to the gym. *...Only Tuesday...can still make this a good work out week...*

She was anxious to get started. Nodding off with these more pleasant thoughts, she suddenly jerked awake; tears springing up again with the thought of her dad pinning on her lieutenant's bars at her West Point graduation.

...All right, stop it...! She gave her head another shake.

Looking out the plane's window, she noted the appearance of the Tampa neighborhoods: forming uniform patterns. In a surrealistic vision, she was reminded of the aligned crosses over the graves at the Arlington National Cemetery.

She recalled her mom saying, "I think military burial ceremonies are so beautiful...the honor guards...the symbolic rifle fire...the bittersweet sounds of Taps." But, the ceremony for her dad had been different – it was personal.

When the honor guard officer had handed Jenny the ceremonial flag from the coffin, she had almost lost it. "Ma'am," he'd said, "on behalf of a grateful nation, please accept our deepest sympathy..." It was overwhelming.

She remembered the procession of well-wishers, "He was a good man...such a shame...so very sorry..."

The follow-on reception Saturday afternoon at her dad's house was not as difficult. Being away from the formality of the Mass and the graveside ceremony, she began to feel more herself. Two of her favorite people were present. General Stan Greene and Sergeant Major Jim Cavanaugh wouldn't leave her side.

The general had reminisced about Fort Leavenworth. 'Uncle Stan' and his wife 'Aunt Judy' did not have children of their own. "We sure enjoyed having you kids around," he'd said. "I think we had more fun than you did. Unfortunately, I don't think your T-ball team ever won a game. I wasn't much of a coach."

They all got a big chuckle over the memories. The Greenes had almost adopted the O'Shane clan when her dad was assigned on the faculty of the Command General Staff College at Fort Leavenworth, and General Greene was the Assistant Commandant.

She was really touched when Uncle Stan told her, “Jennifer, I want you to call me if you need anything.” He’d given her his business card, writing his home number on it. He’d said, “I mean it, young lady.”

She’d dutifully responded, “Yes Sir.” But, she couldn’t help smile at the thought. *…How could a lowly major be calling the Chief of Staff of the Army…? Fat chance…*!

Jim Cavanaugh, the second of the twosome, had held forth on her dad as a young officer. Some of the stories were hysterical and Jenny couldn’t help but laugh. “You should have seen him as a lieutenant and captain. He was so straight laced we used to call him Serious Tom.”

Cavanaugh and her dad had served in many of the same units and Army posts as they’d progressed through the ranks. They became unlikely, but fast friends. Cavanaugh was often at the O’Shane house coaching his boss.

As a Command Sergeant Major, Cavanaugh had served in that capacity for her dad when he was a battalion commander in Desert Storm and, most recently, when he commanded the First Cavalry Division at Fort Hood.

She had thought Cavanaugh a little mysterious during the funeral and the days following. At times he was strangely remote. “Jim, what’s going on?” she’d asked.

He’d shrugged his shoulders and responded, “We’ll talk later.” She’d concluded that his behavior was probably his way of coping.

Her reverie on the plane was disrupted when the landing gear bumped into the Tampa International runway.

As the plane rolled toward the terminal, she remembered some of the comments from friends and family. “General O’Shane was a superb leader…a bright future…the best boss I ever had…" These comments and thoughts were a small solace.

The plane braked at the gate, and the passenger door opened. She gathered up her belongings and waited for front passengers to file out. Standing in the aisle, she noticed a magazine someone had left on a seat. It headlined an article about Admiral Samuel Collins. She picked up the magazine and glanced through it.

With a start, she read that the Chairman of the Joint Chiefs of Staff had passed away the same night her dad had been killed in the car accident. *...That's a coincidence...* she thought.

While waiting in line to disembark, she read excerpts of the article. *...A Medal of Honor winner...Vietnam veteran...Navy SEAL...Wow...!* As a SEAL, Collins had been among the military Special Operations' elite. Impressed, but preoccupied, she tossed the magazine back on the seat as the aisle began to clear.

Chapter Fourteen

Knight Uncovered

Jenny's watch read 2:30 p.m. Tuesday afternoon. She was anxious to get back to the office and get busy. Her mind was racing, forming a to do list. The slow pace of the passengers disembarking in front of her was frustrating. *...Doesn't anybody else have someplace to go...?*

In the midst of that thought, she heard a familiar voice calling her name. She looked around, and standing across the aisle was Gary Patten.

She and Gary had begun seeing each other when they were stationed in Korea together. Their relationship was blossoming into something serious. But, she hadn't expected to see him at the airport.

She asked, an unexplainable abruptness in her tone, "What are you doing here? I didn't tell anyone I was coming home today."

"Your brother called. He said you were cutting your time short in D.C. and might need some help."

Annoyed, she headed toward the baggage claim area. Gary caught up to her at the stairway.

She turned to him and said, "If I'd wanted help, I'd have asked for it. Tom is always trying to run my life!"

Almost stamping her foot in frustration at a feeling of interference in what she viewed as her personal affairs, she turned again and started to step onto the escalator.

"Hey, Jenny, don't get mad at me," Gary said moving in front of her. He put his hands on her shoulders and turned her toward him, "Jen, I know that's not what you're really upset about."

He pulled her close to him and said in her ear, "Listen, I'm only the best friend you have here, and I'm the one your big brother thought to call. It was a good thought. For that matter, he and I are both trying to be nice, you know?

"Aww, look. I know you're still totally sick about your dad. Who wouldn't be? I'm really, really sorry. He was a good man."

She felt a crushing sadness return, and deep sobs tore loose, tears streaming. She hugged Gary close to avoid making more of a scene.

Gary continued, "You know I was out of the country or I'd have gone to D.C. with you. If there's anything I can do, please…?"

Wiping her eyes on his shirtsleeve, she tried to choke back her emotions. "I know, I know," she said, "give me a little time. I'm sorry to act like such a bitch. It's just been so overwhelming. Thank you for being here. I'll try to do better."

She broke away and they started down the escalator.

Trying to laugh she said, "My brother really does try to tell me what to do all the time. He's a big busybody. How did he even know your name?"

Handing her his handkerchief, Gary smiled and reminded her, "You remember, when he visited you in Korea, we all had dinner together at the Sum Choyee restaurant in Seoul?"

"Oh yeah. We drank too much of the fake Korean champagne. Boy, did that give me a headache!" They chuckled at the memory.

"Come on," Gary continued when they reached baggage claim, "let's get your bags, and I'll give you a lift home. I have my wheels out front. Let's go before I get a parking ticket."

The baggage claim station for her flight was not crowded. The plane had only been two-thirds full.

She searched for the suitcase containing her dress uniform she had taken for the funeral. She thought she saw it come out of the chute and pointed to it. "I think that's it," she told Gary.

Just then, a man in a dark suit walked up and grabbed the bag off the carousel. At first she didn't think anything of it since so many bags look alike. She started to look for another. Almost as she completed that thought, she remembered, she'd tied a pink piece of yarn to her bag. *...That bag had a piece of pink yarn...!*

She looked in the direction the man had gone. Seeing him as he climbed on a nearby elevator, she yelled, "Hey, Mister, that's my bag!" Turning to Gary, she said, "I think he picked up the wrong bag." The man had ignored her, and by then the elevator doors had closed.

"Let's hurry," Gary said. "I think we can catch him."

"You go ahead," she responded. "I might be wrong, and maybe his bag just looks like mine. I'll wait here and pull off either his or mine, whichever comes out. You just tell him, and you can both meet me here."

"Gotcha," Gary answered. "See you back here." He then took off running to the elevator bank.

Ten minutes later, she watched the luggage carousel grind to a halt. There were no more bags.

"Just great," she fumed to herself. "It'll take hours to fill out the stupid baggage claim forms. Damn, am I hexed or what?"

She hoped Gary had had better luck. *...I'd better wait by the elevators or for sure we'll miss each other...* After ten more minutes, she began to pace. Ten minutes became twenty. She began to worry. *...He's been gone way too long...*

She was bending over the drinking fountain when she overheard two women as they came out of the restroom next to the elevators. They were talking about someone being mugged in the parking garage. "Not even safe in a uniform around here," she heard one of them say.

Just then two Tampa Airport Security Police came running up, and climbed on an elevator. Over the static of their radios, she heard a cryptic message, "Have victim down. Looks like mugging. Victim wearing Air Force uniform." Jenny pushed her way onto the elevator with the policemen.

"Lady," one of cops said, holding the door open, "you can't come up with us just now. Please get off the elevator. We're going to the seventh floor and it's closed to the public for the next few minutes."

She responded, "I heard about the mugging, and I think that the victim may be my friend. I'm a Military Policeman." She flashed her badge. "Please?"

The cop who had stopped her winked and said, "Hey, I used to be an MP." Then into his radio he said, "Lieutenant, we have someone with us who's a relative of the vic, and is also a cop. We're bringing her with us."

After a short pause, Jenny heard a voice crackling on the radio, "OK. Looks like the perp bugged out anyway. Come on up."

The elevator opened on the seventh floor and the police led Jenny around the elevator building to where a uniformed person was sitting up on the floor. What appeared to be a medical technician was bending over him. Getting closer, she saw it was Gary.

"Gary, what the hell is going on?"

He replied, "Think I was mugged. Almost caught up with that guy with your bag. Somebody just slugged me from behind. Got my wallet, too."

She knelt beside him, gave him a hug, and kissed his cheek, "Oh, Honey. Are you all right? I'm so sorry."

"I think so," he answered. "I like this attention, though…"

"Stop it. You have a one track mind!"

One of the cops cleared his throat and said, "Ma'am, would you please see if anything is missing."

She then noticed that her luggage was sitting wide open beside Gary, and her things were strewn on the ground. *...Embarrassing...! Dirty clothes and lingerie...Great...!*

She did an inventory and told them, "It looks like everything's here."

As she started to stuff her clothes back in the bag, the first cop said, "I'm sorry, Ma'am. We'll have to keep that for evidence. We'll get it back to you in a few days."

She sat down next to Gary, and shook her head, "Just great. Welcome home!"

The police lieutenant asked Gary, "Want me to call an ambulance? I'd recommend you get checked out." Gary assured them that he would be fine in a few minutes.

"Would it be all right if we go home?" Gary asked. "We'll come by and provide a statement tomorrow."

The lieutenant answered, "Sure. But you each need to do so." They both nodded in agreement.

Out of professional curiosity, Jenny asked, "Do you have these things happen here often?"

The lieutenant said, "We've had other muggings in the garage, but we've never had perps lure a victim upstairs using stolen luggage as bait. I think I'll station a security officer at baggage claim for awhile to be sure the thugs don't try this scam again."

At that point, Gary stood up, swaying. Jenny asked him if he would be okay.

"Hell yes," Gary said. "I've had worse knocks than this driving my F-15 in rough weather. I'll be fine. Let me walk it off." With one more caution from the lieutenant about getting checked out, she and Gary were released.

"I'm for sure going to have a parking ticket now," grumbled Gary as they headed back to the elevators. "I should never have parked on the curb."

One of the security police walking back with them couldn't help overhear and said, "I'll call down and get it pulled. No problem."

When they exited the airport terminal, a cop had just stopped his three-wheeler beside Gary's car. He scowled while listening on his radio. He then pulled the ticket off the windshield, and broke into a smile, "Hey Colonel, don't take so long next time, huh?'

Gary laughed, "Thanks, Officer. We had a minor problem. It won't happen again." The cop waved him on.

Jenny had to laugh at Gary's comment. *...Minor problem...good Christ, his girlfriend throws an emotional fit in the middle of the airport terminal...someone steals her luggage...and he gets mugged...some minor problem...!* But, at least the airport events had given her some relief from thoughts about her dad.

Chapter Fifteen

White Rook Moves

The harsh florescent lighting glared off the white walls of the basement offices of the Pentagon. As Sergeant Major Jim Cavanaugh walked down the corridor, the click of his heels echoed in the empty hallway.

It was his habit to arrive before the other staff on Mondays, giving him time to get the faxes off the machine, and to distribute any mail that had been dropped off over the weekend. Today he had other motives. He wanted to check the office safe for fingerprints.

On Friday afternoon he'd made a show of putting a computer disc in the main safe. It was a blank, but he'd told everyone in the office, "The general said to lock this puppy up. He thought it might be hot. He took the original with him."

Cavanaugh had actually put the original in the general's personal office safe.

He didn't feel good about a charade, but after General O'Shane's accident the previous Wednesday, Cavanaugh had become paranoid. His senses told him something wasn't right.

When the task force office was being 'stood up,' Cavanaugh had detected an overriding feeling of tension. He'd thought, *...just people learning to work together...* Now he wasn't so sure.

His antenna first went up when General O'Shane told him to secure the disc and not to share the contents with any of the staff, "...until I tell you it's okay..." That was an unusual comment coming from Tom O'Shane, who was seldom secretive with immediate staff.

Cavanaugh had only known the people in the office for a few months, but he and General O'Shane went back over twenty years.

Besides the unexplained sense of tension in the office, Cavanaugh's suspicions were aroused because of the general's briefcase. It was missing.

When he'd asked the Virginia State Troopers if he could retrieve the briefcase from the general's car, he was told that there wasn't one.

"It must have burned up," the trooper said, "that fire was intense. Another car had the remains of a briefcase on the front floor, but not the Camry."

...That's not right... he thought. The general's briefcase had a nice leather cover, but it also had an interior of a special steel alloy. He'd gotten it as a farewell gift. It was a little heavy, but he liked it to carry classified material. *...Should have survived...something's wrong...*

Reflecting on his friend's death reaffirmed his determination. *...Maybe with my little cloak and dagger operation...*

...His plan that morning was simple. He'd brought a fingerprint dusting kit from home that he'd had from his early days in the CID.

To set up the opportunity, he'd wiped the face of the safe clean before leaving Friday night.

If anyone fooled with the safe over the weekend, he was betting they wouldn't clean off their fingerprints.

He applied the fingerprint dust to the face of the safe. *...Bingo...two good prints...!*

He was pulling the prints off when he heard footsteps approaching in the hallway. *...Damn...! Who'd be in this early...?* He wiped the safe off with his handkerchief and stepped to his desk just when the task force XO walked in the door.

Colonel Foreman was tall, and wore a wide array of decorations from two tours in Iraq. From the shoulders down, he epitomized the poster-boy looks of a Marine. But, worry lines creased his face, and his nose was a bulbous rose red. His eyes were always bloodshot. Cavanaugh suspected that Foreman had a drinking problem.

"Morning, Sir," Cavanaugh called out as he busied himself at the fax machine. "What brings you in so early?"

Colonel Foreman responded with a smile, "Morning, Sergeant Major. This is early, but General Grantley caught me at the funeral on Saturday and asked me to stop by his office this morning. In that the President just appointed him Chairman of the Joint Chiefs to replace Admiral Collins, I didn't think it would be politically correct to say no."

They both grinned at that thought. "You know, Sergeant Major," the XO continued, "General Grantley was pretty much out of the loop on this investigation, even though he was the vice chair. He'd asked me a couple of times to spin him up. General O'Shane told me he would deal with General Grantley, but I don't think he ever got around to it, do you?"

Cavanaugh responded, "No Sir. I think he was waiting to get clearance from Admiral Collins."

Grimacing, Foreman commented, "Well, this is awkward. I'll have to fill him in on the status as best I can. I came in early to draft up some comments.

"Let's have an all-hands meeting at zero nine hundred to review what we have. By the way, have you looked at that disc that Frisk sent?" Foreman had asked casually, but his eyes never left Cavanaugh's face.

"No Sir. I haven't had much time with the funeral and all," he'd answered.

As Cavanaugh said those words, it dawned on him *...Christ...haven't even looked to see if the blank disc is in the safe...what if someone found disc was empty...crap...not thinking...better get act together...* He tried to keep a straight face as those thoughts flashed through his mind.

Foreman was also distracted. "Yeah, I understand," he'd replied. "Today I'll just tell Grantley what we are about and what the task force organization looks like. We'll follow up with a full-blown briefing in a couple of days. What do you think?"

Cavanaugh was relieved that Foreman hadn't pushed for the disc. "Sounds good to me, Sir," he'd responded. "Frisk will be back soon. With his help, we should be able to put something together."

Foreman thought about it for a couple of seconds and then nodded his head. "Yeah, that'll do. Grantley's a little frustrated that he wasn't in the loop on this one." At that point, Foreman walked into his office. In seconds, he returned to Cavanaugh's desk.

"Something else occurred to me Sergeant Major," he'd continued. "Do you know where that folder is that Admiral Collins gave to General O'Shane? I only saw it briefly, and I think it needs to be in the material we review for our formal brief for the new chairman."

"Sir, I think I saw General O'Shane put it in his personal safe in his office."

"Well, how about getting it for me today?"

"No sweat, Colonel. The Pentagon security staff will have a copy of the safe combination. I'll get them up here to open it up."

It was common practice for general officers in the Pentagon to maintain a private safe in their offices, and to keep only one record of the combination within Pentagon security files. Cavanaugh just didn't mention the rest of the story – that he knew the combination. For some reason he couldn't explain, he felt a need to stall for time.

Foreman returned to his office, and Cavanaugh pondered their conversation. *...Most interesting...the general showed the files to me and Frisk...why wouldn't XO be in loop...?*

The staff meeting was painless. Foreman asked about the folder, but Cavanaugh had responded, "Sorry, Colonel. I haven't gotten to the security offices as yet."

One of the investigators, Lieutenant Colonel Crenshaw, commented, "Sir, I thought I should mention, I came by the office on Saturday to do some work. I hope that's OK? I just couldn't handle the reception after General O'Shane's funeral."

Foreman responded, "I understand. It's not been easy, but we do need to refocus on our mission."

Cavanaugh thought,*...there goes my fingerprint idea...She just covered her butt...Oh well...pretty amateurish anyway...*

When Foreman left for his meeting with the new chairman, Cavanaugh decided he needed to get some air and a coffee. "Can I bring anybody something from the snack bar?" he'd asked.

Andy Cohen had piped up, "I'll come with you, Jim. I need to stretch my legs." As they walked to the snack bar exchanging light chatter, Cavanaugh did a mental critique of the task force team. His first thoughts considered Cohen.

"He's a career Navy man that Admiral Collins hand picked to help on the administrative side of the task force operation," General O'Shane had told Cavanaugh. "He's smart and knows the Pentagon backwards and forwards." Cohen and Cavanaugh had struck it off right away.

Also helping on the administrative side was a civilian, Ginger Albright. General O'Shane had briefed Cavanaugh about her. "She's from the Pentagon secretarial pool. She's a thirty-five year old divorcee with two teenage boys." Cavanaugh thought she was smart and nice to look at, too.

In fact, they'd been dating since they'd first met. He liked having another Black person around, and appreciated that Ginger was a pleasant companion. At any rate, he had discounted both members of the task force administrative staff from his mental list as potential problems.

The team of task force investigators was different. He only trusted one: Commander Adam Frisk. General O'Shane was high on him. That was enough of a recommendation for Cavanaugh.

There were five other investigators, but none of them was worth salt as far as he was concerned. They each had a personal agenda of some sort. He was unaccustomed to working with staff that didn't view the unit mission as a first priority.

All of these thoughts were going through his mind as he sat at the snack bar with Cohen. He was sure Cohen considered him rude because he was only half listening to the conversation and was responding in monosyllables.

He tried to focus on what Cohen was saying. He finally said, "Andy, I'm sorry. I've got a lot on my mind right now. My head just isn't here. General O'Shane's accident hit me pretty hard."

Cohen had responded, "No sweat, Jim. We'll have a lot of time for coffee talk. Let's head back."

With that, they walked out of the snack bar. When they arrived at the office, Foreman's door was closed. Cavanaugh asked Ginger what was going on.

"Well," she'd answered, "Colonel Foreman came back fired up from his meeting with General Grantley! He called the investigators into his office as soon as he got back. I have no idea what's going on."

...Great... Cavanaugh thought. *...Something big breaks, and I have to be getting coffee...!*

Just then Foreman's office door opened, and the staff hustled out with varying looks of pleasure on their faces. Cavanaugh overheard a snatch of one comment.

Crenshaw had said, "...Well, I for one can't wait to get back to MacDill. At least that's a real job!" It wasn't long before Foreman called Cavanaugh into his office.

Foreman was excited. "Sergeant Major, I've got some news you may not like. We're shutting down the task force. The new chairman thinks this investigation belongs with Army CID, and he directed me to begin shifting the operation to them."

Taken aback by the suddenness of the move, Cavanaugh said, "Isn't that pretty short notice? He can't possibly know the details of what we've been doing."

Foreman bristled, "I gave him a good thumbnail of what's happening. But, to maintain continuity, he wants me to head up the investigation on special assignment. He offered for you to join me if you like?"

Cavanaugh wasn't ready for any commitment given his rising suspicions. He delayed an answer, "Let me think on that, Sir. You know, since General O'Shane's accident, I've been giving serious thought to retiring."

Cavanaugh sensed that Foreman could have cared less, and his feelings were confirmed with Foreman's retort: "Well, I could use your help, but do whatever you want. I'll need you to help pack the office files by the end of the week."

Cavanaugh responded, "You got it, Sir."

Mental alarm bells again chimed as Foreman added, "Get me the computer disc and folder that we spoke of this morning, as soon as possible. I've got an appointment at sixteen hundred hours with the Director of CID, and I'll want to review them with him."

"Yes Sir," Cavanaugh responded. "And, if you don't mind, I'm going to go over to the MILPERCEN this afternoon to check my options."

Foreman didn't even look up from his desk when he replied, "Sure, go ahead."

When he left Foreman's office, staff had begun to clear out for lunch. As he reflected on all that had happened, he made a decision. He hoped it didn't mean going to jail.

He'd promised to take Ginger to lunch that day. When he saw she was getting ready to go, he asked, "Hold on for a few minutes."

Waiting until Foreman left, Cavanaugh retrieved the 'Commander Frisk' disc and the 'Admiral Collins' folder from General O'Shane's safe, and then made two copies of each.

Sitting at her desk, Ginger's eyes never left him as he moved around the office. Finished copying, he put a copy of each in his briefcase and a second copy in a FedEx envelope, and then he put the envelope in Ginger's purse.

"What in the hell are you doing?" she asked, and started pulling the material out. "You trying to get me fired? I can't take that crap out of here!"

He answered, "Ginger, I need some help. If anyone asks, I'll say I put it in your purse when you weren't looking. Trust me, it's important.

"I want to mail this package to my goddaughter on the way to lunch. If what I suspect is bogus, the copies will be destroyed, and no one will be the wiser. We can talk more at lunch. Please."

She looked at him for a couple of seconds and then seemed to come to a decision. "I'm a fool," she said. "But God, you're nice looking!"

He couldn't help chortle. He was risking their careers, and she makes a wise crack. He gave her a kiss.

He then put the originals of the Frisk disc and Collins folder in the office safe and removed his fake disc. Next, he penned a note to Foreman and told him where the originals were. “Okay,” he said, “let’s go to lunch.”

Unbeknownst to him, all he’d done had been recorded by a camera hidden in the ceiling fascia.

Chapter Sixteen

Knight Time

The twists and turns of the exit from the Tampa airport occupied Gary Patten's attention. He was quiet for the five minutes it took to leave the terminal area and head onto I-275. His silence allowed Jenny a moment to reflect on their relationship.

...Really nice of him to pick me up...this guy is becoming a permanent fixture...his California, blond good looks...what am I doing...?

Entering the highway, he interrupted her reverie and asked, "Hey, you want to come over to my place and chill for the afternoon?"

Jenny smiled and asked, half serious, "Are you hurt and needing to rest, or are you horny?"

"Both," he laughed. "But, I was actually trying to help keep you from fretting about your dad."

"Keeping busy will be the best medicine," she responded. "I plan to go home, change into my uniform and then head over to the office to get a jump on my in-box and e-mails. I also plan on hitting the gym this evening to get in a good work out."

Gary's body language told her that he didn't approve, but he was smart enough to keep quiet. His silence gave her time to think more about their relationship.

...Such an incredible sweetheart to arrange his assignment so he could be with me at MacDill...what am I doing...?

He'd taken a non-flying maintenance job to make the assignment work. The job wasn't glamorous, and it was a major sacrifice for a career Air Force pilot. Jenny was touched.

She loved having him nearby – not only was it nice to have a familiar face around, he was a lot of fun to be with. It didn't hurt that he was also great in bed.

Using the Dale Mabry exit off the highway, they were at her apartment in a few minutes. Driving into the entrance, Gary asked, "Why did you ever pick this place? It's pretty low rent."

"It's just temporary," Jenny answered. "I'll scout around and find something better."

"Well, you've been here two months. Maybe it's about time."

"I know. I know. I still have some hope of getting into bachelor officer's quarters on MacDill. This is okay for now. I can even bike into the office in good weather."

"Hmmm…" was Gary's response.

Just as they pulled into the parking area for her building, Gary's cell phone beeped. He was the Operations Officer for Wing Maintenance and was on call twenty-four/seven for maintenance emergencies.

After he answered, she overheard a couple of "Uh huhs" and "OKs." Then he said, "Be there in a few minutes." As she expected, when Gary disconnected, he told her, "I gotta go. Something's come up. I'll give you a call. Will you be all right?"

She hopped out of the car and grabbed her carry-on. "I'll be fine," she assured him, "I'm a big girl. Thanks for the ride. Go do what you have to do. Talk to you soon." She waved as he pulled away.

Jenny's apartment was only one flight up. She got her keys out of her purse and started to unlock her door. As she pressed the key to the lock, the door opened.

…Strange… The door wasn't locked nor fully closed. *…Sheila…probably tending to Nikki's litter box…* She heard noise in the bedroom.

She called out, "Sheila, it's me. Thanks for taking care of Nikki. Just leave what you have, and I'll get it later. Where is that mangy cat?"

The noise stopped, and it was then that Jenny noticed that the front room was a mess. Her desk drawers were out, and all the papers were scattered.

...Whoa...! She could see through the arched kitchen doorway and adjacent pass-through. The counters and eating area were trashed. "Hey," she yelled, "what's going on?" There was a loud crash. Her police training took over.

She dropped her bag and backed out the door. Crouching against the wall beside the door, she reached in her purse for her pistol.

"Damn!" she muttered, "gun's locked up at headquarters!" *...Great...!* She only had a collapsible nightstick. Taking it out, she pressed the extend button. *...Better than nothing...*

Just then she heard a car engine start and tires squeal out of an adjacent parking area. The apartments had open-air walkways, so she could peek over the railing. She did so in time to see a white car turning the corner of the parking lot. She hadn't looked fast enough to get a make or model, or a license number. *...Wonderful...some cop I am...!*

Not taking any chances, Jenny returned to crouching next to the doorway wall. Reaching into her purse again, she got out her cell phone and dialed 911. "This is Army Major Jennifer O'Shane," she told the police operator, "I'm a Military Police officer. I'd like to report a robbery in progress." She gave the apartment address.

Within three minutes, a patrol car was in the apartment parking lot and two policemen, one African-American and the other Hispanic, were beside Jenny, weapons drawn.

She showed them her badge and explained the situation. Over one of the cop's hand held radios, she heard a report that another patrol car had arrived at the back of the apartments. One of the officers said, "Wait here, Ma'am. Let us make sure the apartment is clear."

They stepped into the apartment as an Air Force Air Police patrol car from MacDill arrived. At the same time, her neighbor's door opened, and Sheila asked, "Jenny, what's going on?"

"Sheila, go back inside your apartment. I'll explain later," Jenny told her.

As Sheila's door closed, a nice looking Air Policeman wearing Air Force Staff Sergeant's stripes walked up to Jenny. "What's going on here, Lady?" the sergeant asked.

Jenny identified herself, "I'm Major Jennifer O'Shane, an Army Military Policeman."

She showed her badge and ID. She further explained, "My apartment appears to have been burglarized. I think I surprised the burglar when I came home about twenty minutes ago. The Tampa police are inside checking out the apartment."

While she was explaining the situation, the Tampa police officers returned and told Jenny, "We checked, and it's clear. Looks like the burglar exited through the bedroom window."

The Air Policeman introduced himself; "I'm Sergeant Miller from the MacDill military liaison team for police matters."

His tone of voice was not friendly. Nor did he bother shaking the offered hands of the Tampa officers.

He said to Jenny. "Lady, you wait here. I'm going to check the apartment myself."

Unbelievably, Jenny heard him say in an audible undertone as he walked in, "Don't trust goddamn niggers and wetbacks. They probably stole anything missing."

It didn't take more than a split second for her to be furious with embarrassment. She followed him into the apartment, and caught up with him as he entered the kitchen.

"Wait a minute, Sergeant Miller," she ordered. "Don't go any further. You go out and apologize to those police officers right now. You're way out of line."

Miller whirled, his blue eyes smoldering. At that moment, she was very glad he hadn't followed police procedure. His pistol was still holstered. At well over six feet tall, he was an intimidating figure.

"What is it, Lady?" Miller responded, "you some kind of do-gooder, nigger lover?" Then he made his biggest mistake. He put his left hand high on her chest and began to push, starting to say, "I'm not apo…"

Jenny had already had a way bad day. Her Tae Kwon Do training went into automatic. Using her right arm from waist level, she swept an over and downward stroke, knocking his left arm down. Allowing her momentum to turn her around, she spun one hundred and eighty degrees.

With her back to him, she used her right arm again and she elbowed him in the solar plexus. She turned again, facing him. He was bent at the waist, gasping, surprised.

Jenny reached up and grabbed his upper lip and twisted as hard as she could. He screamed in pain and fell to his knees. She said, "As I said earlier, I'm a major in the U.S. Army. I expect you to demonstrate appropriate respect. For sure you don't put your hands on me. Do you understand?"

"Yeth, Ma'am," was all he could manage, tears streaming down his face. The police officers ran back into the apartment, hearing the yelp from the sergeant.

Still squeezing his lip, Jenny continued, "You were discourteous to these officers. You owe them an apology. What do you say?"

He answered, “Ah’m thorry.”

She asked, “Will that be all right, Officers?”

The policemen were grinning at the sergeant’s predicament and nodded their agreement. “Do you think you could improve your behavior in the future?” Jenny asked Miller.

She got another, “Yeth, Ma’am.”

“Officers,” Jenny said to the policemen, “we are going out to Sergeant Miller’s car. I’ll be right back. Would you mind taking the handcuffs off his belt and putting them on his wrists behind his back?” They did so without fanfare.

Jenny then led a subdued Miller out to the Air Force sedan. She took his keys from his belt, unlocked the car, took the handcuff key off the key ring, and put the car keys in the ignition.

She then took his pistol off his belt and threw it onto the back seat of the car. She told him, “Lay face down in the driver’s seat.”

He did so without resistance and she unlocked one of his wrists and cuffed it to the steering wheel. Throwing the handcuff key into the back seat, she said, “Sergeant, I’ll be at your squadron headquarters in the morning at zero nine hundred hours. You will be there. Do you understand?”

Sergeant Miller had scrambled up onto the seat by then, and looked at her with hate filling his eyes. His upper lip was red and swollen. He said, “Yes, Ma’am.”

“Good,” Jenny answered, “I’ll see you then.” She then went back to her apartment to deal with a police report for the second time that day.

...Damn...getting to office today is out of the question... Jenny surveyed the rooms and saw only one thing missing – the rack of CD discs that she kept beside her computer was gone. *...Strange...*

Jenny didn't mention the missing discs to the police. *...It's not worth hassle...*

As she finished filling out the police report, there was a knock on the apartment door. Sheila was there with Jenny's mail and Nikki. Jenny thanked her for watching things.

Sheila responded, "Obviously I didn't do a very good job. Looks like someone got into your place. I didn't hear or see a thing. I'm really sorry."

Jenny hugged and reassured her. "Don't worry. I don't think you could have done anything. I'd guess the thieves were after something specific. They were probably looking for household drugs."

Sheila stayed after the police left to help pick up the mess. They'd just started when she announced, "Oh yeah. You got a FedEx package this morning that I left in my apartment. Let me get it for you."

Jenny didn't open the package right away. It was from Jim Cavanaugh. She figured it was the latest Tom Clancy book he'd promised to send.

It took only a few more minutes to put the apartment in order. As they finished, Sheila asked, "Would you like to come over to my place for a pick up supper? Won't be much, but better than you have here."

"No thanks," Jenny said. "Maybe later. I need to call the apartment maintenance staff about the bedroom window, and I want to lodge a complaint about that Air Police sergeant. I also want to get in a workout. Sorry."

Sheila left with a parting, "No sweat. That's fine. The offer is always open. If you need anything else, call me."

Jenny was flirting with depression when Sheila left. *...What a friggin' day this has turned into...capping a horrendous week...*

"Well," she said to herself, "I have way too much to do to sit around feeling sorry for myself. Let's get with it." Her first phone call was to the maintenance people.

They were responsive. "We'll have someone over this evening to get it closed up," the supervisor said.

Pleased at her first effort, Jenny next called the Air Police Squadron. The squadron commander was gone for the evening, but Miller's flight commander was in. She was connected to a Lieutenant Ferguson.

The lieutenant stated, "I've been briefed on the problem. I must tell you that the behavior you report is very unlike my experience with Sergeant Miller."

"That may be," Jenny responded, "but I plan to be in the squadron's offices at zero nine hundred. We can talk about it more then."

He answered, "I'll try to arrange for the squadron commander to also be present."

Jenny provided a curt, "Thank you," and hung up.

She wasn't impressed by the lieutenant's attitude. He seemed almost insolent. *...Probably your imagination...you're looking for a fight...need to burn some of this stress off...the gym...*

Determined to salvage something from the day, she donned her gym clothes, crammed a clean outfit into her backpack, and began pedaling her bike the two miles to the MacDill gym. She was looking forward to a good workout.

Not being accustomed to the vagaries of Florida weather, she failed to notice lightning bouncing off thunderheads in the eastern sky.

Chapter Seventeen

Black Rook Threatens Knight

Jim Cavanaugh was hungry when he and Ginger left the Pentagon for lunch. They took the shuttle bus over to Crystal City, where there was an Italian eatery they both enjoyed.

During the walk from the bus stop to the restaurant, they stopped at a FedEx sidewalk mailbox. Cavanaugh liked the FedEx mailbox service where he could just key in the address, drop the mailer in the slot, and use his credit card to pay the freight charge. In minutes, he had his package off to Jenny.

At the restaurant, the owner met them at the door with a hearty, “Ahh, Mr. And Mrs. Cavanaugh. How are you? It’s good to see you again. Isn’t this a beautiful Monday afternoon? Let me find you a table.”

They both grinned at Angelo’s greeting. It was always the same, even though they’d explained their relationship several times. Angelo was trying to be hospitable and they’d given up trying to disabuse him.

They were soon seated, and it didn’t take long for Ginger to ask Cavanaugh to explain his behavior in the office. “The thought of taking classified material out of the office makes me crazy,” she said.

Cavanaugh went through his story, closing with his feelings about the office staff, “I don’t trust anyone in there besides you and Andy Cohen.

“I want my goddaughter’s thoughts, and I need some time. Will you help me on this?”

They ordered a pizza while Ginger considered her response. In the quiet, Cavanaugh sweated. *...Up a creek if she’s not a willing partner...*

That thought no more than crossed his mind when it dawned on him...*Took this woman for granted...arrogant of me...jeopardizing her future...oh man...what must she think...?*

Cavanaugh started to apologize, taking her hands, “Ginger, I’ve put you in a terrible position with this and I’m very sorry. I’m not thinking clearly...” Ginger held up her hand, stopping him.

“Relax. I understand,” she said. “Actually, I’m okay with it all. It’s just that I was trying to get up the courage to ask if you see us as more than casual friends. I think you do, or you wouldn’t have trusted me to help you like this. Anyway, I hope you do because that’s how I feel about you.”

Cavanaugh was speechless. He wasn’t accustomed to women being direct. Unprepared, his mind went blank.

Ginger added, “Jim, I’m unsure about us because you’ve been so ‘gentlemanly’. A light kiss on the cheek at the end of the evening...

“You and I have been seeing each other for almost two months, and all I get is a handshake. Am I turning you off somehow?”

“Ginger,” Cavanaugh answered, taking her hands again, “you haven’t turned me off in any way. In fact, I’m very attracted to you.”

He paused to gather his thoughts. “I’m just trying to show you some respect. Serious dating is not something I’ve ever done before, and I didn’t want to spoil a good thing. I’m sorry. I obviously don’t know how to communicate my feelings very well.”

He chuckled out loud and added, “I’ve been a happy bachelor for 48 years and suddenly I’m confused and tongue-tied.”

As their pizza arrived, Ginger said, “Okay. We’ll work on your personal communication skills. In the meantime,

I'll do what I can to help you with your little project. I have to tell you, though, I think you're seeing goblins."

Cavanaugh thanked her as sincerely as he could in public, squeezing her hands. Then he started to serve.

Ginger stopped him with, "You know I'm not very hungry. And, I have a confession to make. While you were mailing your package, I called Andy Cohen on my cell phone. I told him I wasn't feeling well and that you were taking me home."

Cavanaugh put down his slice of pizza and looked up with concern. "My God, Ginger. You should have said something earlier. I had no idea you weren't feeling well." He was surprised when she burst out laughing.

"Boy, are you dense! Jim...think about it...I told you earlier that my mom is with a client today. My boys are in school until 4:30. Hello…"

Ginger burst out laughing all over again. "And, I believe you're blushing," she said. "Why don't you get us a cab, and I'll pay Angelo for the pizza."

Cavanaugh couldn't get out of his seat fast enough. He felt like a teenager on his first date. The ride to Ginger's apartment was the longest twenty minutes of his life.

The next thirty minutes were among the most enjoyable. They started kissing as they went up the stairs to her apartment. Ginger's coat and blouse were off before they got the door closed.

Cavanaugh unhooked her bra and held her away from him to admire. "My God, you're beautiful," he said. He began to unbutton his shirt.

"Please let me do that," Ginger said as she led him to her bedroom....

Chapter Eighteen

Pawn Threatened

In the Argentinean embassy, fifteen miles away from Jim and Ginger's entwined bodies, Colonel Enrico Histaves' private cell phone chirped.

When Histaves answered, a breathless voice blurted, "Rico, it's spinning out of control. Seven people died on the highway because of one briefcase. It can't go on."

Recognizing his congressional friend, Histaves lost patience.

"Senator," he said, "we already discussed the collateral damage. As I told you, the highway accident was not my plan. Some friends of ours made those arrangements. It seems extreme, but it looks like it will blow over. There is no investigation.

"If you've called to harp on old business, I have many things to do. Please do not call about this again. Good bye."

As he started to hang up, Histaves heard a faint "…wait, don't hang up…"

He put the receiver back to his ear. "What is it now?"

"We have another complication that I was informed of over lunch. You will want to deal with it right away. If I tell you, though, you have to promise not to kill anybody else."

"Senator, I don't even know how to respond to that. What has happened?"

"Uhh…you know that Army sergeant that I…uhh…told you about in the task force office? Well," he continued in a rush, "my sources tell me that he made copies of the material in the Collins file and copied the Frisk computer disc this morning."

Histaves exploded, "*Madre de Dios*. I thought you told me your group could control these people after Admiral Collins and General O'Shane were out of the way? I'm losing my confidence in your usefulness. You've got to get a grip."

The senator went silent. Histaves heard only shallow breathing in the phone's earpiece.

During the pause, Histaves realized, *...cell phones...can be monitored...amateurs...! Americans are driving me crazy...!*

Before the senator could speak again, Histaves told him, "Wait. Stop talking. Don't say anything else. Call me at my embassy number."

Histaves broke the connection – too late. Miles above them, a National Security Agency cellular intercept satellite had just recorded their conversation.

Unaware of the interception, they soon continued conversing on a landline. During the break, the senator had regained his composure.

"Sorry about that, Rico," he said. "I'm sure my call was too short to be monitored. No harm done." Trying to defuse his blunder, the senator hurried on, "I do have some good news. For your information, I arranged for the task force investigation to be shut down by the end of the week."

"That ***is*** good news," Histaves answered. But, he was not appeased. "What about those damn files and the disc? You assured me that you could secure the copies in that office. Now I'm hearing that not only were you unsuccessful, but that there are additional copies. Have I got it all about right?"

"Yes, but you don't need to get sarcastic. It isn't my fault this sergeant turned maverick on us. I thought he was just a glorified clerk. No one could have predicted his actions."

The senator continued, a whine creeping into his voice, "I ***have*** arranged for the admiral's original files and the original Frisk computer disc to be secured today. That's a big help. With the people you know, surely you can arrange to get the new copies?"

"Yes, I'm sure I can. But, it could be complicated and messy. Please note that I will hold you personally accountable if this screws up the operation. I *will* find you…"

Histaves paused to let the threat sink in. He then continued, "I'll need more information. What do you know?"

He heard nothing but silence overlaid by heavy breathing. He lost all semblance of patience. "Please don't drag this out any further, Senator. This is turning into a bad day."

"Well," the senator started talking, panic edging into his voice, his words coming in a rush, "it seems that this Sergeant Cavanaugh showed a lot more initiative than anyone would have expected…" There was another pause.

"Please get on with it…"

"Uhh…it also seems that Cavanaugh took both copies of everything he made out of the office. He was heard saying he was going to FedEx a copy to a 'Jenny.' Apparently, she's a junior officer in the Army. A major, I think. And, she's the daughter of General O'Shane."

"My God in heaven," said Histaves. "Can it get worse? We'll have to assume he mailed the package. What a mess! We need to find this 'Jenny.'" He thought, *…this name is familiar…how…?*

"This might help," offered the senator. "Cavanaugh said something about MacDill Air Force Base. I'd guess that's where she's assigned…"

"Okay. We should be able to find her with that. Once we know, we'll intercept the FedEx envelope. Do you know Cavanaugh's address?" asked Histaves.

"No, but he should be local…"

"Fine," Histaves interrupted. "I'll have someone get on it. Anything else?"

"Yes. Sorry, but it appears that O'Shane kept a journal as to the status of the investigation. No one knew about it before today. It was among personal effects that Cavanaugh gave to the daughter. He thought the journal was General O'Shane's personal diary. Assuming it offers compromising data, we need to acquire that journal."

"You have an idea of how to acquire it…?"

"It's just a thought," the senator answered, gaining back his confidence. "My information is that the daughter is planning to return to Tampa tomorrow. I'd guess she would pack that material in her luggage. Maybe someone could steal her luggage?"

"Thank you for your suggestion. I'll think about it. Are there any other gems of information I should know? This conversation has been <u>so</u> enjoyable."

"No, Rico. But, please remember that I'm just a messenger. You shouldn't be so angry…" He stopped talking when he realized he was speaking to a dial tone.

Upon breaking the phone connection with the senator, Histaves dialed Lieutenant Fernando's number. *…We have a lot of planning to do and very little time…*

Once Histaves heard the beep indicating a secure link, he gave Fernando the details. He then instructed, "Find out where this Jenny lives at MacDill and intercept that FedEx package.

"Also, she will probably have her father's journal in her luggage. She'll be at Tampa International tomorrow. Find her flight, intercept the luggage, and get that journal.

"At the same time, have someone track down Cavanaugh and his briefcase. Can you handle all that? Any questions?"

"*Si, mi Coronel*. No questions. We're on it."

"Good." Histaves added. "Steal what you need and get away. There's been enough killing. Eventually it will draw attention to us. Do you understand?"

"*Si, mi Coronel*. I understand. We will be careful."

Chapter Nineteen

Knave Attack

While Histaves and Fernando talked, two other people were enjoying the afterglow of their lovemaking. Ginger was lying with her head in the crook of Cavanaugh's arm. "That was very nice, Mr. Cavanaugh," she said. "Obviously you are a seasoned veteran."

Cavanaugh laughed and said, "Well, I am a military combat veteran, Ms. Albright." Then he added with a straight face, "and this was exceptional. But, I have to admit, this was the first time I've ever had sex."

Ginger responded with a small shove, "That's BS and you know it!" They both chuckled, enjoying the moment.

Ginger sat up and said, "I hate to be a party pooper, but Mama will be here in about an hour and I want to straighten up this room before she gets home. I don't want her to get ideas."

Cavanaugh leered at Ginger's bared breasts and responded, "You keep waving those around, and I may have to force myself on you again…"

Ginger punched him on the arm with a twinkle in her eye. "You've already had seconds, Big Boy. No more today. Let's go," she said, pulling off the blankets.

As they were dressing, Ginger asked, "Would you like to come to dinner tonight? I think the boys and Mama would like to get to know you. They've only seen you pick me up and drop me off at the door."

"I'd love to. That sounds great." He was pleased to have an opportunity to meet her family.

Ginger continued, "I would appreciate it if you would leave now and come back in a couple of hours so we give all the right signals. Would that be okay with you?"

"I understand. I want to go over to the military personnel assignment offices anyway. See you soon."

Cavanaugh had a cab drop him at the Pentagon so he could pick up his car. It was a thirty-minute trip to MILPERCEN. A brief conference with his assignment specialist revealed several possibilities.

Cavanaugh parted with a promise, "I'll call in a few days to let you know my preferences."

He then headed over to his apartment to freshen up. He didn't want to wear his uniform to Ginger's place for dinner. He toyed with what shoes to wear, but finally opted for his cowboy boots. They were nice looking and went with his gray trousers.

Cavanaugh was back at Ginger's by 6:30 p.m. Although he felt silly, he'd kept his briefcase with him.

"Where would you like me to put it?" he asked Ginger. "I didn't want to leave it sitting around at my place."

"Set it in the foyer. Nobody will bother it there."

The evening went better than Cavanaugh could have hoped. Ginger's two teenage boys were well behaved and polite. They were avid Washington Redskin fans, and the discussion was heated as to whether the team would make the playoffs.

"Have you fellas ever been to a home game at the new FedEx stadium?" Cavanaugh asked.

Looking over at their mom, one of the boys answered, "Those ticket prices are way beyond our allowance." Ginger grinned and didn't say anything.

Cavanaugh also remained quiet, choosing not to share that he was a friend of one of the Redskin coaches. They'd played high school football together. He'd periodically sent Cavanaugh offers of tickets whenever there were games near where he was stationed. *...see if he can score some tickets for these guys...*

Besides the boys, Ginger's mom was also a treat. "Call me 'Mama'," she'd told Cavanaugh. "Everyone else does."

Mama was born and raised in Louisiana, and the cooking was Cajun – hot and spicy. She beamed when Cavanaugh told her, "This is the best home cooked meal I can remember. It was delicious."

Besides being a great cook, Mama also showed that she was the matriarch of the family. With a nod from her, the boys were excused from dinner and began to clear the table.

She called out to the kitchen when the table was cleared, "You boys go in and see to your school work. I'll clean up the kitchen."

With that Mama excused herself, leaving Cavanaugh and Ginger at the table sipping ice teas. They had a relaxing conversation about everything but work.

Cavanaugh didn't leave until after 10:30 p.m. He told Ginger, "I don't recall a better evening. Thank you." As he gave her a proper kiss on the porch, he added, "I'll see you tomorrow."

Ginger handed him his briefcase and gave him a hug. "You drive carefully going home, Big Boy. See you in the morning."

Cavanaugh drove into his apartment complex, and found all the parking spaces near the entrance to his building were taken. "Well, I can use the walk," he muttered to himself.

The weather was warm, the snow turning to slush. Already wearing a sports jacket, he didn't bother with his overcoat. "This is a strange weather pattern for February," he muttered out load again.

As he got out of his car, lethargic from a pleasant evening, Cavanaugh didn't notice that another car parked a short way from his apartment entrance had started up.

At first, he also didn't notice a man in dark clothes approaching at a fast pace. When he did see the man, he tried to step aside to let him pass.

Instead of going around Cavanaugh, the man collided with him and, at the same time, tried to grab his briefcase. Another man stepped around a parked van, swinging something at Cavanaugh's head.

The timing of his assailants was off by a fraction of a second. Whatever the second man swung hit Cavanaugh on the shoulder. The blow stung, but it wasn't damaging.

Cavanaugh figured he was being mugged. He decided the muggers were going to pay hell. He kicked out with his hard-soled boots and connected with the knee of the first man. The man crumbled, moaning in agony.

The second man had raised his arm again. In that instant, Cavanaugh thought he saw a sap. He raised the briefcase to absorb the blow.

Cavanaugh was pleased to see the look of surprise in the eyes of his assailant. *...He probably expected a scared, pushover pedestrian...*

At that point, Cavanaugh became the aggressor. He charged the man. Swinging the briefcase, aiming it at the man's face.

A corner caught the man on the cheekbone. Surprised and off balance, the man grabbed his cheek in pain and stumbled back.

His heel caught on a wheel stop in the parking area, and he fell backwards. Cavanaugh heard the guy's head thud against the pavement.

Unrelenting, Cavanaugh followed up intending to smash his assailant again. Cavanaugh's blood was up, and he was going to see that this guy stayed down.

When he reached the mugger, Cavanaugh saw there was no need to hit the man again; he was out cold.

Cavanaugh turned to the first mugger who was still writhing on the sidewalk. He was surprised – in the very brief seconds of the attack, he hadn't realized that both assailants wore balaclavas. ...*What the hell...?*

He walked over to the first man and pulled off his mask. The man looked vaguely familiar. "My God," Cavanaugh said, "you were standing outside my apartment when I left to go to Ginger's. Who the hell are you?" he demanded.

As the words left his mouth, Cavanaugh heard a 'pffft.' Something slammed into his shoulder, hurting like hell and spinning him around. Another 'pffft,' and the lights went out...

Chapter Twenty

Knight Captured

Histaves answered his secure phone on the first ring in the very early hours of Tuesday morning. "Did you get it?" he asked.

"*Si, Senor*," answered Fernando. "It was as you said. We have the file folder and the computer disc."

"*Excellente*! What about the sergeant?"

"He's dead. I had to kill him."

"You what? That is the very thing I ask you to avoid. What were you thinking?" As he asked that question, Histaves realized the obvious…

He said, "If *you* shot him, that means *you* went on the mission. Do you have any idea the risk you took by personal involvement? If you'd been caught, you could have compromised the entire operation."

Fernando answered, "*Mi Coronel*, you instructed me to ensure this mission was accomplished, and to keep my eye on the staff. I felt I had little choice."

Hearing the response, Histaves relented. *...He's right...no loose ends...so close...*"You had to kill him?" he asked.

"*Si*. He was strong and fast. He overpowered two men and was about to compromise a team member. I had to make a decision."

Realizing there was no benefit in arguing right or wrong about an on-the-scene decision, Histaves asked, "What did you do with the body?"

"We hid it in alley trash. If the weather stays this cold, he won't be found until summer."

Histaves' instincts were not satisfied, but he realized there wasn't much he could do. *...Sloppy work...*

He switched subjects. "What about the FedEx copy at MacDill?" he asked.

"Not good, *Senor*. We searched O'Shane's apartment. No luck. We had the same results with her luggage. It was bad timing. We should have waited until she came home. We are watching her apartment and will try again."

"No. Don't," Histaves instructed. "Doing anything now may put her on guard, and we'll have a different situation. I'll develop an alternate plan. Bring the agent home. We're stretched too thin. For now, you need to focus on getting the shipment ready."

With those words, the Argentinean officers signed off.

They had no more than hung up when Histaves' phone rang again. Thinking Fernando forgot something, Histaves answered, "*Hola*." He heard another familiar voice.

"*Hola*, Rico. Did you get what you were looking for tonight?" the voice purred.

"*Senor*, Minister," answered Histaves. Unaccountable fear clouded his mind, and sweat formed on his brow. "I'm still working on obtaining some of the material, *Senor*."

"Hmmm. Sounds like failure to me, Rico. *Explemente, por favor*."

After Histaves told of the evening's events and the results of the O'Shane search, he heard, "Rico, you'd better hope my son dealt with this sergeant's body better than you did with the sergeant on the Chilean border. We don't need a trail back to you, do we…? Dr. Ami and Commander Garcia are looking for justification to take over your operation. It will not be a pleasant experience. *Comprende?*"

"*Si, Senor*," Histaves heard himself say into a dead connection. *...Shit...!*

Chapter Twenty-One

White Knight Threatened

Late Tuesday afternoon, unaware of the shooting of Jim Cavanaugh, Jenny was trying to put some order back into her life. A workout at the MacDill gym was on her list of priorities.

She'd biked over in her gym clothes, so she went right to work as soon as she arrived. She started with stretching exercises. They seemed to help get her mind focused – she liked following a standard regimen.

After five minutes of stretches, she started on the elevated treadmill for a fast one mile walk. That got her heart rate up, and between the bike ride to the gym, the stretches, and the fast walk, she felt ready to start working out in earnest.

She moved over to a stair stepper, set it on hill climb at level six, and punched in twenty minutes on the timer.

At the halfway point, her sixth sense vibrated. She felt like she was being watched. Looking around the room, she saw a nice looking young man sitting on one of the exercise bikes staring at her. She was disconcerted when the man didn't look away upon making eye contact.

Being attractive had benefits, but being stared at wasn't one Jenny enjoyed. *...Wearing sports bra...tights...shorts...nothing to see...needs to get a life...* Her mind drifted.

Finishing the stair stepper, Jenny was winded. She decided to cool down with some time on free weights.

She liked to do arm curls and the bench press because they helped with upper body strength. Bench presses translated into doing more push-ups, one of the basic three exercises required in the Army's annual physical fitness test. *...Scored a maximum on last test ...gonna do the same on the next one...*

She started the arm curls at ten pounds. Her standard was two sets of ten repetitions. She picked up the weights from the rack and moved to an exercise bench. *...That man still staring...silly ass grin...scratched crotch again...disgusting...letters AP on gym shorts...must be Air Policeman...he should know better...asshole...*

Jenny did the ten-pound curls and then another two sets of ten lifts with the fifteen pound weights. She thought, *...that's good enough at this point...*

She moved over to the bench to do presses and put fifteen pounds on each side of the bar. It was a light start. *...Don't need to pull a muscle getting back into routine...*

Completing two reps of ten, she decided to put on heavier weights. She used the twenty pounds on each side, and again had little difficulty finishing two sets.

The man walked by her work out bench as she lifted the twenties. His eyes gave her a once over and then dwelled between her legs, obviously looking up her gym shorts. She was on her back, straddling the bench. She stopped lifting and sat up when he came by a second time.

His behavior was rude. "You got a problem, Buster?" she asked.

"No problem, Lady," he answered, "I just like looking at good-looking girls."

"Well, I don't like it. Go stare at someone else." Jenny talked loud enough that others in the gym looked over. The young man at least had the good grace to blush. Nonetheless, he gave her another bold once over and walked away with a smirk on his face.

She put away the weights and moved to the speed bag. It helped a lot with hand and eye coordination. The rhythm was mesmerizing. It was a great upper body work out, and after only a minute, her shoulders burned with fatigue.

The heavy bag was next. She liked it for practicing Tae Kwon Do kicks. She'd found that men who were inclined to be pushy or otherwise bothersome soon became more respectful when they saw her pop the big bag a few times. Glancing over at her voyeur, she was pleased to see the smart-ass grin was gone.

Deciding she'd had enough of him, and a good enough work out, she picked up her backpack and went into the women's locker room to shower and change. She didn't note that the gym was now empty.

As she was showering, she heard someone moving around in the locker room. Not giving it much thought, she finished rinsing and turned off the shower. She opened the shower curtain, and…

…Sitting on a changing bench not more than ten feet away was the voyeur, his smirk back in full bloom.

"What the hell!" She exclaimed, startled. She pulled her towel off a nearby hook and covered herself.

He grinned as if it were some kind of joke and said, "You're even prettier naked. You have beautiful tits, and I love natural red-heads."

She lost it. "You perverted bastard. Get your fucking ass out of here before I kick it from here to Sunday!" She started walking toward him with her fists clenched, dripping wet, intending to beat the crap out of him if she could.

He stood and backed away, laughing. "Don't worry, Lady. I'm leaving. I just wanted a good look." With that he turned and ran out the locker room door.

Her bare feet slipped on the tile floor of the shower room, and she realized that giving chase was fruitless.

She pulled out her cell phone from her gym bag to call the base air police. That's when she noticed that the man had gone through her belongings. Her clean underwear was gone. *...What a perverted prick...!*

Of all people, Lieutenant Ferguson answered her call. After identifying herself, she explained the situation.

"Major," he responded to her complaint, "you seem to have a lot of trouble with men. Would you like me to send a female patrol officer over to escort you home?"

For the second time in less than five minutes, she lost control. "Of all the dimwitted, nincompoop responses I've heard, that sets new standards. Lieutenant, I want you to find that shit head. He's wearing gym shorts with the letters AP on them. And, he's carrying my bra and panties. How about sending a patrol out to find him? Do you think the Air Police could handle that request?"

After a brief pause, the lieutenant answered, "Major, I don't have to put up with your abuse. I think you've got serious paranoia problems with men and you need some anger management counseling. I'll make a note in the duty log and pass your report to the patrols. If we find anyone matching your description, I'll notify you." Jenny then heard the phone buzz. He'd hung up.

She pulled the phone from her ear and stared at it for a full minute. Her mind seethed; She'd never been so pissed. *...What kind of zoo have I gotten into...?*

She sat on one of the locker room benches trying to settle down. After some deep breathing, she calmed enough to get dressed.

...This will go into my report to squadron commander tomorrow...So much for MacDill being a great assignment... She packed up her backpack for the trip home and walked out of the gym…into a pouring rain.

She pinched herself to see if she was in a nightmare. Not! *...This is such crap...!*

She'd heard some thunder while working out, but she hadn't expected a downpour. She waited for a few minutes for the rain to let up. No such luck.

Dejected, she started out. She was going to get soaked. She tried to put a positive spin on her predicament. *...The good news is that the sun hasn't set yet, so there's still some light...*

Pedaling toward her neighborhood, she turned onto a side road that was a shortcut to her apartment complex. The roadside swale was full and the berm of the road was covered with water from the rain. With little traffic on the back street, she rode her bike down the center, out of the standing water.

Hearing a car approaching behind her, she pulled off onto the berm and stopped. Visibility was bad in the continuing downpour, and she didn't take any chances. A white car moved past her at a slow speed. She waved indicating she appreciated the courtesy of the driver not splashing her.

After the car passed, she moved back out on the road and started toward home again. She'd gone another two hundred yards when she heard another car. This one was moving fast. She hustled to the side and turned to watch the approach, preparing to jump into the swale if the driver lost control.

She saw that the car was going to miss her. *...That's a relief...what an idiot to drive fast in this weather on a side road...*

As the car got closer, she could also tell she was going to get splashed. Starting to duck, she glimpsed a face in the open passenger car window and an extended hand giving her the finger.

"Fucking nigger-loving bitch!" she heard a voice yell as a wave of water deluged her.

The car sped by - gone. She was sure she'd heard the voice of Sergeant Miller, her Air Police 'friend.' This time she'd had the presence of mind to get a make on the car. It was a white Mustang.

She boiled in anger for the third time that night. *...What is it with this place...some kind of hell...? That was intentional...know it was Miller...fucking pig...!* She promised herself that she would fix his wagon. She fumed the rest of the way home.

Arriving at her apartment complex, she wiped down her bike and put it back into the storage area. Covered with road yuck from being splashed by the car, she peeled her clothes off at the doorway. She put everything in a plastic bag for laundry.

Going into her bedroom, she noticed that the apartment maintenance staff had bolted a piece of plywood over the broken window. There was a note saying they would have it replaced within the next week. *...At least something's going right...*

Chapter Twenty-Two

Knight Surprise

Arriving at her office at 6:30 a.m. Wednesday morning, Jenny had hoped for time to catch up before the official day started. However, there was a 'sticky' note on her computer screen telling her to see her boss as soon as she got in.

"Ohh, ohh," she said to herself, "Something must be hot. He's usually not in this early." She went down the hall to his office, grabbing a cup of coffee on the way.

Cox was a good boss. She'd enjoyed working with him. However, he didn't look happy when she knocked on his door.

"Come on in and sit down, Major," he'd said. "I thought you were going to stay in D.C. longer?" She explained that she could only take so much hugging, and felt she needed some space.

"I understand. Again, you have my sincerest sympathies about your dad. I know it must be hard."

"Thank you, Sir."

With the pleasantries over, he told her what was on his mind. "O'Shane, it pains me to tell you that I had a complaint about you from the Air Police squadron commander. He called me at home last night. You want to tell me what's going on?"

Jenny was stunned. Given the circumstances, a complaint was the last thing she'd expected. She said, "Uhhh…Sir…I can explain…" She told her story and assured Cox, "I'm positive the cops at the scene will verify what went down."

Cox was silent for a minute, and then said, "Well, I have to tell you, that's a different version than the one I heard.

"Sergeant Miller claims that you hit him with no provocation. He went to the hospital last night complaining of shortness of breath, and a swollen upper lip. The squadron commander also says he spoke to the Tampa police officers, and they declined to make an official comment."

Jenny was beside herself. "Colonel Cox," she began, her voice trembling, "do I look like I would instigate a confrontation with an air policeman who was armed, outweighs me by eighty pounds and is almost a foot taller than I am? That's just ludicrous!"

"I know, Jenny," Cox said. "But you have to put yourself in my position. He claims one thing and you claim another. It's your word against his. The Tampa cops refuse to take sides. There are no other witnesses. You both have good records. What do you expect me to say?"

He took a deep breath and continued, "Jenny, our assignment into this Air Force sand box pissed off some people, the Air Police squadron commander being one."

Cox let that sink in for a few seconds, and then added, "It doesn't matter that they aren't staffed to handle additional security requirements. They feel like the Army's infringing on their turf. Your conflict with this sergeant puts me in a crack. We need to get along with these Air Force guys. We're on their base. Now what would you do if you were in this chair?"

"Sir," she began, her face flushing, "you probably don't need to do much of anything but to tell that Air Police squadron commander that he needs to clean house. His guy is a raving racist. If he keeps acting out like he has, he'll cause a riot. And, his disrespect of me was inexcusable!"

"O'Shane, your feelings are noted," Cox responded in an exasperated tone. "I understand. But, I'm not in a position to tell the squadron commander to do anything. You aren't either."

Jenny started to interject a comment, but Cox interrupted, "No more discussion. I need you to smooth this over and do so before it gets any higher up the command chain. You have an appointment this morning with the Air Police squadron commander. Be there and help me make this problem go away. Do we understand each other?"

Jenny ground her teeth together, and gave the politically correct, "Yes, Sir." She stood and asked, "May I be excused, Sir?"

"Of course. I'll see you later." As she left the office, he added, "Let me know how the meeting goes."

Jenny was so hot, she wondered if her hair was on fire. Her mind was racing. *...Cannot believe this crap...place is crazy...going to lose my mind before done...!*

She stepped outside to try to calm down. She must have looked as pissed as she felt because a couple of other MP's on the security detachment walked by without saying anything, only rendering a salute. They usually exchanged pleasantries, but not today. *...Great...get a reputation as a bitch to boot...Wonderful...!*

As instructed, at the appointed time, she was in the outer offices of the squadron commander. She received a cool reception from Lieutenant Ferguson, who waited with her. She consoled herself by observing, *...mousy bastard...wouldn't last ten minutes in the Army...*

As they waited, Jenny heard a familiar voice. She glanced across the office and saw Sergeant Miller. At a desk with him sat the voyeur from the gym. They both wore insolent grins. She seethed. It was all she could do to keep from going over and trying to punch their lights out.

In a few minutes she and Ferguson were ushered into the squadron commander's office. He introduced himself as Lieutenant Colonel Adams. He was a black man. *...Oh Christ...talk about mission impossible...this can't go anywhere but downhill...!*

Adams started off hostile. "So you think I have a racial problem in my squadron, do you?"

Jenny replied, "Sir, I'm not sure about the rest of your staff, but you have a problem with Sergeant Miller."

"Well, I think I'm probably in a better position to judge whether or not my personnel are racists, don't you?" Adams retorted, "And, there have been no such indications from Sergeant Miller.

"He's an upstanding airman with a superb record. I'm sorry, but I think you're out of line. And, I don't appreciate your manhandling one of my sergeants. He tells me the only reason he didn't defend himself was because you are an officer and woman. He was afraid he'd hurt you."

She lost it. "Sir, that's just bullshit! He put his hands on me before I did anything. I was the one on the defensive. *And*, on top of that, I'm pretty sure he tried to run me off the road last night while I was riding my bike. AND, the airman with him was in the women's locker room at the gym spying on me as I showered."

"Major, I've heard enough. First of all, watch your mouth around me. I don't appreciate foul language. Secondly, Sergeant Miller's record has no indication of ever putting his hands on anyone, nor does it have any indication of racism. Lastly, Miller and his patrol mate, Airman Andrews, were on duty in their patrol car last night. I'm certain the dispatcher on duty can vouch for their periodic radio checks..."

"Colonel, I'm sure the dispatcher would verify radio checks. But, that doesn't mean those two didn't do as I claim. Sir, if I spoke to the policemen who responded to my call at my apartment yesterday, I think they'd support my allegations and..."

Adams interrupted, "You'll do no such thing. I'm responsible for military liaison with the local police here, and I'll not have some maverick Army officer out there stirring up trouble for me. The police told me that they have no further comment on the matter, and that's it. Now you will leave it alone. Is that clear?"

Almost sputtering in anger and frustration she got out the requisite, "Yes Sir," but she felt compelled to add, "I think you're making a huge mistake."

Adams stood, his chair hitting the wall behind him. "I don't need some wet behind the ears Army officer telling me anything!" he yelled.

"Now get out of my office. I don't want to see you here again." Jenny saluted, did an about face and marched out of the office, her face burning in humiliation.

Ferguson escorted her to the door of the office area. Miller was standing near the exit. She heard him say in an undertone, "Nice try, Bitch! Come back any time."

She glanced at Ferguson. He was oblivious. *...Well...shouldn't expect much more from these idiots...how the hell explain to Cox...?*

Chapter Twenty-Three

Rook Recovered

Jim Cavanaugh was certain that he was dead. His eyes wouldn't open. He couldn't see a thing although he did hear faint sounds of traffic.

He thought, *...Probably cars in heaven...or hell...* He felt an incredible pain in his head, and then blessed darkness returned.

He awoke again, feeling something skitter across his hand. He heard the patter of small feet when he jerked in reflex, and his movement caused his head to feel like it would explode. But, he stayed conscious this time, and the pain eased.

His breathing came in short, shallow gasps. His breathing was what convinced him that he was alive. As he came to that conclusion, it also registered that he was cold, shivering. *...Typical D.C. weather...turning from warm to freezing in hours...get up...hypothermia...die...*

Beginning a body inventory, he tried his fingers, and then his hands. They moved without much difficulty. Just stiff. He tried his arms, moving with care; his right arm was okay, but his left arm wouldn't move.

Trying again resulted in another bout of excruciating pain. *...What the hell...? Must have twisted it falling...Falling...?*

He decided he'd have to worry about his shoulder later. He tried to move his feet. They moved, but prickled like they were asleep. *...Just so cold...!* Slowly, lest he start his head pounding again, he moved his legs. They worked. *...Thank God...!*

Reaching out with his right arm, Cavanaugh tried to get a sense of where he was. He could feel a hard, concrete-like surface where he was lying, and there seemed to be a wall behind his back.

He pushed with his good arm and tried to sit up. He knew he had to move. He was shivering like crazy.

He made it to a sitting position. As he did so, he felt something brush the top of his head. He reached up and could feel a covering of some sort over him.

He pushed upwards. The covering fell away, and he heard what sounded like cardboard boxes tumbling over one another. A wave of cold air engulfed him. *...Must have kept pocket of warmth with that stuff...*

"What's going on with eyes?" he muttered to himself. He reached up and touched his face. It felt like putty over his eyes. He rubbed, and whatever it was started to come off. He rubbed again, and his eyelids cracked open.

Relief surged through him. *...Judas Priest...can see...!* Using his shirtsleeve, he wiped his eyes clear of the gunk that was over them.

Carefully moving his head, he looked around. Boxes and miscellaneous trash surrounded him.

He tried to stand. The movement caused him to become nauseous, and he vomited. The dry heaves caused almost unbearable pain. He faded to the edge of consciousness, sagging against the alley wall on his hands and knees, his head resting on the ground.

As the pain subsided, he again used the wall as a brace, and slowly pushed himself upright, shoving more cardboard boxes and other trash away from him.

He could see streetlights. He tried to keep his head level as he stood and shuffled forward like an old man.

He reached the corner of the building. In the streetlights, he looked at his watch. It was 10:00 p.m. *...Damn...must have been out almost 24 hours...!*

Parked cars lining the street reminded him of what had happened. The recollection hit him with a jolt. *...My God...damn thieves shot me... stole briefcase...!*

With an even bigger jolt, Cavanaugh recalled the entire scenario. *...Men wearing balaclavas...was silenced pistol...professionals...not thieves...*

In shock, he began muttering, “They were after my briefcase. The stuff in there must be hot.” His mind then jumped forward. *...Got to warn Ginger and Jenny...grave danger...need phone...* He pushed off the building, starting to walk. Light-headed, he almost fell on his face.

Grabbing the edge of the building again for support, he let the vertigo pass. He looked around, desperate, panic edging into his mind. He saw that he was in an alley. He didn’t recognize his surroundings; he was lost.

It was then that he noticed an off-duty cab parked at the curb fifty feet away, the driver taking a break. He muttered to himself again, “If I can make it to the cab before he goes back on duty, I’ll get him to take me to Ginger’s house.”

Moving with care, he pushed away from the building, and shuffled toward the cab. He felt like he was moving in slow motion, teetering on a tightrope.

The engine of the cab started up. The cab light went back on. *...Oh shit...he’s pulling away...*

At that moment, a car came down the street, and the cabbie waited for it to pass. It was just enough delay. Cavanaugh opened the cab door and fell into the back seat, gasping in relief.

The cabbie turned in his seat, startled. He said, “Hey Mister, what’re you doing out here in this cold? You almost scared me to death.” It was dark, and the cabbie hadn’t gotten much of a look at Cavanaugh as yet.

“Listen, Buddy,” the cabbie said, “you sit up back there and tell me where you want to go. You don’t sit up, we don’t move. This ain’t no bed waiting for you to take a nap. Now you sit up, or I’ll be throw’n you out of my cab.” Cavanaugh sat up, his head spinning from exertion.

It was then the cabbie got a good look. “Whoa,” he said. “You get out of my cab. I don’t need trouble. You’re bleed’n all over my seats. Now get out!” He then pointed a large pistol in Cavanaugh’s face.

Cavanaugh said, “Please, I need your help. I’ll make it worth your while.” He started to reach into his jacket pocket for his wallet.

The cabbie cocked his pistol. The sound reverberated in the confined space of the cab. “You better be bringing your wallet out of that jacket or you’re a dead man,” warned the cabbie.

Clumsy with only one good hand, he fumbled through his money. He peeled off one hundred dollars and gave it to the cabbie. He gave him Ginger’s address. “Please. You take me there, and I’ll have another fifty for you,” he told the driver.

The cabbie stared first at Cavanaugh and then at the one hundred dollar bill.

“This is probably the dumbest thing I’ve done.” He took the money, lowered the pistol, and put the car in gear.

“Alright,” he said. “But, please don’t die on me, and *please* stop bleed’n on my seats.”

Cavanaugh laid his head back against the seat and drifted off, exhausted.

He was awakened with severe pain in both his head and shoulder. The cabbie was shaking him. “Stop,” Cavanaugh yelled. “You’re killing me!”

The cabbie said, “Sorry, but you were so quiet. I thought you’d died. We’re at your address. Let me help you out of the car.”

“Thanks,” Cavanaugh said. He paid the driver, and struggled up the stairs to the stoop for Ginger’s apartment.

He pushed the door buzzer. No answer. He pushed again. He was freezing and faint. *...Please, please,* *someone answer this thing*... He pushed the buzzer again, waiting…

He heard a faint, "Hello?"

He thought it was Mama. He said, "Mama, this is Jim Cavanaugh. I'm downstairs and need help." With that he passed out, falling in a heap at the threshold…

Chapter Twenty-Four

White Knight Takes Pawn

Jenny stormed out of the Air Police building after her meeting with Colonel Adams. She'd never felt so angry. She was muttering to herself, "This is crazy. No one is listening to reason. How can so many people be so stupid?"

It was almost 11:00 a.m. She decided that it would be best not to go back to her MP headquarters for a while. *...Need some time to figure out how to explain this mess to Cox ...*

Instead, she headed over to Gary Patten's office thinking, *...maybe he's got some ideas...*

"Hey," he said with a smile when Jenny walked in. "You never get over this way. What's up with the glum look?"

She unloaded. Gary became more and more pissed as she explained what had happened.

"That damned Adams," he said. "He's so GD hard headed. This isn't the first time he's been known to go off half-cocked. I've heard some talk about problems in his outfit.

He got up from his desk, and started out of the office. "Come on," he instructed.

"Where're we going?" Jenny asked. Gary was moving fast and was gone before she heard him respond.

"We're going to drive over and talk some sense into that hare-brained Colonel."

Jenny hurried after him and tried to calm him down. His reaction was more than she expected.

She said, "Sweetheart, I think this is a bad idea. In fact, I think it's going to make things worse. Please, shouldn't we…uhh…maybe talk about this over lunch?"

Gary wouldn't be detoured. In short order they arrived at the Air Police building.

As they pulled into the parking area, Jenny glanced over at two men in civilian clothes walking out of a nearby barracks. She recognized Sergeant Miller and Airman Andrews. They climbed into a white Mustang. There was another person already in the car.

She grabbed Gary's arm and pointed. "Sergeant Miller just got into that Mustang. I know I'm being paranoid, but his car looks identical to the one that almost ran me off the road last night."

They watched as the car pulled out of the parking lot. She got a good look and added, "It may also be the car that was in my apartment complex yesterday."

Her comments perked Gary's interest. He asked, "How about we follow them for a few minutes and see what they're up to?"

"Great idea," Jenny said, trying to mask the relief in her voice. She thought, *...anything's better than confronting Adams right now...*

Soon it became obvious that Miller was headed to the Tampa airport. The Mustang headed up the blue ramp for departing flights.

The car stopped at the American Airline terminal doors and, as Gary rolled by, they saw a tall, rugged looking man get out and limp into the terminal.

"That wasn't very exciting," Gary said. "I guess sleuthing isn't my thing."

Jenny patted him on the arm and said, "Let's just keep following them for awhile longer. I wouldn't mind seeing what else Miller's up to. It's lunch anyway; what else are you going to do?"

Gary muttered, "...it's a waste of time, acting like a couple of Dick Tracy's." But, he pulled out behind the Mustang as it re-entered the traffic stream.

It wasn't long before they arrived in downtown Ybor City, the seedier side of Tampa. Gary was providing color commentary on the community when they saw the Mustang pull over and park. Gary did a U-turn, and found a parking space on the other side of the street.

Miller and Andrews got out of the Mustang and approached a young couple handing out leaflets on the sidewalk. They shook hands as if meeting long-time friends, and then they went into nearby building that had whitewashed storefront windows. Soon, the couple came back outside, and continued handing out leaflets.

Jenny started to get out of Gary's car, saying, "I want one of those leaflets."

Gary pulled her back. "Wait a minute," he said. "You're not thinking. That uniform you're wearing is a dead giveaway. If they or their friends see you, we're busted. Let's think of another way."

Just then two Hispanic boys rode by on skateboards. They'd already made a couple of passes on the sidewalk beside Gary's car. That gave Jenny an idea.

When the youngsters approached again, she asked one of them over to the car window. "Would you boys like to make twenty bucks?" she asked.

"Hey Lady," one of them answered. "We don' do nothin' kinky. We jus' out here havin' fun."

She couldn't help but laugh. The boys didn't look a day over ten years old. She responded, "It's nothing bad. We just want you to go across the street and get one of the leaflets those two people are handing out. What do you think? Here's ten dollars. You bring me a leaflet and there's ten more in it for you."

Both boys grinned. This was easy money. They jaywalked across the street and then skateboarded up to the couple, taking one of their handouts. The boys were back to Jenny in two minutes.

She gave them another ten dollars and opened the leaflet. "My God, get a load of this!" She handed it to Gary. It read:

White Power Unite

Have you had enough?

Tired of being pushed around?

UNITE WITH US TONIGHT

Do you see the power vacuum?

UNITE WITH US TONIGHT

8:00 PM 1712 East Avenue, Ybor City

As they read in astonishment, Miller came out and began to put a banner across the front of the building. On the banner a face was outlined beside a raised fist. In bold letters it said, “White Power, Unite with Us Tonight. 8:00 p.m.”

She looked over at Gary. “I’m going to that meeting.”

“No way! You are <u>not</u> going to that meeting! At best they’ll beat you senseless if you’re caught. What would Cox say then? If you think you’re in trouble now, wait until he finds out you went to this thing without talking to him, and with no back up. He’ll have a cow!”

They got into a shouting match.

She soon realized how ridiculous it was for them to be yelling at one another sitting in a car in the middle of one of the rottenest parts of Tampa. She couldn’t help but burst out laughing. That made Gary madder. He clammed up and wouldn’t say anything more.

She thought, *...maybe I should try a different tack...* She took a deep breath, put on a big smile, and gave him a wet smooch on the cheek.

She said, “Sweetheart, I need to go. Please, please, please help me…” She nuzzled his neck and put her hand on his thigh, adding, “I’ll make it up to you.”

He knew her well enough to know that she’d go with or without his ‘permission.’ He sighed in exasperation saying, “Oh, alright damn it. But, if we go, you have to promise to follow my lead. OK?”

She smiled and kissed him again. “Of course, Gary. You’re the boss.”

“Right!!” he snorted.

Chapter Twenty-Five

Knight Attack

Jenny had on a black wig, heavy make up and oversized glasses. She also wore leather low-rider slacks, a 'bare midriff' blouse, and no bra.

Gary wore jeans, boots and a cowboy hat. He brought two big, brawny looking characters from his Maintenance Squadron. Both had buzz haircuts, cut off T-shirts, and leather vests.

...We should fit right it... she thought. Her mind then shifted to a vivid recollection of her conversation with Cox that afternoon. *...Was he ever pissed about my meeting with Adams...big time...maybe this will help with damage control...can't get much worse...*

Gary interrupted her train of thought by announcing that he'd brought a miniature video camera. "I bought this when I was in Japan," he said. "I never expected to use it on a spy mission. Ha!"

"Very funny. But, it would be great if you got some good pictures. Does it pick up sound?"

"Yep. It sounds tinny, like there's an echo, but you can hear it. And, I just charged the batteries."

"Super. I also brought a tape recorder in my purse. I hope Miller says something to hang himself."

They were outside Miller's building by 7:30 p.m. and watched as others went in. Jenny remarked, "Those turkeys sure look the part – hard case troublemakers. My guess is that most of the crowd at the meeting will be street people with nothing better to do, hoping for a free hand out."

There were police patrol cars parked at the curb, and young Black and Hispanic men had gathered on the other side of the street.

When Jenny and her group did go into the building, she kept her head down, and squeezed between her big escorts. They found seats in the rear of a large area filled with folding chairs, and fronted by a raised platform. It was apparent that there would be speakers.

Just as they sat down, she saw Miller. He and Andrews were circulating, introducing themselves to attendees and handing out literature. They were wearing confederate flags as bandanas, and T-shirts imprinted with a raised fist beside the words ‘United We Stand.’

She thought, *...dressed as would expect...didn’t think they’d rove around...not good...if get close...recognize me...trouble...! Need to hide...*

As Miller approached, she edged out of her seat, whispering to Gary “Going to rest room…” He nodded in understanding.

She was sure that Miller was staring right at her as she got up. She expected him to call out at any moment. He didn’t seem to recognize her, but she decided to wait in the rest room until the speakers started.

She was looking in the mirror, and was fiddling with her wig when an attractive young woman came in.

The woman was almost bubbling with enthusiasm. “Isn’t this a wonderful idea for a little get together?” she asked Jenny. Then she introduced herself. “Hi. I’m June Bergstrom. Everyone calls me ‘Jitterbug’. I guess it’s because I’m always just flitting around,” she said, giggling. “Do I know you?”

Jenny answered, “I don’t think we’ve met. I’m Jennifer.”

Jitterbug paid little attention to Jenny’s response, and prattled on, “You sure look good in that outfit. By the way, I’m the fiancée of one of the organizers for this event. Do you know Jimmy Miller?”

Jenny kept a straight face. She asked, “Is he a sergeant in the Air Force?”

“He sure is. He’s such a neat guy. I just adore him.”

Jenny reached into her purse and turned on her tape recorder. She said, “I think I might know a Sergeant Miller. From the airbase, right?”

Jitterbug giggled, “Right. I wouldn’t be surprised that you’d know him. Jimmy’s a real big shot over there. He told me he has his colonel tied around his little finger.

“You know,” she continued, “I really shouldn’t say this, but with you already knowing him and all…well…he was telling me that he pulled a slick one today on some Army Major. Jimmy convinced his colonel that the major was a loon and his colonel threw the guy out of his office. Isn’t that a hoot?” Jitterbug asked, laughing out loud.

“You just hav’ta just love him! Well, gotta’ go. They’re gonna’ start giving speeches pretty soon. Jimmy will be speaking. I can’t wait!”

…Me either… Jenny thought. She followed Jitterbug back into the main room.

Walking out of the rest room, Jenny saw Andrews standing in the hallway. *…Oh boy…not good…!*

“Say, don’t I know you?” he asked.

”I don’t think so,” Jenny mumbled, keeping her head down as she started to walk by him.

“Hey, wait a minute. You’re that Army bitch. What are you doing here?” His voice was rising as he spoke. He grabbed Jenny’s arm, saying, “I’m going to kick your…” He didn’t get any further. Jenny hit him in the throat.

It wasn’t a killing blow. She struck with the web between her thumb and forefinger. It paralyzed his windpipe for a few seconds. Andrews gagged, “Aarggh!”

She stepped to his side, kicked his leg out from under him, and pushed him toward the floor. He fell, landing on his back, his head hitting with a thump. Dazed for a split second, Andrews lay unmoving.

In that instant, she pulled his belt off his pants and turned him over. She twisted the belt around his hands behind his back. Next she tied his shoes together with his shoelaces. Andrews started to regain his voice.

"Hey, what are you doing?" he asked. "Let me loose, you cunt. You'll never get away with this…"

She pulled his bandana off his neck and gagged him with it. He could now only mumble, "Umm, uhhh, issh."

She dragged him out a side exit of the building and propped him against an outside wall. She headed back into the building saying, "See you, Asshole."

Andrews glared at her with hate blazing from his eyes.

She looked up on the stage as she found her way back to her seat in the main room. Miller was there. *…Damn…he's looking right at me…!* Jitterbug was talking to him and pointing toward Jenny. *…Oh crap…that can't be good…*

Sitting down, Jenny told Gary what had happened outside the rest room. "We may have to boogie out if Miller heads back here. By the way, did he say anything to you?"

"Yeah. He told me that if I ever got tired of you to give him a call. He'd like to try you on. Wasn't that sweet?"

She felt her blood begin to boil again. "I can't wait to bust this punk. He's history!"

Changing the subject, she asked, "Did you get any good video yet? It would be way cool having one with him right under that banner over the stage."

Gary smiled and answered, "Relax. We got some great pictures. There's no mistaking who's doing what."

"Awesome. If he makes remarks, I also want a picture of him at the podium." As she spoke, Miller walked up to the microphone on stage. He was everything she expected.

His comments included racial and ethnic slurs, and he used preposterous examples of minorities, "...taking over the world..." He also offered theories of evolution that were ludicrous.

He concluded with, "...whites need to join forces and eliminate everyone else from the U.S. Deport every one that doesn't belong!" There was polite applause. Another speaker headed to the microphone.

She told Gary, "I've had enough. Let's go before I get physically ill."

Gary motioned to his cohorts and they started toward the main door. At the same time, four burly men gathered at the exit, looking at Jenny's group as they approached.

"This isn't good, guys. Please try not to get in a brawl," she asked.

She had her hand on Gary's arm and could feel him tensing. *...Oh shit...going to get the Wing Maintenance Operations Officer in a fight in downtown Ybor City...great...!*

Just then three black youths came bursting into the room through the main door. They ran down the center aisle yelling, 'racist pigs!' They began throwing water balloons at the participants. Jenny was sure the youths were going to be killed.

Fortunately, officers from the Tampa City Police came in right behind the boys, corralled them, and escorted them out. In the melee, the four burly men at the doorway were distracted and pushed aside; Jenny's group was able to squeeze out the exit with the police, unscathed.

Hearing yells in the background of, "Hey, Lady, wait a minute," they ran to Gary's car. Jenny thought, *...it's a miracle we got away...Thank you, God...never do something like that again...*

As they pulled away from the curb, several of the youths who had gathered on the opposite side of the street began to move toward the building where the meeting was being held. More police cars arrived.

Jenny commented, "The police are going to have a tough time maintaining order in Ybor City tonight." All nodded in agreement.

They were in a euphoric high as they drove back to MacDill. Jenny was so excited she felt like a child. *...Out of the doghouse for sure...hot damn...!*

She asked Gary, "Look for a Photomat or Office Max. I want to have copies of those pictures you took on the desks of Adams and Cox first thing in the morning. I'm making a copy of my tape recording for both of them, too. This will be sweet."

After dropping the pictures off for processing, Gary stopped by Jenny's place for a beer. As she opened the bottles in her kitchenette, Gary stepped behind her. "I can think of something special we could do to celebrate," he said as he nuzzled her neck.

The excitement of the night acted as an aphrodisiac, and she felt her heat build. He caressed her shoulders and arms, his breath warm in her hair. She leaned against him. The night was having the same effect on him.

Breathing deeply, Jenny murmured, "Man, I think that's a great idea!"

She turned, and they shared a passionate kiss. She ran her hands over his back and pressed her hips into him with uninhibited desire. "Come on," she panted, pulling him to the living room couch, "let's get naked."

Gary lay back and watched as she stripped off her blouse and pants. The anticipation on his face as she undressed made her even hotter.

She stepped out of her bikini panties and…

…His cell phone rang.

"Christ," Gary groaned.

"Don't you have someone to cover that for you?"

"Sorry Tiger, you know the deal. Planes break. We're on high alert. They only call when it's serious."

She heard a couple of "Uh huhs" and "OK's," as Gary responded to the phone conversation. Then she heard the inevitable, "Be right there."

Growing up in the military, she knew how important it could be. *...It's just so aggravating...!*

Sighing with pent up frustration, she began gathering her clothes as Gary pulled on his pants and boots. "Do you want me to come back?" he asked.

"It's getting late, Hon. Thanks, but I think I'll hit the sack. See you tomorrow."

Locking up behind him, she padded naked into the bathroom. *...A hot bath...chill out...*

She got out scented candles and bath bubbles, and unwound in the warmth of the bathwater. She soaked for an hour before drying off and climbing into bed. Dreamland was almost instantaneous.

Chapter Twenty-Six

Knight Retreats

Jenny felt as if she'd just closed her eyes when she heard the phone ring. She looked at the clock. *...Two a.m....God...not on call...can't be important...answering machine...*

Jenny was dozing off again when she recognized her brother's voice on the machine saying, "Pick up, Jenny. If you're there, pick up. This is an emergency." She was awake and out of bed like a bolt. She grabbed the bedside phone. *...Trouble...he wouldn't call at this hour...*

"What's wrong, Tom?"

"It's Jim, Sis. Jim Cavanaugh. It looks like he's been shot. He's hurt bad."

"My God! What happened?"

"I don't know. His girl friend called me about thirty minutes ago. I just got here, and I'm looking at him as we speak. I have to go. Let her tell you..."

"Wait..." Jenny said. Then she heard a woman's voice on the phone.

"Hello, Jenny. ...I'm so sorry..."

"Yeah. Me too. I mean...really. I don't know what to say..."

"...This is so awkward," Ginger said. "I guess I should tell you that Jim and I have become close friends over the last few months. My name is Ginger Albright. You may not remember, but I met you briefly at your dad's funeral."

"I don't remember much about that day. My apologies..."

"Of course. I understand. Why don't I start with the little I know?"

"Sure...that'd be good, I think."

"Well, as crazy as it sounds, Jim arrived at my doorstep at about 10:30 p.m. last night. He'd lost a lot of blood and was almost incoherent. He told me not to call the police or a doctor, and not to take him to the hospital. Then he passed out."

Ginger paused for a breath and then continued. "As improbable as it sounds, I think he was attacked Monday night."

"My God. That was two days ago. What…?"

"I know. He was here for dinner that night, and then he didn't show up to work the next day. I can't imagine where he was or what happened in the interim. My mom's a nurse, so he got good care.

"He's been out of it, and we haven't been able to learn much more. When he woke up late this evening, he gave me numbers for you and Tom. That's how we reached you. I'm sorry to ramble on. It's just been so insane…"

"That's OK. I understand. Thank you for taking care of him. Is he going to be alright?"

"Here, let Tom tell you. He looks like he's about finished."

Tom didn't waste any time, "It looks like he may have a concussion from a gunshot that creased his skull. Another bullet went through soft tissue in his shoulder. It missed the lung by about a quarter inch. Ginger and her mom did a super job taking care of him. Here's Ginger again. I need to finish up."

Ginger said, "Jim woke up two hours ago a lot less groggy. He told me that we're all in danger, but that you would know what to do. He's been looking into some conspiracy theory. I don't know the details.

"He also told me to tell you to read your dad's journal, and to look at that FedEx package he sent. He said to tell you, 'It's Korea in reverse,' whatever that means."

Jenny said, "I understand what he meant. Tell him I'll be flying in tomorrow. I'll get a cab from the airport." She jotted down Ginger's address, and they disconnected.

Hanging up the phone, she thought, *...Can't imagine my helping...what's he thinking...?*

She called the airlines and booked a seat, and then she began to look for the FedEx package. Finding it under the pile of mail, she ripped off the fastener. Her mouth dropped open.

...Holy shit...this is all marked compartmentalized top secret...what the hell has Jim gotten into...? She scanned the pages. *...Remington...dated 1980's...something twenty years ago that important...?* She decided to read the reports in more detail on the plane.

She then booted up her computer, and slipped in the disc that was in the package. The information on it was not any clearer to her than the reports in the folder. It appeared to only contain a paragraph narrating the theft of secret weapons from Smith & Wesson. *...This is clear as mud...it doesn't make sense...Jim will have to explain...*

Tired, figuring she was wasting time, she decided to shut down and go to bed. Her screen suddenly filled with columns of data. She'd hit the wrong key.

With a start, Jenny realized that she'd pulled up another section on the disc. It was a chart labeled 'Redstone Arsenal, Access Records, Secure Storage Areas.' There was a subtitle labeled 'Smith & Wesson.'

She muttered to herself, "Jesus, Mary and Joseph. I bet this is what some of the excitement is about. Hmmm…some kind of code…I'll need help unscrambling this thing." *...Maybe Jim will have some ideas...wait until get to D.C....*

Shutting off her computer, she realized she'd been putting off the hard part. It was time. She called Cox.

Sleep fogged, he answered, "Hullo."

"Uhh…good morning, Sir."

Recognizing her voice, Cox responded, "O'Shane, you're turning into a real pain in the ass. What in the hell is so important that you call me at home at this hour?"

"Colonel, I'm really sorry to bother you, but I have another family emergency in D.C. I need to go back. It shouldn't be but a few days."

"You serious?"

"Yes, Sir. Sorry…"

"I see. All right…well…I'll assume you have a good reason. Tell me later. I'm too tired right now. Is there anything I can do?"

"Uhhh…Yes, Sir. There is one small thing…"

"Okay. What is it? Come on, it's late…"

"Sir, I'd like to check out my sidearm."

"What? You're kidding me? You want me to authorize what? Come on. Even though you're a federal officer, carrying your weapon off post is almost unheard of. What kind of family emergency is this?"

"Sir, I think it's necessary, and I know you have the authority. I…uhh…I can explain…"

"Wait. Wait…this is going to be another doozer. Don't say any more. Just be quiet for a minute and let me clear the cobwebs." She heard silence in the receiver.

After what seemed like an eternity, she heard, "O'Shane, this is against my better judgment. If you hadn't had such glowing performance reports, and if I hadn't known your dad… Pick up your weapon in the morning. You can explain when you get back. It had better be good."

"Thank you, Sir. I appreciate your trust. I won't disappoint you."

"OK," he replied, after another pause. "Now look…I don't like your being gone again. How about getting it all over with this time so you can get back to work?"

"Yes, Sir. I'll make it quick. I'm sorry to run out on you."

"These things happen. And…we'll put the problem with Sergeant Miller on hold until you return," he said, a renewed frost in his voice.

"Sir, you'll find information on your desk when you get in tomorrow morning. I think it will help clear up the misunderstanding."

"We'll see. It's going to take a lot to make Miller go away. Let's talk another time. Right now, I'm going back to bed. Good night." She heard a dial tone.

…Jesus…he's really pissed…got to get that material to him…!

She dialed Gary's number. He answered on the second ring, accustomed to all hour calls. "What?" he mumbled.

"Gary, it's me."

"Jesus Christ, Jenny, I just got in bed. What's going on?"

She explained about Cavanaugh. Then she asked, "Would you pick up those pictures and get them and the audio tapes to Cox and Adams first thing in the morning? It's really important to me. Please."

"Sure…No sweat. Of course I'll get the stuff. Don't worry about it. You get back to D.C."

After a brief exchange on how Gary would pick up and deliver the materials, she closed with, "Thanks, Hon. I promise I'll to make it up to you."

"Right…"

Hanging up the phone, she began to pack.

Chapter Twenty-Seven

Knights Joined

Even though exhausted from the excitement of the late night, Jenny was too wired to sleep on the plane.

She pulled out the material Cavanaugh had sent, first reviewing the Remington papers. She noticed that a Sam Collins, a Navy Commander, had signed each report.

...Be damned...wonder if he's the same Admiral Collins who just died...this is getting twisted...

She made a mental note to verify the author when she saw Cavanaugh.

There were four different memos. One outlined progress that Remington had reported about research they were conducting on small arms laser technology. There was a lot of technical jargon, but it copied an upbeat status report provided in a letter to the Pentagon. It announced the corporation's intent to begin marketing products in the near-term.

A second memo noted that prototypes, research material, and test equipment were missing from a Remington research lab.

The memo went on the say that a mysterious fire had destroyed the research lab, killing the leading scientists for the program. There was a penciled margin notation that Krueger, a firm in Germany, had begun marketing the weapons that Remington had developed.

Another memorandum reported names of several people who had access to the prototype weapons. Included was a similar list of people who had access to the top-secret lab.

...Wonder how that checks with the names on Smith & Wesson e-mail listings from computer disc...might be

interesting...has to be some reason there are two sets of documents...

The fourth and final memo was a synopsis of the earlier information and a narrative expressing chagrin about being ordered to close down the investigation. Another margin notation commented that Remington officials, who had been cooperative in the initial review of circumstances, would no longer discuss the matter with Commander Collins.

...Why wouldn't corporation leaders discuss any more...? Weird...

She put the memos away, feeling nervous about them being visible to the other passengers around her. The big "Top Secret" stamp on the top of each page was difficult to conceal.

She next pulled out her dad's spiral notebook that Jim had given her after the funeral. She'd brought it to MacDill with her in her carry-on luggage. She hadn't felt up to looking at it at the time, and hadn't really given it much thought since. Now, with Jim's message, it had a whole different meaning.

The first page of the notebook was simply an insert for the reader indicating that the material was classified top secret and the contents should be returned to military authorities unopened. She was saddened, looking at her dad's handwriting.

...Reading this is going to be hard...

The second page of the notebook was titled 'Background'. It was a diary of events by her dad describing a task force and his assignment. Included were general observations about guidance Admiral Collins had provided in directing the investigation.

...Well now...wondered why Dad was in D.C. instead of deployed at some military post...he <u>was</u> working for Collins...be damned...shouldn't be surprised...Jim gave

me this stuff – ergo, he was working on same investigation…this is wild…!

The next page was titled, 'Remington Theft'. It listed what appeared to be a synopsis of key points of the incident, most of which were in Collins' reports. After the key points was a series of questions and other notations that were listed as one subject area per page:

Page one had two questions written in bold print – 'Who had access to the labs? Did anyone make a special request for access and weapons shipment schedules?'

Beside these questions were some margin notes: 'Crenshaw reviewing all military personnel assignments to the Remington lab to see if any prominent names surface. Who in Pentagon connected to project?'

On the same page, there was also the note: 'Crenshaw found sixty-eight names of personnel who were active duty military, either assigned to the lab or the Pentagon, who were involved in some way with the development cycle for the weapons -- sixteen are still on active duty. To Do: Find out where are they assigned. Have Cohen run down military records.'

She thought, *…Crenshaw…Cohen…don't recognize the names…probably investigators…wonder if they got answers…? How contact…? Jim will know…*

Page two of the journal had one question printed in bold – 'Who would profit if Remington did not produce the weapons? (Another arms firm!)'

Beneath the bold print were some notes: 'Wusacki looked up the firm noted in reports. Krueger – a German company. They marketed weapons in early 1980's, soon after Remington lab destroyed. To Do: Find connection.'

Page three had multiple questions – 'How did Krueger get the technology? Were they working on the project with Remington? Who in Krueger developed project? To Do: Try to access Krueger weapon development records.'

Only one question was highlighted on page four – 'Are there records of unusual shipments out of U.S. to Germany during this time frame? To Do: Assign to Frisk when he returns.'

The following pages were similar with questions, but there were no notes underneath – 'Were there unusual events involving any Germans in U.S. at time of theft? What about U.S. military liaison staff in Germany? Why did the Remington executives stop cooperating? Names? Where are they now? Who in the White House ordered the investigation shut down? What benefit was there to end the investigation? Political?'

The last page had editorial notations: 'Civil strife in West Germany at the time; East German refugees; Berlin Wall; immigrants from other countries; sluggish economy; Baader Meinhoff terrorists; Red Army Faction.'

Leaning back in her seat, she closed the notebook. She allowed her mind to absorb what she'd learned, and to reflect on recent events. *...This is connected...how...? Jim almost killed...what's going on...? Hope he's OK...couldn't stand losing him after Dad's accident...*

Her mind paused in its tracks for a second. *...Accident...? Was it...? Had to be...! Hundreds of people involved...Come on, Jennifer...! You're seeing ghosts...*

Chapter Twenty-Eight

Clear Knight

In the Albright apartment, a beam of sunlight broke through a gap in the bedroom curtains. It struck Cavanaugh directly in an eye.

Startled and awakened by the sudden glare, he didn't recognize anything at first. He looked around in momentary panic.

Then a sigh of relief *...apartment...boys' room...whew...!* Memories came flooding back.

...Shot...Ginger and Mama helped...Tom, Jr. here... Called Jenny...

He then remembered the most important thing. *...Told Ginger to find place to hide...what's going on...?*

Then his body started sending signals. He had to pee, and he was ravenous. *...First things first...*

He got up and found his way to the bathroom. His mind took a quick physical inventory, *...head stopped hurting...not so dizzy...on the mend...*

As he walked down the hallway, the smell of cooking wafted through. *...Man, don't ever remember being this hungry...!*

Ginger came down the hall as Cavanaugh left the bathroom. "Well good morning, Big Boy," she said. "Glad to see you up and around. Tom, Jr. said you'd feel better soon." She gave him a little pat on the behind and a brief kiss.

"By the way," she added, "you might want to get dressed. Mama stayed home today to be sure you had 'proper care'. But, I don't think she expected you to be padding around buck-naked. I put clothes on the dresser for you. My ex left them." She turned and headed back toward the kitchen, laughing.

Groggy from painkillers, it was only then that Cavanaugh realized he was walking around without any clothes on. *...Holy cow...!* He hustled toward the bedroom.

Ginger couldn't help but offer another whispered jibe. "Don't worry, I've seen it before…ha, ha!"

Handicapped by the bandages on his shoulder, he struggled to dress. Finally successful, he followed the scent of food. It looked as good as it smelled. Mama had grits, sausage and scrambled eggs.

He dug in. However, he soon found that his appetite had vanished; he finished only half his plate, but drank three glasses of juice.

"Normal," Mama said in her role as nurse/advisor. "Your stomach has shrunk and you've got to replace the fluids you lost bleedin' all over the place!"

Fatigue enveloped him. He almost dozed off at the table. Ginger helped him up and back into the bedroom. On the way, she told him, "Jenny is on her way and should arrive later this afternoon." She told him three more things that broke through his lethargy.

"Commander Frisk is back in town. He's still convalescing from his injuries, but he agreed to come over to the apartment when Jenny arrives."

She added, "I know you told us we had to leave the apartment, but Mama refused. She told me, 'I won't be run off by a bunch of hooligans.' She wouldn't be convinced otherwise!"

Lastly, Ginger told him, "I sent the boys to be with my ex-husband, Robby. He sent two of his associates to keep an eye on things around the apartment complex."

By that time, he had collapsed on the bed and was nearly asleep. Ginger pulled off his slippers, put a blanket over him, and returned to the kitchen.

Chapter Twenty-Nine

Knights United

Ginger's comments to Cavanaugh coincided with Jenny hailing a cab at Reagan International. She'd made a brief stop at the air marshal's office to retrieve her sidearm. Its weight in her shoulder holster was comforting.

Distracted by thoughts of Cavanaugh and her dad's investigation, she ignored her surroundings until she climbed the steps to the stoop of the Albright apartment complex. As she started to ring the door's security buzzer, two black men walk up. They were not friendly.

One of the men was the biggest person she had ever seen. He towered over her and he'd only come halfway up the steps. "Missy, my name's Bubba. What you want here?" he asked. "Ain't you in da wrong 'hood?"

The other man, almost as big, stood off to the side in the street fifteen feet away. His hands were in the pockets of a long trench coat.

She stared up at the man beside her. *...Damn...should have called ahead...don't need trouble...Oh boy...!*

"I'm Jennifer O'Shane," she answered, forcing any quaver of fear from her voice. "I'm here to visit a friend in apartment sixteen named Ginger Albright. She's expecting me."

The big guy responded, "Robby said no one goes into dat buildin' who don' live dere less'n he says. You don' live dere. And, he ain't said. Scram, Missy." He put his hand on her shoulder.

Stepping away, she told him, "Don't touch me, mister."

"What you gonna do, Missy? Hit me wit' your purse? Ha!"

He reached under her arm to move her out of the entryway. She stepped into him and grabbed his pinkie finger and bent it back. It felt like she was wrestling a Mack truck.

"Ahh…Hey…Ouch!" he exclaimed, kneeling on the stairs. "Owww! Stop!"

In the same instant, she had her Beretta in her hand, and had it shoved it under Bubba's chin. Just as quick, the man in the street had a shotgun pointed at her.

"Wait a minute," she quickly said. "That scattergun will kill your friend, too. Just put it down, and I'll put mine away. Please.

She let that sink in for a second and then added, "I don't need any trouble. They really do expect me in there. Can't you at least ask?"

The shotgun disappeared in the folds of the trench coat. "Okay, Missy. Let him go," the man in the street instructed. To his partner he said, "It's OK, Bubba. Come on down here. We'll call upstairs and check her out."

He pushed auto-dial on his cell phone. Jenny heard a female voice answer, "Hello?"

"Ms. Albright, it's me. Robby said not to bother you, but dere's a white lady out here calls herself Jenny something. You know her?"

"Yes, please have her come on up. Thank you, Big John."

The man motioned for Jenny to go on in when the door buzzer sounded. As Jenny entered the apartment building, the man called Big John said to her, "Das a slick move on Bubba, Missy. I may use it sometime…"

"Uhh, thanks, I think…" Jenny answered.

A gorgeous Black woman greeted her from the top of the first flight of stairs. "Hi," she said. "I'm Ginger. Thanks so much for coming."

They hugged as if long time friends. Jenny responded, "I just wish it were under different circumstances. I hope I can help."

They walked into the apartment, and Ginger introduced her to a woman who looked like an older sister.

The older woman told Jenny, "Call me 'Mama'. Everyone else does." She added, "You're sure a pretty little thing. You don't look like no cop to me!"

Blushing, Jenny explained that she was a military policeman, not a cop in the normal sense. Mama began, "Well don't tell those young punks downstairs, they'll probably just shoot you out of hand. They're a…"

Ginger interrupted, "Now Mama, don't get started. For once I'm glad they're here. Let's not frighten our new friend."

Jenny laughed, "Those two downstairs don't need anyone to say anything to scare people. They're a couple of tough looking characters."

Mama dismissed that with a wave of her hand and said, "Don't let them scare you, Honey. I practically raised those boys. When they were younger, they were here more than in their own house. They better behave or I'll be gittin' my broom out after'em again!"

Jenny started to laugh, but thought better of it. Mama was serious. Instead she changed the subject.

"How's Jim doing?" she asked.

Ginger answered, "Much better. He's getting his strength back. We'll wake him for lunch. He's been napping for over an hour.

"He told me to ask a Commander Frisk to come over when you got here. Will that be alright with you?"

"Fine by me. Wasn't he working with Jim and my dad?"

"Right. He's on the task force."

"Great. I've got a couple of things I want to ask him."

After Ginger called Frisk and alerted Big John that they would have another visitor, she and Jenny got acquainted while Mama started making lunch. The fact that they thought so much of the same guy made for great chemistry.

Frisk buzzed at the entry within twenty-five minutes. Walking with a cane, he struggled up the stairs. Ginger went in to wake Cavanaugh.

In the time Ginger was gone, Jenny learned that she and Frisk had a lot in common. He was a Naval Academy graduate and was assigned to the Naval Criminal Investigation Service. He had been a member of the Navy's Master at Arms organization. They performed many of the same functions as the Army's Military Police.

Frisk asked her to call him 'AD.' "All my friends do."

Jenny decided she liked him. He was good looking and carried himself with quiet confidence. He wore a polo shirt that showed off a great build. As those feminine observations were running through her mind, Cavanaugh walked into the room.

Jenny jumped up and gave him a hug. "Jim, I'm so glad to see you. You sure had me worried. You still look pretty rough," she said.

As he shook hands with Frisk, he answered, "Hey, you should see the other guys." Everyone gave his weak humor a half-hearted laugh, knowing that the circumstances could have been quite different.

Mama served sandwiches and sodas. He wolfed down two sandwiches as he recounted what had happened to him. He ended his report with, "We have to be very careful. These guys are playing for keeps."

Even with the seriousness of Cavanaugh's story, Frisk gave the situation an exclamation mark. "I haven't made it official through U.S. channels as yet, but you should know that my accident was an attempt to kill me."

"What? Are you serious?" Jenny exclaimed.

"Absolutely. I was scuba diving at about one hundred feet with two buddies. We were looking at an old sunken ship off St. Thomas. We got separated briefly, and someone swam up behind me and cut my air hoses. I had to make an emergency surface.

"I got a severe case of the bends. We had no decompression equipment on board our boat, and it was thirty miles back to St Thomas. The doctors tell me only time would determine whether my knees will recover. I'll be on a cane for a while."

"Does anyone else know you're back in D.C.?" Jenny asked.

"No one besides Petty Officer Cohen and you guys. I've asked him to keep it quiet. I'm still listed as a patient at the hospital in St. Thomas."

He continued after taking a breath, "I feel somewhat guilty. The doctors had me doped up on the islands. I only heard about General O'Shane and Admiral Collins last week. I just wish I could have gotten back here sooner."

"Well, it's nice of you to be concerned AD, but the services for them were…" Jenny paused and looked off into space. A silence enveloped the room.

"What's the matter, Jenny?" Cavanaugh asked.

Tears stung her eyes as realization dawned. She said, "I discounted this during my plane ride, but now I'm becoming convinced that my dad and the admiral were murdered!"

"What? I don't see… You must be…" Everyone exclaimed at the same time. And, then silence filled the room again. They all looked at Jenny, stunned, not wanting to see the obvious.

Ginger broke the silence. "What kind of freaks would do something like that?"

Jenny answered in a barely audible whisper, “We’re dealing with fanatics. There’s no other explanation when you add up what happened to Dad, the admiral, Jim, and then AD.”

After a short pause, Frisk asked Cavanaugh, “Didn’t you say your briefcase was stolen when you were attacked?”

“Yep. And, it had copies of the Collins memos and your disc. And, guess what. The general’s briefcase was missing from his car…it had the same stuff...”

Jenny interrupted his comment, “That’s got to be it. Whoever is doing this is trying to disrupt or halt the task force investigation. And, they’re trying to obtain all copies of incriminating material.”

She paused as she thought through her comments. “I brought the copies Jim sent me. We need to keep an eye on them. It’s clear that these people will resort to anything to accomplish their goals. They already broke into my apartment and stole my luggage in Tampa. We’re dealing with dangerous people! They’re organized and seem to have unlimited resources.”

Ginger commented, “All of this over a stupid investigation of the Remington operation 20 years ago? They must be desperate to cover their ass!”

“No,” Frisk and Jenny almost simultaneously corrected.

Frisk continued, “You’re half right. There was a theft from Remington many years ago and that was the main impetus for starting the task force. But, as we spun up that investigation, thieves stole Smith & Wesson prototype weapons from Redstone Arsenal. It was a copycat operation.

“Seeing a connection, Admiral Collins sent me to investigate the Smith & Wesson theft at Redstone. I uncovered information off of Redstone’s main server that I copied on to the disc that I sent to General O’Shane.

"Wow! Two identical thefts… That's ballsy," Cavanaugh broke in. "But, still, why are they reacting now, in such drastic fashion?"

"Well, I think I can guess several reasons," Jenny said. She began to tick off points, "There's billions of dollars involved – Careers and reputations are at risk – The Smith & Wesson operation is nearing completion – Dad and Admiral Collins were about to uncover the culprits.

"Any or all of these factors could have caused them to take desperate measures. Additionally, I'd bet a paycheck there have been other people murdered in these operations that we have no idea about. These guys don't have a conscience."

Jenny paused for a minute. Then she added, "I'm thinking that we should request that the bodies of Dad and Admiral Collins be exhumed. An autopsy could confirm our suspicions."

Steel came into her voice as she added, "Using that, and the information we know, we're going to find the guilty bastards and bust their ass! They're not going to get away with this. I don't care what it takes."

A murmuring from the group conveyed similar feelings from each of them. There was another silence as they all reflected on the enormity of the situation.

Jenny broke the spell by asking Cavanaugh, "How do you suppose they knew that you sent the reports to me? They had to have had you under constant surveillance."

"By God, you're right. The office must be bugged."

"Yep," Jenny answered. "We have to assume that these guys are deep into the system. I'd guess they have complete Pentagon access. The phones are probably tapped, too."

Jenny turned to Frisk, "Not letting anyone know you're back in D.C. was a smart move. We need you to stay invisible. We're going to need you to move around town without undue suspicion. They won't be looking for you, but the rest of us will be under a microscope."

She then asked, "Just out of curiosity, how did you keep the goons in St. Thomas from following up and finishing the job while you were recovering in the hospital?"

"I told my diving buddies what happened. They could see that my air hoses were cut. Most of us have been diving buddies since high school. Four of them stayed in St. Thomas while I was recovering."

"Wow, some friends. What about the local police? Didn't you contact them?"

Frisk smiled. "Oh yeah. You have to report all diving accidents when anyone is injured. But, like most police in the region, they're understaffed. They get similar reports daily. It simplified their lives to conclude I'd cut my own hoses on the wrecked freighter."

"How did you get out of the hospital and St. Thomas without detection?"

"The same way we got there. One of the guys has a private plane. And, I was very careful. In fact, a couple of my diving friends who are retired stayed down there, and are pretending to still be watching over me in case the place is under surveillance. I left from a back door."

"Sounds like you covered the bases," Jenny commented. Turning to Ginger, she asked, "As long as we're clearing up questions, I was curious about those men downstairs. Who are they?"

Ginger started to explain when the door buzzer sounded. Mama answered. It was Big John.

"Mama," he said, "I got a couple of men down here that Robby said I should bring up. He thinks you folks will want to talk to them. You want to buzz us up?"

Mama turned to the others.

Jenny responded, "If he says we need to talk to them…"

Chapter Thirty

Knight Attack

Across town, Lieutenant Fernando called Colonel Histaves. The lieutenant reported, "*Mi Coronel*, it looks like the chickens have come home to roost just like you thought they would."

"Esteban, you have learned your American idioms well. It's no longer amusing. Please tell me why you called. I'm very busy."

"*Si, mi Coronel*. As you instructed, we've been watching the apartment building of that Albright woman who worked in the task force office. By the way, there are two very big men guarding the entry to the building."

"OK…So what? My patience is wearing thin. What's your report?"

"*Pardon, mi Coronel*. What I wanted to tell you is that the 'Jenny' woman showed up at the apartment about thirty minutes ago. Also, another man just arrived, using a cane. Our operatives didn't recognize him. He's not the same one that was there last night."

"You're right to call, *Teniente*. I expected Cavanaugh's girlfriend to reach out after his disappearance. I thought she might include the O'Shane woman. Let's hope that O'Shane brought the files. We should know soon enough."

Histaves mulled over the circumstances before continuing. "Keep an eye on the apartment. I sense that O'Shane is the remaining link. The others are inconsequential. We need to focus on her until we get those files."

"*Coronel*, do you want my team to break in and get them?"

Histaves reflected for another moment. "No, not yet. Let's watch and wait for now. My guess is that she will make a move soon, and we will have her and the files."

Changing subjects, he asked, "Have you heard from our agent in St Thomas?"

"*Si, Senor*. It appears that Frisk is still hospitalized."

"Hmmm. Have your man recheck his information. We only have a few more days to shipment time. We need to keep a rein on all the players and Frisk is one. We don't need any of them complicating things. Let's hope Cavanaugh's body doesn't surface for a few more days."

Histaves changed subjects again. "Have you made the arrangements for the U.S. Customs inspection of our shipment?"

"*Si.* It's done."

"Good. Good. Anything else I should know?"

"*Si, Senor.* Nothing to get alarmed about as yet, but the operatives outside the Albright apartment aren't responding on their cell phone. I think it's probably low batteries,"

"Well, check and let me know. Please be very careful, my young friend."

"*Si, Senor*," responded Fernando and disconnected.

Chapter Thirty-One

Pawn Question

At the moment Histaves put his phone in its cradle, Big John and Bubba hauled two men into Ginger's apartment, holding each by the collar. Both were semi-conscious, and one was limping.

Big John said, "We found these 'honkies' hangin' 'round. When we axed'em what was happenin' dey din't have no good answers. Fact is dey got hostile. Bubba quieted 'em down."

Handing a small device to Jenny, he continued, pointing to the older of the two, "Dat one was wearin' dis here phone. And, dey bot had shooters. When you done wit'em, give a call. We best be gittin' back."

Mama called after him, "Big John, here's some sandwiches and a thermos of hot soup. You boys stay warm down there now, you hear?"

"Yes Ma'am. Thank you." With that he left the two men lying on the floor.

Jenny was the first to move. She checked the bindings of each of the men, and then said to Ginger, "Whatever you were saying about those two on your doorstep doesn't matter too much. I think they may have saved us a lot of grief."

Ginger responded, "Well, I'm embarrassed to admit that Robby is a leader of a local group of thugs. His gang is the main reason that I left him. Right now though, I'm almost grateful he's a hoodlum."

Jenny shook her head. *...Crooks are protecting us...! No one will ever believe this story...* All she could manage to say was, "At this point, I'm glad they're on our side."

As Jenny turned the men onto their backs, Cavanaugh peered at them. He exclaimed, "Hey, that older one is one of the men who attacked me. I yanked his mask off before I was shot! You saw him limping. I'd bet that's from me kicking his knee."

Color drained from the older man's face as he recognized Cavanaugh. He said in shock, "You're dead!"

"Not quite, but nice try," answered Cavanaugh.

Jenny asked the men, "What were you two doing outside the apartment?"

The older man answered, "We're not saying anything to you. You have no right to keep us here. This is kidnapping."

Jenny straddled and sat down hard on the man. Leaning into his face, she said. "You don't answer my questions, kidnapping will be the least of your worries."

She studied his face for a minute more, and then slowly smiled, "Hey, didn't I see you in Florida at the Tampa airport? Do you know Sergeant Miller?"

Another look of surprise crossed the man's face, but he quickly recovered gasping, "Hey, I can't breathe. You're killing my wrists."

"Too bad. Maybe we can have the big guy come up and sit on you for a while."

He wheezed an answer. "Look, we're just keeping an eye on the place and reporting comings and goings to a voice on the phone. And, yeah, I might have been visiting some friends in Tampa. So what? You've got no right…get off my chest!"

Jenny stood up partway and then dropped all her one hundred and twenty pounds back on the man's chest.

"Oops. Sorry, lost my balance," she said. "Now listen to me you bonehead. One of you, or one of your friends, killed my dad. I'm a cop, and I promise you that I'm going to make sure you pay.

"I've got you at least for attempted murder. Look at that man there," she said pointing to Jim. "He'll testify in court that you attacked, robbed and shot him. You guys are either going to jail, and we can tell the judge how you cooperated, or we'll let those boys downstairs deal with you! It's your choice."

Jenny let her comments sink in. Then she added, "And, you know what? I hope you don't say anything because it will give me pleasure to think of concrete pouring over your heads at one of the downtown construction sites."

With that she stood, and moved to the kitchen table. She turned back to the two on the floor, the older one now lying in a fetal position, retching. "You have one minute to make up your minds."

She took off her watch in an exaggerated motion, making her point. The two men looked at one another, then back to Jenny.

At the one-minute mark, she told Mama, "Please ask Big John to come up here and get rid of this trash." Mama picked up the phone.

The youngest man blurted, "Wait a minute. I'll tell you what I know. It's not much, but I don't want anything to do with those guys downstairs."

The older man glared at him. "Keep your mouth shut. They don't have anything." The younger man shook his head.

"No way! I don't care what they have. I didn't do nothin' and I ain't going to jail for you or anyone else. And, I sure as hell don't intend to get killed.

"My name is Bryan Dees. I left the Army after four years in the Rangers and have been sort of bumming around. Last month I read an ad in a men's magazine recruiting ex-Rangers. I applied and was called a couple of days ago."

Dees took a breath and then continued, "I was told to come by a warehouse at the Reagan Airport. When I got to the warehouse, a man in a balaclava directed me into a van. We talked for a few minutes and he told to go back to my hotel, and someone would arrange to pick me up.

"Two days ago, this guy (pointing to the older man) showed up and gave me five hundred in cash. He said his name is Zucher and that he's an ex-Air Force Air Commando. I've been on stakeout outside this apartment ever since I was hired. That's all I know."

Jenny's group digested the information for a few minutes. She pointed to Zucher, "He's the man I saw in Tampa. He probably burglarized my apartment and stole my luggage."

Frisk asked, "You have anything to say, Zucher?" The guy shook his head.

Dees added, "It just occurred to me, Zucher spoke on the phone in Spanish. I speak a little, so I recognized the language. He spoke so fast I didn't pick up what he said."

After a moment more, Jenny asked Mama to call Big John up to get the two men. Dees became agitated.

"Relax," Jenny told him. She asked Big John when he got upstairs, "Do you have a place to keep these two off the streets for a while?"

"We have a couple of places we can use," he responded.

Jenny pointed to Dees and said, "This guy is helping us out. Don't be too hard on him. We'll need him later."

She said to Dees, "I'll want you to show us that warehouse. After that, we'll let you go. I'd recommend you be a lot more careful of the company you keep."

Then she pointed to Zucher. "He's being hard-headed. I don't care what you do with him for now, but don't hurt him too bad. He's going to jail."

"We got just the place for them both, Missy," Big John said. He and Bubba picked the men up by their coat collars and hauled them out of the apartment.

At that point, Cavanaugh indicated he needed to lie back down. He said, "I'm exhausted. But, don't do anything serious without me. I want in if we go after these punks."

"Go ahead, Jim. We'll catch you up," Jenny said. Then she asked Ginger, "Do you have a computer in the house?"

"Sure. The boys have one in their room they use for their homework."

"AD, let's look at this together," she said holding up the computer disc. "I've got some questions. I also want you to read the journal my dad was keeping."

Chapter Thirty-Two

Pawns Block

As Jenny booted up the Albright's computer, Fernando made a call he did not want to make.

"*Teniente*," Histaves answered when he picked up the receiver, "this is becoming irritating."

"*Pardon, mi Coronel.* I…I thought you…you would want to know…"

Histaves had little patience for the fearful stutter. "What is it, for God's sake?" he snapped.

"Uhhh, *Senor,* it seems that our two operatives outside the…uhhh…the Albright apartment have disappeared. Their car is still there, but the…uhhh…the operatives are gone."

"*Madre de Dios!* Your 'hot shot' operatives got careless," Histaves exploded. "Damn it! What did they think…that those men watching the apartment were there for window dressing?"

"My apologies, *Senor,*" Fernando answered hurriedly. "I have no idea what happened."

"They just got too close. That's what happened, you stupid man. I tried to tell you they were amateurs. Do your so-called operatives know anything?"

"*No, Senor*. Those two have never been to the actual warehouse. I had them report to a dummy address at the airport. Also, neither one has seen me, or you, without our balaclavas. And, they definitely don't know why they were ordered to do what they've done."

"What about their cell phone?"

"It operated through several switchbacks and is untraceable. Nonetheless, I canceled the service."

"You'd better hope it's untraceable," Histaves snarled. "What about their car?"

"It…it was a stolen vehicle, *Senor.* The plates were also stolen. It can't be connected to us."

Somewhat mollified, Histaves said, "Well, that's not as bad as I thought. But, it's still a dangerous situation. Have someone else watch the apartment, and tell them to stay off the nearby streets.

"We have only two more days. If they move before then, we will need to stop them. If they wait longer, it will be too late."

Histaves decided he was wasting his breath. Too angry to speak to Fernando any longer, he banged the phone down in its cradle, his frustration bubbling over.

Taking deep breaths, he tried to calm his nerves. He knew he needed to contact his congressional friend to coordinate any response to a move by the O'Shane woman. Forcing himself to relax, he dialed the number.

The senator picked up. "Rico, why the hell are you calling me on my private office line? This is not smart!"

"I needed to speak with you without delay. I thought you would appreciate an update on our 'files' situation. At least I didn't call you on your cell phone."

The senator started to retort but Histaves interrupted, "There's no point in sniping at one another. The operation is almost complete. You should know we captured the file from that sergeant."

"Well, that's a relief!"

"It's not over yet. We were unsuccessful with the girl's copy. But, the good news is that she's come back to D.C., and I would expect that she's brought that file with her.

"I intend to get it so that it doesn't incriminate you, your friends, or my country after I return to Argentina.

"I may need your help. Call me immediately if O'Shane contacts any of your group." He hung up before the senator could respond.

Chapter Thirty-Three

White King Castles

Back in the Albright apartment, Jenny and Frisk looked at the maze of data that appeared on the computer monitor. It seemed indecipherable.

Jenny said, “It’s coded. But it’s probably just the way the software records the information. I’d bet we can figure it out. See…these columns look like…maybe dates… Let’s print this out so we won’t bother Jim.”

They sat in the kitchen to review the data. She said, “Look at the other columns. Weirdly enough, they look like reversed e-mail addresses. Wonder how that would match up with names in the Remington files? How’d you get this stuff?”

“I played a hunch,” Frisk answered. “I logged onto the main server at Redstone, and asked for a listing of dates and times for anyone accessing the Smith & Wesson storage facility. I didn’t expect anything, but then this popped up.”

“Whew! Good work. The bad guys were bound to make a mistake. Whoever was doing this probably didn’t get it erased fast enough.”

As Jenny made that observation, Mama came in and announced, “Sorry to desert you, but I have a client this afternoon.” She explained that she was an in-home nurse. “I need to get back into my rotation.”

Ginger asked her to be sure Big John had someone drive her. “You don’t need to be riding a bus today, Mama. Please.” Arrangements were made and she headed out.

For some inexplicable reason, the closing door reminded Jenny that she had unfinished business with

Lieutenant Colonel Cox. The issue with Sergeant Miller was still a nagging worry.

When she called, Cox answered his phone on the first ring. "I saw the information you sent me," he said. "And, I listened to the recording. I've also had a talk with Colonel Adams. He extends his apologies. It looks like you're off the hook. Good job."

"Thank you, Sir. That's a big relief."

"Yeah, well…I'd be interested in knowing how you came about that information."

"Yes, Sir. Uhhh…I can explain…"

"Wait…wait." Cox interrupted. "Don't…don't tell me right now."

Jenny heard a loud breath as he exhaled. Then he said, "Let's leave it as a good job, and we'll talk later."

He paused again, and then added, "For your information, Sergeant Miller and his friend were found dead in an alley in Ybor City last night. The police apprehended two suspects this morning. They were Arabic. Strange. The police don't have much in the way of evidence and indicated they will be releasing the suspects tonight. You know anything about these guys?"

"Uhh…Not really, Sir. I may be able to explain…uhh…later."

"Hmm. Right. You're full of surprises, aren't you? I should have figured. Well, I'm sure you'll let me know. On a more pleasant topic, you mentioned getting back. What's the plan?"

"I'm aiming for next Monday. Will that be all right?"

"Make it as soon as you can. I'm anxious to get back to Bragg. Talk to you soon." With those words, he disconnected.

…Well, a perverse, but pleasant surprise…Miller's history…now I can really focus…

Returning to the kitchen, she saw AD leafing through her dad's journal. He looked up.

"Hey, I was reading your margin notes. A quick answer to a couple of your questions: Commander Collins was definitely Admiral Collins. And, the names you had question marks beside – all task force investigators."

"Yeah. I figured as much. But, what about those sixteen names Dad mentions? Someone named Cohen was supposed to check that out."

"That's right," Frisk noted. "Petty Officer Cohen. We'll call him at home after work hours. It's probably not smart to contact the office at this point."

They scoured the remaining bits of information and then discussed their findings with Cavanaugh and Ginger over dinner.

"You know," Jenny offered. "We should see if there are any unusual shipments scheduled out of Reagan National. That's where the warehouse is that Dees mentioned, so you'd assume they'd be moving the stolen weapons out of there. If we find the warehouse and/or unusual shipments…"

"That's a great idea," Cavanaugh responded. "First let's call Cohen about those sixteen names. He should be home by now."

Ginger dialed his number and pushed the speakerphone button. They all heard a voice, "Petty Officer Cohen's residence."

Cavanaugh recognized Cohen and didn't waste any time. "Andy, it's me, Jim Cavanaugh."

"Man, I thought you'd disappeared off the face of the earth. Where you been? Colonel Foreman is hopping mad."

"I'll explain when I see you. But, right now I need some help. Would you do some nosing around for me?"

"Of course. What do you need?"

"Don't be hasty. This could get ugly."

"I already figured as much. The ID designator on the phone showed it was Ginger calling, and I was hoping that maybe…well…I don't know. I just know I don't like what's going on."

"What are you talking about?"

"Well, since Ginger was reassigned back to the secretarial pool, they've just about closed down the investigation. I'd guessed you were AWOL because you might be trying to unscramble this mess, and I was hoping you'd ask me to help."

"Good guess, Andy. There are others involved. You're on speakerphone with Commander Frisk, Ginger and my goddaughter, Major Jennifer O'Shane."

"Is Major O'Shane the general's daughter?"

"Yes, and I'm going to have her jump in. I'm a little out of it. As I said, I'll explain later. She's got some questions for you."

Jenny picked up the conversation. "Hi, Petty Officer," she said. "I'm Jenny O'Shane. I think we met at the funeral."

"Yes, Ma'am. We didn't have much time. Ma'am, I want you to know that I thought your dad was a prince of a guy. He was a good man. I'm sorry…"

"Thanks very much. I appreciate your thoughts, and we all *really* appreciate your offer of help. But, watch your back. These are some bad people."

"No sweat. Don't worry about me. I've been involved in a little sleuthing before. What do you need?"

"Do you remember a list of sixteen names you were given? It seems that a Colonel Crenshaw identified them. Did you ever find anything on them?"

"I think so. I remember looking up the names. But, I packed all the files for storage, so I think I can find the information. I'll also see if there's anything else that looks interesting. How do I get it to you?"

“I hadn’t thought that far. Getting the information here may be tricky. Don’t come to our location. I think some bad guys are watching us… How about e-mail...?”

”Of course,” Ginger interrupted. “Use the boy’s address. It’s 2redskin4u@aol.com.” Jenny repeated the address for Cohen.

“Okay,” he said. “How much time do I have?”

“Unfortunately, we need it like yesterday,” Jenny answered.

There was a short pause and a muffled conversation in the background. Cohen came back. “I’ll go back into the office tonight. My wife said she’d fix me a sandwich that I can eat at my desk.”

They disconnected with Cohen saying, “I should be able to send you something in a couple of hours.”

Afterwards, Cavanaugh slumped with fatigue. “I’m going to lie down again,” he said. “Wake me up when Andy’s stuff comes in.”

Ginger walked him back into the bedroom. She said, “That Jenny is something else. What a dynamo. Wow!”

“I told you. She’s gonna figure this thing out…”

Chapter Thirty-Four

A Rook Falls

Histaves watched the jiggle of Kandi's naked backside as she walked to his office bathroom; the welts from his belt crisscrossed her butt and thighs.

He stretched out on the couch, overcome by a drowsiness brought on by his sexual pleasure. A sense of warped satisfaction enveloped him. His feelings were short-lived.

It seemed only minutes later that, over the office intercom, Kandi's voice announced, "Your congressional friend is on line one."

...Madre de Dios...what is it now...? Histaves thought. *...Will this never end...*

"What is it today, Senator?" Histaves asked in a sarcastic tone.

"Don't be rude, Rico," the senator answered. "You suggested we wiretap Albright's phone. It's provided information that you will want to deal with right away."

"I don't think I'm going to like this..."

"It's not good, but I think you can finesse their little game. It involves that other administrative serviceman on the task force. The one named Cohen. O'Shane asked him to go to his office tonight and e-mail her a list of names her dad investigated in association with the Remington theft. We need to stop him."

"Just great! Where's this office? Don't tell me it's in the Pentagon..."

"No. It's not, thank God. It's in a small office building called the Pennsylvania Building. It's behind the Smithsonian, and the only occupant is the Army's CID headquarters. I have the code to get in the building after hours." The senator provided the information.

"Fine. I'm on it. Stay in touch." Histaves hung up and called Dr. Ami.

Forty-five minutes later, Cohen was preparing an e-mail. He'd found the files. It seemed to take a lifetime to copy the information from the scanner to his hard drive.

The list of names was easiest to convert, and he started with it. He typed, "Here's the list you asked for. I've annotated a couple of names. More information to follow…" Just as he pushed the send button, he heard a noise. It sounded as if someone was in the corridor.

Attaching two more memos, he quickly typed another message: "Heard a noise. No one should be around. Am checking and..." For reasons he would never know, he sent the unfinished message.

At the same instant that he sent the second e-mail, an electric jolt surged through his body. He was paralyzed, unable to resist; a silenced pistol barrel was jammed into his mouth; his own hand gripped the weapon. He heard an explosion, felt brief, excruciating agony, and then nothing…

Commander Garcia stripped off the light plastic garment he was wearing over his Wackenhut uniform. He checked himself for splatter with a handheld mirror.

...Nothing...perfect... He gathered up the copies of memorandums that Cohen had been working on and stuffed them into his jacket. Next, he put a memory stick into an external port of Cohen's computer. Pressing several keys on the keyboard, Garcia accessed a program on the memory stick that erased everything on Cohen's hard drive.

Garcia then typed a sentence that appeared on the computer monitor, 'Dear Danny. My wife - the love of my life. Please forgive me…I can't take it anymore…'

Afterwards, Garcia opened a heavy briefcase, and placed it at the foot of the computer stand. Embossed on the briefcase lid was the name, 'Tom O'Shane.'

Lastly, Garcia pressed a small remote control device that was a video scrambler. He stepped out of Cohen's office, and ran down the corridor to an alcove. He then spoke into a walkie-talkie.

One floor down at the reception area for the CID headquarters building, a Wackenhut guard watched his camera monitors go blank for the second time that night. *...Must be power surges...* the guard thought.

On his walkie-talkie he heard, "This is dispatch headquarters. Shots reported on second floor, room two three one. Check it out."

The guard pushed the transmit button and responded, "Roger, on the way." He then pressed a switch on his console that alerted the Capital Police of a possible emergency. He charged up the stairs to the second floor.

The first thing the guard noticed was that the corridor lights were out. Toward the end of the hall, he could see the blink of a computer monitor. He called dispatch, identified himself, and said, "Am on second floor. Lights are out. Recommend you send back up before proceeding." He heard the response...

"This is dispatch. We have no report of activity in your area. Please inform us of the nature of your emergency."

"Wait a minute," he answered. "You guys called me. I'm checking the second floor like you told me to do. What the hell's going on?" At that moment, two Capital policemen showed up at his elbow.

The Wackenhut guard asked them, "How the hell did you get into the building?"

One of the policemen answered, "Your buddy downstairs let us in and told us where your were."

"God damn it, I don't have a buddy downstairs."

As the guard was saying those words, Garcia was throwing his Wackenhut uniform jacket and hat into a dumpster two blocks from the CID building. He climbed into a nearby car and drove off into the D.C. traffic.

The next morning, the *Washington Post* ran a story under the fold on the front page of the local section. The story was headlined with, 'Navy serviceman commits suicide at CID.' The article read, 'Police report that a Navy petty officer killed himself under mysterious circumstances last night in the Army's Criminal Investigative Division Headquarters building on Pennsylvania Avenue.

A security guard for the building notified police of an emergency at approximately 9:00 p.m. Responding police found the body fifteen minutes later.

An unnamed source at police headquarters informed this newspaper that, although there was some confusion among the security agency staff, the petty officer had the pistol in his hand, and had written a suicide note to his wife. It appears to be a case of suicide over remorse about the tragic death of a co-worker.'

Chapter Thirty-Five

Checked

Earlier that evening in the Albright apartment, Jenny was talking to Frisk. “We need to locate that warehouse,” she said. “Why don’t you take that Dees kid over to Reagan and see what you can find?”

“Yeah. I was thinking the same. If those goons are still watching the apartment, my leaving shouldn’t cause much of a stir. The real me is supposed to be in St. Thomas.”

She nodded her agreement and called for transportation. “The Commander needs to take that Dees fellow with him,” she told Big John. “Can you manage that?”

“Sure, Missy. Gimme ‘bout ten minutes.”

Frisk got his coat. “I’ll call if I find something.”

Soon after Frisk left, the apartment phone rang. Ginger answered. It was Mama, and Jenny couldn’t help but overhear her strong voice over the receiver when Mama asked, “Girl, can you give me a hand with Fred tonight? He’s being a little cantankerous.”

“Just a minute, Mama,” Ginger answered. She explained to Jenny that Fred had advanced Alzheimer’s, and could be difficult to manage in the evenings.

“Sure, go ahead,” Jenny answered. “We’ll be fine. Things are good here, and I can crash on the couch. And, with you going to a non-threatening location, it will probably help keep the bad guys off-balance.”

“Mama, it’ll be fine,” Ginger said into the phone. “Jenny said she’d spend the night here.” There was a momentary pause, and then Jenny heard. “Yes, I’ll have Big John bring me over.”

That left Jenny alone at Ginger's kitchen table looking through notes when the computer in the boy's room pinged. The familiar 'aol' voice announced 'you've got mail…' She read the short message from Cohen, and printed the single attachment – the list of sixteen names. Cohen had underlined three, and included notations about their past and current assignments.

Cavanaugh, awakened by the computer noise, followed her to the kitchen and they began to peruse the names. They focused on those that Cohen had underlined. Cavanaugh recognized one name immediately: Colonel Foreman.

Cohen's notes indicated that Foreman was assigned as a Marine project officer in the Remington factory the year that the theft took place. "He's now the XO for your dad's task force," Cavanaugh explained to her.

A Major General Davies was also underlined. Twenty years earlier, 'Major' Davies was assigned as a liaison officer in the West German embassy in Bonn. "Look at that," she said, pointing to one of Cohen's notations. "His current job is Deputy Director of CID. This might be getting somewhere."

The third name was the most senior, a Lieutenant General named Myers who was presently assigned as the Commanding General for the Air Force Reserve. She verbalized the Cohen notes, 'At the time of the Remington theft he was a military White House fellow.'

She added her own thoughts, "Wow. I'd bet a paycheck that, if we can get to these guys, we'll have some answers."

They next compared the three names to the printed list from the computer disc to see if any matched.

"Eureka," she yelled and jumped to her feet. "It's Davies! Look at the e-mail addresses. This one appears the most often." She pointed to one address on the list. "Compare that to his name."

Cavanaugh shook his head. “You’re nuts. What the hell are you talking about?”

“It’s a reversed e-mail address. Ignore the last two letters. Those are probably his first initials. But, spell his name backwards and look again.”

“Damn! You’re right. How did you see that…? Man, it’s no wonder the bad guys were hot to get this information back.”

“Well…I’m not sure they know what’s on here. They’re guessing just like we were. Also, look at these numbers. They look like dates. They’re all run together…like numeric dates and military times.”

“Yep. I see what you mean now that you point it out. Those might match up with the dates of the theft from Smith & Wesson. Good…what about this column?”

“I don’t know. Maybe it’s the codes for entering the secure areas at those specific times and dates. At any rate, I’d bet we’d also find who he sent this data to if we can hack into his personal computer files.”

“Why would he leave this on the Redstone mainframe?”

“He probably didn’t intend to. As AD said, it was all timing. Davies hadn’t gotten around to wiping the server memory. I’d bet it’s not on the system any more.”

“Yeah. Hopefully, he won’t have an opportunity to manufacture an alibi for accessing the information before we bust him. Unfortunately, this is all we have until the bodies are exhumed and/or we find that warehouse.”

“Sadly enough, you’re right,” she answered. “But, this is golden. And, we need to get it to the right audience.

There was silence as they each considered the best approach. She said, “AD and I talked about trying to get whatever we had to the new Chairman of the Joint Chiefs. The whole investigation started in his office. This list of names and this e-mail record would at least get things started again.”

Not bad…" Cavanaugh noted. "But, how do we go about that without getting sidetracked by the bureaucracy. There are so many levels…"

More silence filled the room. She suddenly jumped as if she'd been poked. Cavanaugh looked at her, startled by her sharp intake of breath. "What was that all about?" he asked.

"I just thought of the answer. I'm going to call Uncle Stan." At Cavanaugh's quizzical expression, she explained further. "You know…General Stan Greene. He said to call if I needed anything. Hell, if the Army's Chief of Staff can't set us up, no one can."

"Hot damn! You know, that could work!"

"Let's call him at his quarters on Fort McNair. He wrote his home number on the card he gave me."

"Shouldn't we wait until morning, during business hours?"

"No…no…" she continued, excitement in her voice. "If we wait and call during duty hours, we'll never get through his office staff. It's only 9:30 p.m. It's still early." She scrounged through her purse for the business card General Greene had given her.

Finally finding the card, she took a deep breath and dialed. After a couple of rings, an aide answered. She identified herself, "This is Major Jennifer O'Shane. I was instructed to call General Greene at this number. Is he in?" After what seemed like an eternity, she heard the familiar voice.

"Jennifer, is that you? Where are you? I didn't expect to hear from you so soon after the funeral. Are you alright?"

"I'm fine, Uncle Stan. I'm with Jim Cavanaugh, and we're following up on an investigation that Dad was pursuing before he was killed."

"Okay..." he said, hesitating. Then he asked, "Well... why did you call *me*?"

"Uncle Stan, you'll need to trust me on a lot of this, but the bottom line is that we think Dad and Admiral Collins were murdered because of this investigation."

"You're not serious...? Come on, Jennifer!"

"Uhh...I'm sure it all sounds pretty farfetched at this point, Sir. But, we have verifiable information that we believe should be shown to the new Chairman of the Joint Chiefs. I'm asking you to trust my word and for you to arrange a meeting with the Chairman."

There was a long pause and she heard a heavy sigh. Thinking she'd presumed too much, she started to apologize, "General Greene, I'm so sorry to impose..."

He interrupted, "No, Jenny, you're right to call. I'm glad you did. This is just a lot to absorb. Are you sure you have reliable information?"

"Yes, Sir. I'm absolutely certain. And, with the Chief's help, I believe the whole thing will be exposed."

There was another pause and sigh. "Let me have your phone number, and I'll call you back in a few minutes," General Greene said. She gave him the number and they hung up.

She told Cavanaugh of the conversation. "I just hope we didn't go overboard."

Cavanaugh gave her a thumbs-up sign. "Jennifer, you did the right thing. It's the best move we have. Let's see where it goes from here."

As they spoke, the computer pinged again, and another 'you've got mail' sounded. It was the additional information from Cohen. She noted the abbreviated e-mail message. "I wonder what that's all about? I hope he's alright."

Accessing the attachments to the e-mail they found a memo written by a Major Wusacki. It provided background information on the Krueger Manufacturing Company.

There were two margin notes: "No documentation found that would substantiate weapon research by Krueger…" and, "…tried to reach the two scientists who were advertised as responsible for the breakthrough in Krueger. Both died in a skiing accident."

The second attachment was a memo written by a Lieutenant Colonel Crenshaw. The subject was West German military liaison activity in the U.S. at the time of the Remington incident.

Crenshaw wrote, "…the German Army military liaison officer assigned to their embassy in the U.S. was declared '*persona non grata*' following the Remington episode. That officer returned to Germany and committed suicide soon after he arrived home."

Once again, she and Cavanaugh were stunned by what they felt certain were more examples of cold-blooded murder.

They were still trying to shrug off the ominous feelings when General Greene called back.

"Jenny this is highly irregular," he said. "However, I've arranged for you to see the chairman at 0700 hours tomorrow morning in the Pentagon. I must tell you, he's extremely skeptical. I had to use all my blue chips to make this happen."

She could only think to say, "Thanks, Uncle Stan."

"I've taken extraordinary precautions. Because you indicated there were people watching your building and because of the apparent breach of military security in your dad's top-secret task force investigation, I've asked for special support from the U.S. Marshal's Service. They'll pick you up at 0600 hours. Will you be ready?"

Smiling, she answered, "We'll be ready."

"Great. Bring all your files with you. Okay? See you soon."

When they had disconnected, something was nagging her. It was a thought just below consciousness that wouldn't surface. She sensed that it was something obvious. *...Oh well...I'll sleep on it...*

She called down to Big John. "We're going to have visitors in the morning. You'll want to make yourself scarce at about 6:00 a.m. because they'll be U.S. Marshals, and you might not want to be seen by them."

"Thanks, Miss Jenny. We'll be off in the shadows."

She and Cavanaugh outlined what they would say to the chairman. She summed it up, "It's pretty straightforward. We have the list of names, the e-mail records, and the memos. The only gaps are the warehouse and the exhumation."

They fretted about not hearing back from AD. They felt sure that finding the warehouse would provide a missing link that might trigger the exhumation of the bodies.

Realizing there wasn't much they could do at that point, they decided it was time to get some sleep. She stretched out on the living room couch.

At 3:00 a.m., she awoke with a start. *...Does Uncle Stan know we're at Ginger's apartment? ...Must have told him...can't remember...* With that thought she fell back into a deep slumber.

Chapter Thirty-Six

Knights Captured

Jenny's alarm buzzed at 5:00 a.m. She shook her head to try to clear the cobwebs. Adrenaline brought her out of slumber as she remembered what she had planned.

She went to get Cavanaugh. He'd already managed to struggle out of bed.

"No call from AD yet," she told him. "I'd hoped he'd find something by now."

Jenny glanced out the front window at a little before 6 a.m. She was impressed. Two black four-by-fours pulled up to the curb right on time. Six men climbed out.

"The marshals are here," she told Cavanaugh. She looked more closely at the vehicles.

"Wait a minute," she said. "The Marshals' Service gave a briefing at a law enforcement seminar I attended here last month. Remember, I had that run-in at the airport with those Argentinean idiots. At the seminar the marshals talked about their fleet of vehicles.

"They told us that their cars were always white and most of them were souped-up Buick La Sabres. These cars don't fit the description. Something's wrong."

The building door buzzer rang. "This isn't right. And, you know what? It just dawned on me. I didn't tell Uncle Stan where we are. I think we're busted. Hide the documents."

She slipped off her shoulder holster, and hid it with her pistol under the couch. *...A shoot-out won't work...*

She next stuffed some miscellaneous papers into her briefcase. She ran into the boys' bedroom and picked up one of several computer discs lying on their desk. The Frisk disc was still in the computer drive.

In the meantime, Cavanaugh jammed the evidential documents under the drawer of the oven. He then took a metal, knife-like letter opener off the desk in the front room, and slid it under the sling for his shoulder.

There was a sharp knock on the apartment door. The marshals had gotten through the apartment building entryway without being buzzed in. *...Not good...!* Jenny thought.

She answered the knock. Three men were at the door. "How can I help you?" she asked.

They didn't answer her, and shouldered their way into the room.

One of them showed her something that looked like a badge. He introduced himself, speaking with a heavy accent, "I'm Marshal Fernando. How many of you are here?" Surprise seemed to register on his face when he saw Cavanaugh standing beside Jenny.

"It's just the two of us," Jenny responded. As she spoke, one of the other visitors did a quick walk through of the apartment.

When he returned to the front room, he said, "All clear. No one else is here."

Fernando told Jenny and Cavanaugh, "Follow me." He asked Jenny, "Do you have the files?"

She held up her briefcase and nodded her head, "Right here."

They headed down to the trucks. Cavanaugh was put in the lead vehicle and Jenny was led to the second. She noticed Big John across the street leaning against a doorway.

She looked in his direction, and gave an almost imperceptible shake of her head, intending to tell him this was not right. *...Sure hope he got the message...*

She was put in the back seat of the truck, one man on each side of her. The man who had shown a badge sat in the front passenger seat. As the vehicles pulled away from the curb, one of the men beside her covered her nose and mouth with a cloth.

It was pointless to struggle. She smelled a hint of ether and began to loose consciousness.

Her last thought was, *...Uncle Stan mentioned the task force...how did he know...?* Then there was blackness…then, nothing.

Her subconscious registered a one-sided phone conversation that sounded as if it were occurring in a cavern. She heard her abductor say, "*Coronel*, we got her." And then, "*Si, Senor*. She brought her files.

"By the way," the voice continued. "That man Cavanaugh was with her. He's still alive. I'll find out what happened and let you know when I see you at the warehouse."

Chapter Thirty-Seven

Black Bishop Checks

Jenny woke curled into a tight ball on a hard concrete floor. She was shivering from the cold.

Semi-conscious from the ether, she recalled someone saying, "Take off their clothes and put them in the cold storage room. With no clothes they'll be easier to handle.

She then heard, "She's lied to me about the files. She has to tell me where they are. We need to find them." She also remembered hearing a heavy door slam.

Struggling to sit up, she found herself in a concrete-walled room clad only in a bra and panties. Her mind began to focus.

In the dim light, she saw that Cavanaugh was in the room with her, shoved over in one corner. He wore only his jockey shorts. He was also shivering. She moved to his side, worried about the effects of the cold given his weakened condition.

Movement compounded the ache in her head. The room's chill factor increased as she noticed the grimy walls running with moisture trails; a steel door was recessed into the doorframe.

Forcing her mind into survival mode, she wrapped her arms around Cavanaugh. He was still unconscious, and she assumed he'd also been drugged. She figured that their combined body heat would help ward off the cold.

She lapsed into a cold-induced slumber. Her arms tightened protectively around Cavanaugh. Just as she began to slip into a deeper sleep and blessed darkness, two men stormed into the room, banging the door back.

Heavy boots clumped on the concrete. Both men had holstered side arms. One of them carried a light rope. The other was the man who had introduced himself as Marshal Fernando.

He said, "Isn't this sweet. Sorry we can't let this love tryst continue." Motioning to Jenny, he said, "Stand up. I want to talk to you. You have caused me a great deal of trouble."

"Not nearly as much as I would like," she responded, starting to get up.

Impatient, the first man grabbed her by the arm and shoved her toward Fernando, almost throwing her back to the floor. Cavanaugh didn't stir, still wiped out.

Fernando put his hand out to his compatriot and said, "Careful Jorge, we need her a while longer." Jorge began binding her hands behind her back.

Again, Fernando interceded, "Don't bother tying her. She's such a tiny woman, what's to worry?"

He further instructed Jorge, "Hold her arms for a moment." With Jenny's arms secured, Fernando reached out and ripped off her bra and panties: the material offered little resistance.

He ogled her naked form. "Oh, you're even more beautiful than I imagined. This will be very enjoyable."

Jenny squirmed under his gaze, and attempted a kick at his groin. He laughed as he dodged her futile attempt.

Trying to put on a brave front, she hissed, "You perverted bastard. You touch me and I'll kill you."

He laughed again and responded in a voice low and laced with lust, "I don't think so, little one." He began to caress her breasts. He massaged, as would a lover.

Her nipples hardened involuntarily. Without warning, he twisted and yanked her left nipple. She cried out, gasping from the pain; tears sprang to her eyes.

His casual brutality rekindled memories of her episode with Cross. She was certain this was a much deadlier encounter.

"You sick shit!" she said through gritted teeth.

Jorge smacked the back of her head with the heel of his hand. “Shut up, bitch.”

She turned her head and glared at him. She noticed that Cavanaugh’s eyes were open, and he was watching them.

“That’s just a taste, little one,” Fernando said. “Scream and cry all you want. No one will hear you, and no one cares. We need some answers and you’re going to give them to us.”

Jenny kicked out again, but Fernando stepped aside. He instructed Jorge to let her go, adding, “She’s too little to give us any real trouble.”

To Jenny, he said, “I want to know what you did with the files that were supposed to be in your briefcase. It was clever of you not to bring them. You faked me out. And, I see the man I thought I killed is alive. I’m afraid all your little games are temporary setbacks. They serve no purpose other than to make me angry and to delay the inevitable.

“We are going to kill you both. How well you please me will determine how painful your deaths will be. I need the files. You will tell me where the are, and you will do what I say.”

“I’m not telling you anything, and I’m not doing anything.”

Jorge struck her in the back of her head again. She staggered from the blow.

Fernando pulled a magazine out of his back pants pocket and rolled it up into a tight cylinder. “In my country, I have ways to make you do my bidding,” he said. “Here, I am a little handicapped. But…”

…He slapped her on an ear with the rolled up magazine. It stung. Taken by surprise, she raised her arms to protect her face.

He then struck her right breast with another sharp blow with the magazine. She cried out again from the searing pain.

Fury and frustration welled up in her. *...These turkeys are going to keep beating on me...it's obvious what else they have in mind...this guy's enjoying himself...well...it won't be free...!*

She launched herself straight at Fernando. She felt Jorge start to grab her, but he suddenly stopped and howled in agony.

His eyes were bugged out, his mouth agape. He was scrabbling with his hands, trying to reach something behind his back.

Out of the corner of her eye, she saw Cavanaugh standing behind Jorge. She didn't have much time to see what he was doing.

Overconfident and distracted by the noise from his compatriot, Fernando was unprepared for the fury of her attack.

She struck before he could react. One blow was enough. She hit him squarely in the throat with a closed fist, shattering his larynx.

Backing away, not yet comprehending the death rattle in his throat, he began to draw his pistol. A deafening boom reverberated off the walls.

Fernando hurtled across the room, bounced off the far wall and fell in a heap on the floor. Blood splatter spotted and dribbled down the wall. Big John stood in the doorway, his shotgun smoking in his hands.

Jenny was never so glad to see anyone in her life.

She turned toward Cavanaugh. He was kneeling over Jorge who was on the floor, no longer moving. Cavanaugh pulled out the letter opener from the man's back, wiping blood off on his shirt.

He looked up to Jenny and said, "This is Ginger's and she'd be pissed if I didn't get it back."

They both burst out laughing, in shock from their brush with death.

Big John put his windbreaker over Jenny's shoulders as Frisk came hobbling in. He was also armed. He and Big John exchanged looks. Big John asked, "The others?"

Frisk responded, "Bubba's watching them." To Jenny he said, "Here are your clothes. I found them in one of the offices down the hall."

Dressed and warm, Jenny joined Cavanaugh, Frisk and Big John. They were standing in the middle of the warehouse looking at some shipping crates.

Bubba was nearby keeping an eye on four men sitting with their hands on their heads. Two other men were lying on the floor. It was difficult to tell whether the two were alive or dead. A pile of handguns was in a corner.

Frisk and Big John spent fifteen minutes filling in Jenny and Cavanaugh on what had happened.

"I saw your signal," Big John told Jenny. "We followed you to the warehouse and watched them bring you in. While we were looking the place over, we ran into Commander Frisk."

Frisk continued the explanation. "All the warehouses look alike. Dees had a hard time identifying the area in the dark. At first light we had just about given up, and then we saw the two trucks show up."

"We decided to wait awhile to let the bad guys get settled before breaking in," Big John added.

Breaking into the building had been easier than expected. No one inside suspected they were at risk, and the doors were not secured.

"We split up, with Bubba coming in the back door and me and the commander in the front," Big John continued.

Frisk added, "Six men were sitting at a table playing poker. When I told them they were all under arrest, two of them started to draw weapons. Bubba walked up behind them and cracked their heads together. Those are the two on the floor."

Changing subjects, Frisk asked Jenny, “What happened to the files? Did they get them?”

He was relieved when Jenny explained how they had called ‘Uncle Stan’ and how he had arranged for her and Jim to be picked up. “When our escort arrived, we got suspicious. Jim hid the files.”

Once everyone was updated, Big John called Ginger’s apartment. Mama answered. “Boy, it’s about time! You best be tellin’ me some good news.”

“Yes, Ma’am. Everyone’s OK. We’re headed back to the apartment.”

“That’s just what I wanted to hear. I’ll tell Ginger. We’ll be makin’ you some lunch. You bring those folks straight away, you hear? Ginger’s been real worried.”

Big John managed a “Yes, Ma’am,” before she hung up on him.

Jenny joined Cavanaugh and Frisk in exploring the warehouse while Big John spoke to Mama.

Opening the crates, they found what appeared to be files, test equipment, ammunition and strange looking firearms - ‘Smith & Wesson’ embossed on it all.

“We got these assholes!” Jenny exclaimed.

Cavanaugh was not as optimistic. He said, “This is great. But, we still need to link this to someone…”

Bubba and Frisk had searched the men in the warehouse and had found no identification. The men were being close-lipped, saying only, “We want an attorney.”

A search of the two dead men in the storage room yielded equally frustrating results.

Almost at wits end, Jenny decided to climb on top on one of the crates to try to look at the warehouse from a different perspective.

“Hot damn! Look what I found,” she yelled. Stapled to the top of the crate was shipment information. It had the stamps of the U.S. Customs office.

Chapter Thirty-Eight

Queen Captured

As Jenny was celebrating her discovery, Histaves parked his car two blocks away from the warehouse. He'd decided to make a visit a little earlier than planned.

He'd called Fernando earlier. "I'm anxious to meet this 'Jenny' woman," he'd said. "She's caused me a lot of grief. She might be a fun diversion."

He seldom visited during daylight, but it was time to tidy up loose ends. For one thing, there were too many witnesses. His hired mercenaries needed to be dealt with…

He parked well away from the warehouse. He didn't want his diplomatic plates anywhere nearby. As he started in the warehouse door, he pulled on his balaclava. *...Take no unnecessary chances...*

Walking into the warehouse, Histaves saw his operatives sitting on the floor with their hands on their heads…he saw a giant black man guarding them. His instinct…

...Run...! He bolted back out the door, and ran toward his car…

Jenny had just climbed down from the top of the crate when she heard the sound of the opening door. She saw a masked man enter, and then run out.

"Hey, come back here!" she yelled, and ran after him. Bursting out of the warehouse door, she saw him heading toward vehicles in a far parking lot. She called out again, "Mister, wait a minute. I just want to talk to you."

Histaves didn't stop. But, he was no match for Jenny's speed.

He whirled to confront her as she caught up. “You,” he exclaimed in surprised recognition. “Ha! The airport.”

He pulled off his balaclava. A look came across his features, registering confidence that he would exact his revenge.

Jenny also recognized him, *...Name...?*

Throwing caution to the wind, sensing danger, she attacked without hesitation. *...Well...this is what I got all those bruises for in my Tae Kwon Do classes...*

She remembered her instructor’s words as if he were standing there… “Jennifer, you must think through your attack. Not just the first blow, or the second, but the third and the fourth.”

She launched her body, feet first, kicking. Her right foot caught Histaves dead on the nose, a perfect blow. She bounced off him, using his chest like a springboard.

She landed back on her feet pleased that the blow worked as advertised.

Taken off-guard, Histaves staggered backwards, blood spurting from his nose.

Jenny’s instincts told her that she still faced a very dangerous man.

She spun in her favorite three hundred-sixty degree spin, and kicked the inside of his knee. Histaves collapsed, howling in pain.

Even in agony, Histaves reached for a pistol under his jacket.

At that moment, Big John came running up and put his shotgun under Histaves’ nose. “Don’t even think about it, Turkey!”

Big John and Jenny hauled the limping man back to the warehouse and searched him. They found his identification.

As soon as he was identified, Histaves told them, “I claim diplomatic immunity and demand to be released.”

Jenny responded, “Put a lid on it, Colonel. This isn’t an official police operation. If you’re not quiet, we’ll put a gag on you. Given what I think you’ve done, you may not leave here alive. Now shut up while we think.”

Jenny’s group held a ‘war’ council. They decided that Bubba would stay with the prisoners at the warehouse and keep watch over the crated equipment.

Big John would take Histaves to where Zucher was being held, and then return to Ginger’s to overwatch the apartment. He’d call Robby for reinforcements.

Jenny said, “The rest of us can take AD’s car over to Ginger’s. We’ll brainstorm another approach on how to get this information up the food chain. Someone has to listen!”

Chapter Thirty-Nine

Knight Covers King

When Cavanaugh walked into the Albright apartment, Ginger wrapped her arms around him. Jenny thought it was cute, but Mama kept giving him the fish eye.

Everyone settled down to lunch while they began to strategize. Depression and futility were hard to overcome with their 'ace in the hole' (Uncle Stan) somehow compromised. They were at a loss about how to get into the power structure.

After lunch, Jenny glanced at the *Washington Post* front-page subtitles while the group brainstormed options. Under the fold of the paper, she noticed that one of the headlines announced the appointment of a new ambassador from South Korea to the United States. He was an ex-military officer named Lieutenant General (Retired) Anh Rhee.

Jenny stared at the name for a couple of seconds, not immediately grasping the significance. "I can't believe it," she yelped, interrupting the conversation.

"Sorry," she said at everyone's startled expressions. "I may have something here." She explained how she knew General Rhee. "I'm going to call him and see if he can get someone's attention. What have we got to lose?"

Pulling his business card from her wallet, she dialed the number he'd given her, half expecting a flunky to answer. After only two rings she heard a familiar voice.

"General Rhee," the voice said.

Unprepared for the prompt connection, and unsure of what to expect, Jenny simply introduced herself.

"General, uhh…you probably don't remember me. Uhh…This is Major O'Shane."

"I remember you, Young Lady. My country has a debt of honor with you for which I have responsibility. I assume you called because you heard of my appointment."

"Yes, Sir. That's exactly why I called. Congratulations," she responded.

"Thank you. I sense reservation in your voice. Let me assure you, this new job does not alter my assigned responsibility. How may I help you?"

Not expecting as ready a response, Jenny stuttered through their dilemma and outlined the situation. She ended her explanation with, "Sir, we need an audience with the right authorities without being intercepted. Can you help us?"

Silence. She thought he'd hung up. "General Rhee, are you there?" She sighed with relief when he responded.

"Absolutely, Young Lady. I'm making notes. I'm going to put you on hold. Don't hang up."

After what seemed like an eternity, she heard him say, "There will be arrangements made. I will call you back. What is your cell number?"

When General Rhee didn't call back within the hour, concern began to build. The hour stretched into late afternoon and the tension became thick.

Jenny put their concerns into words. "We're going to have to assume the worst and clear out of here. Staying any longer puts us all in jeopardy." Everyone nodded in agreement except Mama.

"Now I told you all, I won't be run off by a bunch of hooligans! This is my home and I…" She didn't get any farther. Cavanaugh interrupted.

"Mama, we understand. But, it's too dangerous now, and we have to leave," he didn't raise his voice, but there was an edge to his words. He added diplomatically, "It's only temporary, but you have to go."

The silence was deafening. Mama glared at Cavanaugh, her eyes smoldering. He glared right back. And, then it was almost as if a message passed between them – a shift had taken place in the family hierarchy.

Mama said to Ginger, “Don’t just sit there, Girl. Let’s put some things together.” She stood and walked into the back of the apartment.

Ginger sat with her mouth wide open. She looked at Cavanaugh who smiled, nodding his head to indicate she should go help Mama.

As Mama and Ginger went to pack, Jenny called Big John and told him that they would be leaving shortly. Their destination was unknown. “We’ll need some transportation…”

“I got that covered, Missy. Let me know when you’re ready.”

Cavanaugh spoke up again, “I’m worn out and need a nap. I’d like to put off making a firm decision on a destination until I’ve had some sleep.”

Everyone agreed. Each one of them was still hoping that General Rhee would call, but their hopes diminished with every passing minute. They would have to find a place to hide.

While Cavanaugh rested, Frisk and Jenny sat in the kitchen and tried to think of suitable temporary quarters. As they talked, Jenny was idly fiddling with her dad’s spiral notebook. It gave her an idea.

“Why not use my dad’s house? It’s sitting empty and it’s isolated enough so that no one will notice if we minimize our comings and goings.”

Frisk asked, “Where’s the house? We don’t want to be too far away from D.C.”

“It’s in Springfield, about thirty minutes out on I-395.” Everyone breathed easier. It was a good idea.

Jenny explained to Cavanaugh when he woke up. “Great plan,” he said. “Let’s load up and get out of here.”

Jenny was the last to leave. She was walking down the hall to join the waiting group when her cell phone rang.

Answering, she heard General Rhee, "I don't know the full story, but there's an all-points bulletin out for you. You're being accused of stealing classified material from your dad's house. There's an alleged terrorist connection. I am told an FBI SWAT team is enroute. Call me when you clear the building." He hung up.

"Good Christ," Jenny exclaimed as she told everyone the news, "They're pulling out all the stops. Let's get out of here."

Just as they hustled down the stairs, they heard the unmistakable 'boom' of Big John's shotgun coming from the front of the apartment building.

Then there was another loud boom. The 'pop, pop' of small arms, and the sound of automatic weapons quickly followed.

"Ginger, where's the back door?" Jenny asked. "Let's go. Hurry!" They were on the run on foot.

Jenny peeked outside the rear door. *...Damn...!* A black sedan with two men inside was idling in the alley.

The car doors opened when they saw Jenny. She slammed the door shut and asked, "Is there another way out of this building? We're boxed in." Ginger shook her head.

They were stuck. For the second time that day, it looked as if they would become captives. This time the whole group was corralled.

Mama then spoke up, "Ginger, don't you remember that all these buildings are connected at the basement level? There's a fire door that the fire department insisted be installed years ago. Come on!"

Mama led them to a dark, narrow hallway filled with cobwebs and miscellaneous trash. "Down there," Mama pointed.

Jenny led the way in and Frisk brought up the rear. It was hard to see. They groped forward, the light growing dimmer the farther they went.

Ginger let out a yelp when something scurried across her feet.

Feeling her way with her hands, knocking cobwebs aside, Jenny finally reached the end. She felt a solid steel door. She couldn't find a handle.

Mama said, "Look for a breaker bar release."

They could hear more gunfire above them. Jenny couldn't find a door release.

Time was running out.

Cavanaugh asked, "Jenny, is there a handle up high or at floor level?"

Mama responded, "Boy, you're brilliant. I forgot. Kids were setting off the alarm, so the building super put the bar high. Reach above head level, Jenny."

She reached up. There it was!

Jenny pushed. It didn't budge; unused for years. She pushed as hard as she could. With a loud creak, it finally opened.

Surprisingly, no alarm sounded. But, two flashlights blinded them from the other side of the doorway. They all gasped. *...Crap...busted...!* Jenny thought.

Chapter Forty

Only One Move

Big John's voice sounded in the narrow passageway. "Thought you'd come this way, Mama. Follow me. We be goin' through this basement and into the next. I have a van in the alley."

When they had passed through the door, another man with Big John reached into an electrical box next to the door and connected two wires. He then pushed the fire door closed.

Big John explained as the group started through the basement. "We disconnected the wires so the fire alarm wouldn't sound. When those clowns upstairs use the door, it'll go off. They'll initially assume you didn't go that way because there was no alarm. It'll give us an extra few minutes."

They reached the next basement, and Big John led them into the alley. Streetlights revealed a bright yellow van with red racing stripes parked with the engine idling. They all piled in, Big John in the driver's seat.

He explained, "These are Bubba's wheels. I figured he wouldn't mind. Where we goin'?"

"Let's get out of here, and we'll decide on the move," Jenny answered

They drove in silence for the first few minutes, and then Jenny noted, "Dad's house is off-limits. No doubt it's under surveillance given Rhee's information. We'll have to find something else."

"I've got an idea," Mama said. "Big John, let me have your cell phone." She took a small notebook out of her purse, flipped some pages and dialed.

"Wilma," she said into the cell phone, "this is Mama. How's Fred today?"

She listened for a few minutes. “I’m sure he’ll be more comfortable. That nursing home has a nice staff. Will you be staying there with him for awhile?”

Again, she listened. A smile spread on her face. “I think he’ll settle in much better that way. Listen, I have a big favor to ask.”

There was another pause, and Mama said, “Well, I know what you said, but this is pretty special. I need to ask if I could use your house for some friends of mine.”

Another short pause, “Wilma, you are very sweet. Give my best to Fred.”

Hanging up, Mama gave Wilma’s address to Big John. She explained, “Fred’s my Alzheimer patient. We put him in a special care facility this morning. Wilma is going to stay with him for the first few days. Her house is big and empty right now.” There was a collective sigh of relief.

“Great idea, Mama. You saved our bacon on this one,” Jenny offered.

She then called General Rhee. “General, thanks for the heads up. We just made it out of there before the SWAT team showed up. Sir, you have to know that’s a ridiculous story?”

“Believe me Major, we wouldn’t be speaking if I thought there was the remotest possibility.”

He continued, “I’ve arranged for you to speak to some people tomorrow morning. Can you be at the Tyrone Square Shopping Center at 8:00 a.m.?”

“Yes, Sir. We’ll be there.”

“Good. I’ll be in a white Town Car in the middle of the west parking lot. It will be Sunday morning so the lot should be empty.

“There’s one more thing. It seems that your country’s intelligence services are monitoring all cell phones in the Washington D.C. area to try to locate you.

"I suggest that you turn off your cell phones and don't use them until after we meet." Jenny then heard the buzz of a disconnected phone line.

She told the others of the arrangement. She knew her plan put them all out on a limb. They were relying on her judgment, and her trust in the South Korean. "Are we sure we want to do this?" she asked.

"Let's do it," Frisk opined. Everyone nodded in agreement.

After that discussion, Jenny explained about the cell phone monitoring, "I can't believe they're watching every cell link in the D.C. area."

Frisk responded, "You can't imagine the capabilities. They can hear everything.

"The general was right," he continued. "No more cell phones until we sort this out. Fortunately, no one could know who Wilma is, so we should have a safe house for tonight, even if they heard the conversation."

They all became quiet, deep in their own thoughts about what they'd gotten into, and how each of them had gotten there.

Breaking the silence, Jenny couldn't restrain her curiosity any longer. "Big John, what was all the gunfire in front of the apartment? It sounded like a war zone."

"Them shootin' at shadows," he answered. "They showed up at the apartment movin' so fast I wasn't able to warn you. I shot over their heads to slow'em down.

"Sammy here," pointing to the man sitting in the passenger seat of the van, "was 'bout half a block down the street and did the same. That really confused'em; they thought it was an ambush.

"When they started shootin' back, we took off. I called Sammy on his cell and told'm where to meet. I got Bubba's van and parked it in the back alley and came, got you folks. You know the rest."

Mama reached up and patted him on the arm. "You did really good, Big John. Thank you," she said. He beamed with pleasure at her words.

When they got to Wilma's, Jenny told Big John, "Let's park the van in the garage. Someone may have spotted it at the apartment. We don't want some curious neighbor calling the police because a strange car is outside."

They discussed the next day's plans over sandwiches. Ginger offered, "I don't think Mama and I should go. We've only been on the periphery, and we wouldn't have a lot to add." They agreed. She and Mama should stay at the house near the phone. It was as safe a place as they could come up with.

Jenny went outside to coordinate with Big John. "It's important to bring that Argentinean Colonel with us," she said. The plans were set.

When Jenny went back inside, she called Tom, Jr. She knew he would be worried. "Hi, Tom. Wanted you to know everyone's OK."

"Where are you, Jenny. I've been out of my mind. When I went over to the Albright apartment this evening to check on Jim, there were cops everywhere. What kind of mess are you in?"

"I can't tell you very much right now. We can talk more tomorrow." She suspected his phone would be tapped.

"What do you mean? You need to go to the police. I'm your brother…"

"Tom, I…uhh…I can explain…"

"Right. Here we go…"

"I've got to go. Love you."

Hanging up without waiting for a response, she thought *...damn...! Hate doing that...just wanted him to know we're OK...he'll never understand...*

After getting off the phone, Jenny saw that everyone was already in bed. It was late.

Though exhausted, her mind reeled. *...What to include in brief...? Who is audience...? Will they think it's paranoia and imagination...? Who are real players...? How did bad guys know where we were today...?*

Questions kept popping up in her head one after another. Eventually she drifted off, not really resting.

Chapter Forty-One

White Checkmate

They awoke to a cold, drizzly day. Mother Nature was showing her worst side.

After Jenny combed her hair, washed her face, and had a bite to eat, she began to feel almost human.

A car pulled into Wilma's drive. It was Bubba with Histaves.

Histaves looked worse for the wear. There were dark circles under his eyes, and his clothes were smelly and wrinkled. He'd gone from a smartly dressed aristocrat to what could pass for a street person. *...Serves him right...* Jenny thought.

Bubba drove a twelve-passenger van. It bore a sign, "Robby's Limousine Service" on the side.

Big John explained, "I thought we'd need somethin' bigger than Bubba's van for everyone to fit. This van belongs to one of the side businesses that Robby runs."

They loaded up by 7:00 a.m. and headed to the shopping center with Big John driving. He stopped on a side street that overlooked the lot. They could see the Town Car.

Bubba, who'd been following in his van, drove into the parking lot and pulled up to the Town Car. He had barely stopped when three cars came screeching around buildings in the mall, heading toward the van at breakneck speed. A trap!

Smoke billowed from his tires as Bubba peeled away. The cars gave chase, sirens blaring.

Bubba's van was souped-up. It outdistanced the cars and raced down a side street. The white Town Car with its diplomatic plates sat idling.

As the cars chased Bubba, Big John sped toward the Town Car. General Rhee was standing beside it looking at the receding cars. Big John squealed to a stop beside him.

Two other men exited the Town Car. One was a white man Jenny thought she recognized. He was wearing a hunter's cap with earflaps. The other was an oriental man whose overcoat flapped open, and Jenny could see a Stryker machine pistol in a shoulder harness.

Everyone piled into Big John's van, and he raced away. He used double backs and quick turns to be sure no one followed them.

Jenny couldn't help but laugh at the looks she was getting from Cavanaugh and Frisk during the ride.

She explained through her chuckles. "It finally dawned on me last night that Bubba's yellow van was a giveaway. Someone would have seen it at the apartment. The FBI isn't stupid. They would be looking for it.

"Between that and the probability that our phones were tapped or otherwise being monitored, I suggested to Big John that we use Bubba's van as a decoy…"

General Rhee interjected, "Ha! You smelled a trap. Very good."

"Uhhh…Thanks, Sir. It wasn't that big a deal." Trying to deflect attention, she asked, "Would you mind giving the driver directions?"

"Of course," he smiled.

They soon entered a prestigious D.C. neighborhood.

General Rhee also did introductions. He nodded to the oriental man. "This is Sergeant Lee. He is my aide."

The General then turned to the white man who was in the far back seat. "This is Colonel Allen Pitman. Major, I think you might know him."

"Colonel Pitman!" Jenny exclaimed. "I didn't recognize you with that hat. How are you, Sir? How did you get in the middle of this?"

"I'm fine, Jenny. General Rhee, would you like me to explain?"

Rhee responded, "Please do."

Pitman continued, "I was the aide to Admiral Collins before he died. General Grantley asked me to stay on. General Rhee and I are friends, and he called me. When he explained the situation…well, here we are."

"Thank you, Sir. Again." Jenny said. "Looks like I'm in another mess."

Colonel Pitman nodded his head, "Yeah, well…I think we'll soon get to the bottom of it."

By happenstance, Pitman was sitting beside Histaves. The odor was bad. Pitman asked, "Who's the bum?"

Jenny outlined the story.

Big John further explained the smell, "We only have a small place where we were keeping him. It's one of the tenements. He's been in an old bathroom all night where the plumbing kept backing up. I already apologized to him, but he didn't take it very well."

Jenny couldn't help but say, "I can't think of a more deserving person."

Histaves sneered, "I demand to be released. I have diplomatic immunity!"

Big John responded, "Be quiet, or you'll be riding on the roof." Histaves started to retort, but glanced up at the rear view mirror. He could see Big John's eyes. He decided not to say any more.

In twenty minutes they arrived at a nice home, fenced and gated. They pulled up to the gate. A hard looking man, his hands in the deep pockets of an overcoat, approached them from a small alcove next to the gate.

Another man on the other side of the gate stepped out of some trees along the drive. He was armed with an M16 rifle. Two other armed men exited a car parked at the curb. Jenny thought, *…Good Christ, another trap…will it ever end…?*

Chapter Forty-Two

Queen Threatened

Big John reached under the car seat for his shotgun and Sergeant Lee unsnapped his Stryker from its shoulder holster.

Colonel Pitman put his hand on John's shoulder and said, "Wait a minute. It's okay."

The man approaching from the fence alcove looked into Big John's window. He said, "Good morning Mr. Ambassador, Colonel Pitman. You're expected. I'm sorry, but we are going to have to ask everyone to exit the van. You'll have to walk up to the house.

"We're also going to have to frisk those going up. You'll need to leave any weapons here. You can park the van at the curb."

They all climbed out. Jenny asked Big John if he'd wait for them. He agreed and parked the van across the street. He handed Jenny a cell phone. "Call me if you need us, Missy. Just push this button."

Jenny thought, *...talk about being paranoid...* She handed him her pistol.

Rhee said, "Sergeant Lee, you also wait with Mr. John. Keep your eyes open."

Everyone else submitted to a search, and started walking toward the house. There were big rocks and trees lining a long, winding circular drive.

Jenny commented on the pavement edge, "Look at how it's raised. It looks newly surfaced. I wonder what that's all about."

As they continued up the drive, the reason for the steep pavement edges became apparent. Indentations in the middle of the new pavement revealed collapsible 'blow-out' spikes. The spikes could be raised if an intruder approached the house by vehicle.

At the end of the drive, they crossed a wide porch to the main door where another guard stood. Inside, two more guards were standing behind a see-through partition. "Could I see some ID please?" one of them asked.

They each got a hard look from the guard. He said, "You may go in. The secretary is in the dining room."

Jenny mentally asked, *...what the hell do we need with a secretary...?*

Colonel Pitman led them to a room where two distinguished looking men were standing.

Before Pitman had time for introductions, the younger of the two men said, "I think we know who these folks are." He walked over to Jenny and shook her hand, saying, "You must be Major O'Shane. I'm told that you're a very resourceful young lady.

Without waiting for a response, he walked over to Jim Cavanaugh and shook his hand, "You must be Sergeant Major Cavanaugh. Colonel Pitman told me of your injuries. It's nice to see you're recovering."

Again, not waiting for any response, he approached Frisk. "And, you have to be Commander Frisk. I'm glad to see you're recovering from your scuba accident."

Lastly, the younger man walked up to Histaves. "I believe I recognize you, Sir. We probably met at a cocktail party, but I don't recall your name?"

Histaves answered, "I am Colonel Enrico Histaves, military liaison from Argentina. I protest at being held prisoner. I have diplomatic immunity and demand to be released.

"And, I want to press charges against that woman. She struck me without provocation!"

Without responding to Histaves, the man turned to the nearest guard, "Please show the colonel to the next room.

I anticipate we'll be speaking more with him. I assume we'll find out soon enough why he's so disheveled."

He motioned to the chairs around the dining table and said, "Why don't the rest of us have a seat. I understand you have quite a story to tell." They sat with Cavanaugh and Frisk on one side, and Jenny and Rhee on the other. Their hosts sat in two chairs at the head of the table.

A man dressed in a white steward's uniform came in. He asked the younger man, "Sir, can I get you anything from the kitchen?"

"Good idea. Why don't you bring us coffee and some of those sweet rolls you made this morning? We're going to be hungry before this is all done."

Coffee cups and a service tray of rolls were placed on the table, and after the steward excused himself, the younger man said, "Folks, we have about thirty minutes. I'm expecting a phone call, and I've invited some other guests. Colonel Pitman gave me background, but before the others arrive, I want you to tell me what you have."

Jenny took a breath, and began outlining their findings. To start, she slid a copy of the list Cohen had provided. "Here is a list of people we know about."

"The highlighted names are still serving military officers and may be familiar to you.

"Generals Walt Myers and Tony Davies, and Colonel Hank Foreman, are the names we've been able to identify. Each of them was in a key position when the Remington equipment was stolen, and they are now influencing events surrounding the Smith & Wesson investigation.

"The e-mail records we obtained also indicate that General Davies accessed the security information on the Smith & Wesson equipment at Redstone prior to the material being stolen. Here is a printout of his e-mail account." She slid the second document to the men at the head of the table.

"We believe Sergeant Major Cavanaugh and Commander Frisk were assaulted and nearly killed to prevent exposure of this operation. We also believe my dad and Admiral Collins were murdered for the same reason."

She described capturing the two operatives who were watching Ginger's apartment, and the take down of the warehouse, including General Greene's involvement. She handed them copies of the shipment documents from the warehouse.

She decided to leave out any mention of Big John, Bubba and Robby. *...Being allied with criminals might not be well received...*

At that point, the younger man interrupted. "Major O'Shane, let me get this straight. I have to ask...how many men were in the warehouse?"

"Eight, Sir."

"You two were naked, no weapons, and with the help of a man walking with a cane, you overwhelmed eight men and captured the Smith & Wesson shipment. Did I get that right?"

She blushed, and tried to detect a level of sarcasm. There was none. "Well, Sir, we weren't completely naked and we had a little more help, but that's the essence of it." The two men exchanged looks, shaking their heads.

The younger man smiled and asked, "Please continue this astonishing tale."

Again, Jenny tried to detect some sarcasm but could not. She pointed to the bill of lading from the crates. "As I said, those documents were taken off one of the crates in the warehouse. They indicate that the crates have been inspected by U.S. Customs for shipment to Argentina."

Handing over the two memos from Crenshaw and Wusacki, she continued, "These are copies of two memorandums from investigators on my dad's task force. They discuss stolen weapons from Remington, as do

Admiral Collins' reports. We believe the Smith and Wesson theft is a copycat of Remington."

While they were perusing the memos, she explained about Histaves. She said, "I admit to having hit him. I hope it doesn't cause a diplomatic furor." Jenny looked up from her notes.

"We have two requests," she added. "First, you should know that we've been chased by FBI agents based on false allegations. We request that the charges be dropped.

"Secondly, as I said, we believe my dad and Admiral Collins were murdered. To make the case, we request their bodies be exhumed for autopsies."

She put her notes down and looked at the two men again. "Gentlemen, that sums up what we wanted to tell you."

After a pause, the younger man spoke. "Major, you've given us a lot to digest here. It's an incredible story." He turned to the older man, "Horace, what do you think?"

"I think they've done a remarkable job, Mr. Secretary. I'm anxious for your other guests to arrive to assess their reaction."

At that moment the steward came in and said in sotto voice, "Sir, your call is ready."

He responded, "Thank you. If you all will excuse me, I need to take this call. Horace, would you join me?" Both men stood and left the room.

When they'd left, Jenny asked Pitman, "Sir, who are those men? They never mentioned their names."

Pitman chuckled. "You may want to update your military chain of command list, Jenny. The younger man is John Doakes, the Secretary of Defense. The other gentleman is General Horace Grantley, the new Chairman of the Joint Chiefs of Staff."

Jenny's jaw dropped. "Whoa..., I figured the Chairman, but the SECDEF...? That's rich." She started to ask, "How the hell...?"

Colonel Pitman interrupted, "Well, the short answer is that when General Rhee called me, General Grantley and I were already suspicious. We hadn't had time to formulate a plan to investigate when we got the ambassador's call.

"It so happens that General Rhee and Secretary Doakes are friends, so Grantley told me to put Doakes in the loop. That's about it."

At that point, Doakes and Grantley walked back into the room. Doakes waved them to their seats. He said to Pitman, "Allen, our guests have started to arrive. Would you show in the first?"

Chapter Forty-Three

King Threatened

Pitman went into an adjacent room and returned with a man dressed in the uniform of an Air Force Lieutenant General. His nametag read Myers. Jenny wriggled in her seat, anxiety weighing on her mind. She thought *...Oh boy...here we go...hope we have our facts straight...*

Doakes made the introductions and asked Myers to sit at the table. Doakes then synopsized what Jenny had briefed. Myers' face turned pale.

"Walt," Doakes continued, "I know you were a Major and a military White House Fellow during the episode concerning Remington. Maybe you can fill us in what you know."

There was a slight pause. Myers then said, "Sir, I remember that the military aide to the National Security Advisor called me when I was a White House Fellow. I was told that he wanted the various investigative agencies to discontinue investigation of the Remington affair.

"My instructions were to call them and pass on the orders. At the time, I knew little about what he was referring to, and only just now learned the details. It made little difference to me. The aide was speaking on behalf of the equivalent of a four-star general, and I was a Major."

Doakes stared at Myers for a few moments. He then asked, "Who was the military aide?"

Myers answered, "Sir, his name is Stan Greene." Jenny gasped, the implications clear.

"Well, that is an interesting connection. Do you recall the names of those you spoke with from the military services that you told to cancel the investigation?"

Myers thought for a few more seconds and then answered, "Sir, I might have the names in some notes I filed somewhere, but I only recall that I contacted the directors of the various investigative services. They've long since retired from active duty."

Again, Doakes was silent. He looked over at Grantley who shook his head.

Doakes asked Myers a last question, "What do you know about the Smith & Wesson theft?"

General Myers responded, "Sir, I've heard allegations that some technology had been stolen. I don't know much more than what you told me this morning."

Doakes turned to Grantley and asked, "What do you think, Horace?"

Grantley answered, "Mr. Secretary, it sounds about right to me. I don't think we've heard anything indicating Walt is in the middle of this. His personnel file is outstanding, and he has no anomalies in his financial records."

Doakes spoke to Myers again and said, "Walt, I agree with General Grantley. It appears you were only on the periphery. But, would you mind sitting here with us for a few more minutes?"

Myers responded, "Of course not, Sir."

"Oh, one other question, Walt. Who was the National Security Advisor at that time?"

Myers paused briefly before responding, "Sir, I think you know it was Senator James Englewood."

Doakes nodded and then added, "Walt, you'll hear some comments this morning indicating that I'm conducting an investigation of this matter. If I find that you are involved, I ***will*** hang you out to dry. You understand me?"

Myers gulped and nodded his head. "Yes, Sir," he said. Doakes then turned to Pitman again and asked him to see if their next guest had arrived.

Chapter Forty-Four

Check

Beads of sweat formed on the upper lip of Army Major General Tony Davies as he took the seat offered by Doakes at the dining room table.

Doakes repeated what he had gone through with Myers; introducing those at the table; and, then synopsizing the discussion. He said, “Tony, please tell me what you know about this matter.”

Perspiration now ran off of Davies in rivulets. He tried to bluster. “Mr. Secretary, I know little about this. Marine Colonel Hank Foreman has been working in our CID offices as directed by General Grantley for a few days. I’ve overheard some of his discussions, but that’s been the extent of my involvement.”

Doakes leaned forward in his seat, his eyes boring into Davies. “Tony, you were a Military Liaison Officer in the German embassy at the time of a theft of technology from Remington Corporation.

“That technology ended up being produced by the Krueger Corporation in Germany. You’re telling us that you were unaware of that occurring?”

Davies squirmed in his chair, and his face turned pink, but he reiterated, “Sir, I don’t recall hearing anything about that.”

Doakes looked at Davies for a long time. The silence was deafening. Finally, he said sarcastically, “Tony, I have to tell you that I find that a little hard to believe.”

After another pause, Doakes said, “I have data taken from the Redstone master server that indicates that you accessed codes to a Redstone storage area for Smith & Wesson equipment. Any comment?”

Shock and panic simultaneously crossed Davies' face. It was obvious this news was unexpected. He started to stammer an answer, "Sir, I..."

Grantley held up his hand. "General," he said. "Don't say any more. You may incriminate yourself. Mr. Secretary, with your permission?"

Doakes nodded. Grantley continued, "General Davies, you are hereby relieved of your duties. You are placed on administrative leave effective immediately.

"Consider yourself under house arrest. You will not leave your quarters without my personal approval. Lastly, do not discuss this with anyone but your attorney. Do you understand?" Head drooping, Davies nodded.

"You are excused to return to your quarters," Grantley told him. Davies stood, saluted, and left the room.

As Davies left, Doakes said, "Well, that wasn't much fun, but it's confirmed some suspicions. I can hardly wait until our next guest gets here."

Chapter Forty-Five

Check Again

Coinciding with Doakes' comment, another general officer walked into the dining room, escorted by Pitman. It was General Stanley Greene.

When Greene saw Jenny and Cavanaugh, he became visibly shaken. He appeared to be on the verge of collapsing. He held onto the back of a chair to keep his balance.

Looking at Jenny he said with anguish in his voice, "Jennifer, I hope you can forgive me. I had no idea..." Then his voice broke.

Doakes said, "Stan, why don't you have a seat. I need to ask you some questions. Obviously, you know the people here and probably know most of the story. But allow me to review."

With that introduction, Doakes repeated what he had said to the previous visitors. Then he asked, "Stan, why don't you tell us what you know about this situation."

Greene had recovered his composure by the time he was asked to provide a response. Without hesitation he answered, "My initial participation was to give direction to stop the Remington investigation as directed by the National Security Advisor.

"I called the White House Fellow who was assigned to our staff and told him to handle it." Greene pointed across the table to Myers and noted, "The White House Fellow I contacted was Walt Myers."

Greene continued, "Mr. Secretary, I was not aware of any details of the Remington episode when I was asked to turn off the military investigation. I learned of the details afterwards and was appalled."

Doakes looked at Greene for a minute and then asked, “Why didn’t you ask that an investigation continue after you found out the facts?”

“Sir, I was informed that if I didn’t keep my mouth shut, my family would be murdered, and my career destroyed.

“The threats were backed up by pictures of my wife working in her garden and my parents taking a walk outside their home. The blackmailers weren’t kidding.”

Doakes considered Greene’s answer for a few minutes, and then asked, “What do you know about the theft of the Smith & Wesson technology?”

“Mr. Secretary, I have a very limited knowledge of the theft. My information about the incident came from daily intelligence reports given to me by my staff. I’ve heard more about it today than ever before.”

Grantley wore a skeptical look as he asked, “Stan, how did it come about that you set up the kidnapping of Major O’Shane and Sergeant Major Cavanaugh if you weren’t involved in what was going on with Smith & Wesson? I find that hard to swallow.”

“Horace, all I know is that I received a note in the mail right after General O’Shane’s funeral. It was devastating. I thought the Remington issue had long since been buried, but the note started the nightmare all over again. The note said that I was to follow instructions, or the entire Remington episode would be surfaced. It had a phone number to call.

“I called the number. A voice I did not recognize told me to contact the same phone number again if Jennifer tried to reach me.

“Whoever it was assured me that Jennifer would not be harmed if I cooperated. The person on the phone added that if I did not cooperate, she would be killed at the first opportunity. I believed them. So when Jennifer called me, I called the number.

"They gave me the instructions that I relayed to Jennifer. My intent was that once I saw that she was safe I would go to the authorities. Obviously, I'm too late."

With a mixture of anger and resignation, Doakes responded, "Stan, you are way too late." He and Grantley exchanged looks.

Grantley shrugged and said, "Mr. Secretary, we have no choice." He then turned to Greene and told him, "Stan, I'm sure some would probably argue the you had legitimate rationale for your actions by virtue of threats to you and your loved ones. But, from my perspective you failed your country and your oath of office. You also endangered the lives of people you profess to love."

Pausing briefly for effect, he continued, "Frankly, I believe your actions were more a product of protecting your own ass than that of protecting your family. However, I'm not a judge or jury, and we'll leave those decisions to those who are.

"In the meantime, I have the unpleasant task of telling you that you are relieved of duty effective immediately and placed on administrative leave.

"You are to consider yourself under house arrest and you will not leave your quarters without my expressed approval. You are also not to discuss this with anyone except your attorney. Do you understand?"

Crestfallen, Greene could merely nod. General Grantley then instructed, "You are dismissed. Please leave us."

Doakes spoke to Jenny and the others after Greene's departure. "Jenny, I apologize for how unpleasant this must be for you...for that matter, each of you. However, I think you should witness that I am acting on your findings. Rest assured, those responsible will be brought to justice."

Doakes paused to allow those words to sink in. He continued, "There's a couple of other things I should tell you. First of all, I requested that the courts authorize the exhumations you suggested. We need to find out what really happened.

"Secondly, you should know that I had Colonel Foreman arrested thirty minutes ago. Based on what I've heard today, I can't help but conclude that he's involved."

"Also, one of the calls I made was to the Director of the FBI. All charges against you have been withdrawn. Apparently they were operating on an anonymous tip. All of the terrorist threats have them hypersensitive. As of now, the manhunt is called off."

He let his audience digest that information for a couple of minutes. Then Doakes added, "We've got one more guest who will be here in a minute." He then asked, "Do any of you have any questions while we wait?"

Jenny spoke up, "Sir, why didn't the list of names we got from the military personnel files show that General Greene was among those in key positions during the Remington operation?"

General Grantley responded, "That's a good question. The answer is that, for security purposes, the personnel records of four-star generals are sealed. They cannot be accessed through normal channels."

She asked another question. "Sir, doesn't this seem like a sophisticated conspiracy? Even though everything points toward the Argentineans, this seems beyond a military liaison team out of an embassy."

Secretary Doakes smiled and responded, "Very perceptive of you. I've thought the same thing as this story unfolded. I don't know where they got their pool of manpower. We can only hope that we'll be able to uncover all the loose ends when you investigate the situation in more detail."

Chapter Forty-Six

Forcing Check

As Jenny was about to ask the meaning of Secretary Doakes' comment concerning 'continuing investigation,' Pitman came into the dining room with a distinguished looking man dressed in an Armani suit.

Doakes stood and greeted him, "Ahh, Senator Englewood, I really appreciate your coming over this morning on such short notice. I hope it wasn't too disruptive?"

Englewood replied in a gruff tone, "Well, I juggled my calendar because you said this was an emergency. I hope you have a goddamned good reason. My office is in turmoil with this unscheduled interruption."

Shaking Englewood's hand and guiding him to a chair, Doakes offered, "I apologize for the inconvenience. I think you'll find coming here very informative. Before we talk, let me introduce you to my other guests…"

Doakes then proceeded to introduce Jenny and the others. Senator Englewood turned pale when he heard their names.

However, he assumed a more aggressive demeanor. "Doakes, I appreciate meeting these people, but what do they have to do with me? I don't have time for a social. This is bullshit! What am I doing here?"

Doakes smiled affably and said, "Let me explain…" He proceeded to tell the story.

Englewood seemed to get even paler. But, he tried to give the impression that he was simply annoyed.

He stood and said with anger in his voice, "Mr. Secretary, this is a fascinating tale, but it sounds like an in-house problem for the military. It has nothing to do with me. I'm sure you can handle it without my help. If you will excuse me, I have a mountain of work waiting for me in my office." Englewood turned as if to leave.

"Before you go," Doakes said, "let me introduce you to another of my guests."

At those words from Doakes, Pitman brought Histaves into the room.

"Senator," Doakes continued, "perhaps you might know Colonel Enrico Histaves from Argentina?"

Still pretending innocence, Englewood answered, "Yes, I believe we've met at cocktail parties. So…?"

At that point Doakes pulled a sheet of paper out of a folder in front of him on the table. He asked, "Senator are you saying you've only casually met Histaves?"

Senator Englewood almost snarled an answer, "Doakes, I'm not going to play any more games with you. You heard my answer. Now if you'll excuse me…"

"That's strange," Doakes interrupted before Englewood could leave. "Can you explain this cell phone conversation that the National Security Agency intercepted between you and Colonel Histaves? I have a copy of it transcribed here if you'd care to read it.

"The recorded conversation clearly implicates you in the scheme I described. Any comment about that before you leave? Oh…before you answer that question, here's another for you. Would you mind telling us why you ordered the Remington investigation canceled?

"Would it have anything to do with a $500,000 deposit shown in your bank account? The FBI accessed your financial records this morning. Any comments now…?"

Englewood just looked at the people around the table for a moment, his face now red and his body shaking.

He began shouting, "You snot-nosed punks! Who do you think you are? I've given my entire life to this country. You have no right to question me. You piss ants. I'll…ruin every one of you…I'll…"

Spittle was spraying as he talked, his eyes bulging. But, almost as if a switch were turned, he stopped. His head drooped, and he began muttering to himself. He slowly began to shuffle out of the room as if in a trance.

Pitman started to stop him and Doakes shook his head, "No, Allen. Let him leave. He won't go far."

Chapter Forty-Seven

One Move Left

Following Englewood's dramatic departure, Doakes turned his attention to Histaves.

"Colonel, it looks as if you've made a real hash of several lives in our country. You had senior military officers murdered. You probably murdered those Smith & Wesson scientists. You've kidnapped, bribed and blackmailed citizens on sovereign U.S. territory. And, you arranged the theft of classified technology.

"Would you care to share the names of your fellow conspirators so that our investigation will be made easier?"

Histaves stood mute for a moment. He finally responded with his aristocratic nose held high, "I have diplomatic immunity and demand to be released. You have no right to keep me captive. It's against international law."

Jenny couldn't keep quiet any longer. Standing, she said, "It's also against the law to murder people, you sick, demented freak." Her mind was seething. *...I'm going to kick this arrogant prick into next year...*

Rhee put his hand on her arm and pulled her back into her chair. "Jennifer, it won't do any good. Let the courts handle it," he said. She sat back down, quivering in fury.

Just then they heard the ring of a cell phone. It was the one that Big John had given to her. She glanced at Cavanaugh. *...What the hell? No one should be calling me on this phone...* She answered.

Big John said without introduction, "Trouble!! Get out..."

A loud explosion interrupted the connection. The firing of automatic weapons followed. There were two more explosions, one at the front door. More small arms fire...

At first, they all sat too stunned to react. Jenny broke the spell. She leapt from her chair and yelled, “Everyone, out the back. Hurry.”

The steward rushed in. He was armed with a Beretta pistol. He said, “Mr. Secretary, follow me…”

No sooner had he spoken than two Arabic featured men charged into the room, firing Uzi’s. A burst caught the steward in the face. Blood and brain matter sprayed the room. He crumbled to the floor.

One of the attackers yelled at the group in broken English, “Stop. Do not move!”

Myers turned as if to say something. Both Uzis fired. Multiple rounds hit him in the chest. He fell to the floor moaning. Jenny bent to help him.

One of the intruders kicked her in the ribs and yelled again, “Leave him. Sit at the table. Do not move. Do not talk. Anyone disobeys, dies.”

The group returned to their seats. Jenny sat in a chair, gasping for air

Doakes asked, “Who are you? What do you…” both Uzi’s fired again hitting Doakes in the upper chest and flinging him back against his chair.

He collapsed with his head on the table, blood pooling beneath. The man repeated, “No talking. Next one also dies.”

At that moment, two more men entered the room. Histaves greeted them with, “Thank God you’re here. I was just getting ready to phone you.”

Chapter Forty-Eight

First Check

Dr. Ami and Commander Garcia looked at Histaves with bleak faces.

Ami cut the bonds that held Histaves' wrists and said, "You incompetent fool. This would have been unnecessary if it wasn't for your stupidity and arrogance. Now take us to your warehouse. We want our weapons."

"But, Achmad, I can explain…"

"Stop talking, you idiot," Ami said.

He pushed Histaves out the doorway and ordered the brawny guard nearest Jenny, "Ishmael, give us two minutes, and then kill them all."

No sooner had Ami left the room than the 'boom' of Big John's shotgun sounded. They also heard the unmistakable 'bam, bam' of a Stryker machine pistol.

The echo of automatic weapons and small arms fire again filled the air. Then another shotgun 'boom.' They all glanced toward the gunfire.

Jenny used the opportunity to grab a peppershaker off the table. She unscrewed the top.

She looked at Cavanaugh, then over to Rhee and Frisk. She saw that they each were watching her. It was her play. There would be only one chance.

Jenny began coughing. Wheezing and choking, she started to stand up.

The man called Ishmael yelled, "No, you sit!"

Jenny thought, *...hope like hell he won't shoot a coughing woman...*

"My side," she groaned. "I can't breath."

She stood, hacking and gasping. Ishmael walked over and put his hand on her shoulder to push her back down.

She threw the pepper in his face. He screamed at the burning in his eyes.

...Please fellas...get the other guy... For the third time that day, gunfire ripped the air of the dining room.

She flinched, anticipating the thud of bullets in her back. Instead, plaster dust clouded the air.

She risked a glance. Frisk and Cavanaugh were wrestling the second guard to the ground. A burst from his Uzi had punched holes in the ceiling.

It didn't matter if she didn't stop Ishmael.

Though blinded for a second, he was quick to recover. He deflected a knee that she intended for his groin, and swung a backhand that sent her sprawling.

In the instant before she crashed into the wall, she saw Grantley and Rhee try to help.

Grantley grabbed an arm, but the much bigger man shrugged the general off, and hit him on the nose with a roundhouse swing.

Grantley collapsed on the floor, blood streaming.

Rhee leapt from his seat and landed in the middle of Ishmael's shoulders, attempting a chokehold.

Demonstrating immense strength, Ishmael reached around and pulled Rhee off as if he were a fly and threw him against the wall. Rhee lay still.

Recovering in the nana-second that Grantley and Rhee had distracted Ishmael, Jenny jumped back into the fray.

She pushed the barrel of his Uzi up with her left hand, and swung a right uppercut. She put her hips and legs into the blow.

Her fist connected under his chin. It felt as if she'd hit a rock, the shock of the impact traveled to her toes. He didn't even blink.

Instead, his eyes narrowed in contempt as he stretched her up, her hand clinging to the barrel of his Uzi. He paused, a cruel grin crossing his lips.

He then butt-stroked her in the chest with the Uzi, lifting her off her feet with the power of the blow. It felt like a battering ram.

However, his timing was a fraction slow. She'd been able to grasp the rifle grip in the instant the butt spun towards her.

Her finger closed over the trigger.

Centrifugal force pulled her hand. The deafening roar of gunfire reverberated once more.

Chapter Forty-Nine

Second Check

Stunned from Ishmael's crushing blow, Jenny crashed backwards. She stumbled over her chair, landing arms and legs akimbo.

Skidding across the floor, she watched Ishmael jerk like a puppet on a string, a burst of bullets stitching his chest and stomach.

He swayed, and then toppled, a look of surprise etching itself on his face. Jenny had his Uzi.

Breathless, she jumped back to her feet, heart pounding, looking around for the second man, expecting a gunfight in the close quarters.

Across the table she saw Cavanaugh and Frisk, chests heaving, standing over the inert form of the second man.

She said, "Thanks, guys. Great work!"

Her relief was short-lived. She shouted, "Come on. They're getting away!"

She raced out the door and ran through mayhem.

In the dining room entryway, she passed guards and Pitman in pools of blood. On the porch she saw other security guards, and several balaclava-clad men laying over the lawn and drive. In the distance, the body of Rhee's aide sprawled against the entry gate.

In the portico, doors slammed and two cars screeched down the drive. Big John stood in the middle holding the Stryker. It banged two more times.

The windshield of the lead car shattered and the car careened out of control, crashing into trees.

The second car continued to barrel straight toward Big John. He pulled the Stryker trigger again, but it clicked on empty. Out of ammo.

Chapter Fifty

Checkmate

Cutting across the grass island, Jenny ran after the car. It was racing around the circular drive, but she had a huge advantage moving in a straight line.

She could see Big John trying to cram more shells into the unfamiliar machine pistol.

The car cleared some trees. She had a line of sight. She fired two bursts from the Uzi. Her shots shredded the front left tire; rubber blew off in chunks.

She watched in fascination as the car swerved, and the tire rim dropped over the steep edge of the raised pavement. The rim dug into the soft soil of the grassy berm. The car pivoted on the buried wheel.

It did two twisting barrel rolls, skidding to a stop upside down twenty feet from where Big John stood.

Smoke billowed from the engine. Flames began to curl from leaking fuel.

Jenny ran to the upturned car. Wrenching open the driver's door, she pulled a dazed Ami out. Cavanaugh and Frisk collared him while Jenny ran to the other side of the car.

The door was stuck. "I can't get the door open," she yelled. Big John stepped up and practically ripped the door off its hinges. They pulled Garcia out of the smoldering wreckage and dumped him beside Ami.

She saw Histaves in the car. He couldn't get the rear doors open and the collapsed roof prevented him from crawling over the front seat. His face was pressed against the rear window.

"Please help me," he screamed as the flames spread. The heat was too intense when she attempted to get back to the car.

The gas tank exploded and the car was engulfed in flames. The screaming stopped.

She heard sirens.

She put her arm around Big John's waist and gave him a hug. "Thank you for everything, Big John. You've been incredible. But, you best get out of here." She nodded toward the approaching sirens.

"You didn't do too bad yourself, Missy. You pack a helluva wallop. I'll tell Robby we don't want to get crossways with you. Hope to see you again sometime."

Handing the Stryker to her, he sprinted toward his van.

In her mind, several thoughts cascaded over one another, *...Well, size isn't everything...it's what's in the package...maybe terrorists will think twice before taking on the U.S. again...hey Dad...hope you rest a bit easier...we got the bastards...love you...*

General Grantley interrupted her thoughts as he walked up, holding a red-stained cloth to his nose. "Jenny, who the hell was that huge guy?"

"Sir, it's a long story. Uhhh…I can explain."

"I've heard about your 'explanations,' O'Shane."

Just then two police cars and an ambulance pulled into the drive. It was over.

Afterward

Although this story is complete, the lives of many of the key participants continue. Below is a brief synopsis of later events in their lives.

A search of Ami's apartment revealed documents indicating the intent to use the stolen weapons to assassinate senior U.S. government leaders, including the President. There was also a second cell phone conversation intercepted by the NSA in which he was recognized giving instructions for the assassination of Admiral Collins and General O'Shane. Ami was sentenced to death in federal court for his participation in the murders. He is presently on death row at a high security prison.

As Garcia was being transported to jail, he ingested a capsule of cyanide and killed himself.

Further investigation revealed that senior executives from Remington were silenced in their official protests of the technology thefts by award of significant U.S. government contracts for production of small arms for the U.S. and NATO military forces. The executives were also provided lump sum payments into their bank accounts from unknown sources. The executives involved had since passed away from natural causes. When Krueger provided the Remington Corporation a payment of $1 billion in an out-of-court settlement, the matter was dropped.

The Argentine government issued a formal apology to the U.S. government. A sum of $5 million was offered by the Argentine government to each of the families of Admiral Collins and General O'Shane as compensation for their murders.

Senor Flaveo Fernando, the arms manufacturer, was arrested in Argentina. He successfully avoided extradition to the U.S., but was sentenced to prison in Argentina for bribery and tax evasion. As reflected in the story, Jenny killed his son, Lieutenant Esteban Fernando, in the warehouse. At his trial, Flaveo vowed he would avenge his son's death.

Secretary of Defense, John Doakes: recovered fully from his wounds. He ably led the military terrorist campaign for the duration of his tenure. He made a special presentation of the Silver Star to Major Jenny O'Shane for performing the first recognized act of military heroism in the U.S. War Against Terrorism on sovereign soil. He also awarded the Bronze Star with 'V' device to Command Sergeant Major Cavanaugh and Commander Adam Frisk.

Chairman of the Joint Chiefs of Staff, General Horace Grantley: supervised the full investigation of the industrial espionage against Remington and Smith & Wesson. As noted, at the conclusion of the investigation, Krueger paid Remington a sum of $1 billion dollars in an out-of-court settlement.

Colonel Allen Pitman: recovered from his wounds, was promoted to general officer, and eventually led a division in operation Iraqi Freedom.

General Davies and Colonel Foreman: both confessed to receiving bribes for their participation in the thefts. They were found guilty in a court-martial, sentenced to a federal penitentiary, and given dishonorable discharges from military service.

General Stanley Greene: maintained his innocence, but in a court-martial he was found guilty of negligence and conduct unbecoming an officer. He was reduced in rank to Lieutenant General and retired from military service.

General Walt Myers: was exonerated completely, but died from his gunshot wounds.

Senator James Englewood: was charged with receiving bribes while in government service, conspiracy to commit murder, and with participating in the theft of U.S. secret technology. Before he could be tried in civilian courts, he committed suicide by hanging himself in his office bathroom.

Commander Adam Frisk: was medically retired from active duty. He was unable to regain the full use of his legs due to the crippling effect of the 'bends'.

Big John: soon after the attack on the Secretary's house, Big John and Bubba retired from Robby's organization and formed a professional wrestling 'tag-team'. They eventually competed in and won the All-World Tag-Team Wrestling Championship. They are the reigning champions. Fight promoters are unable to find opponents willing to get in the ring with the champs. At a suggestion from Jenny, they are taking up second jobs as security consultants working part-time for Jim Cavanaugh.

Command Sergeant Major Jim Cavanaugh: Jim and Ginger Albright married. Cavanaugh retired from the Army, and he and Ginger moved to Tampa to be near Jenny. He opened and is operating a successful private investigation service. Ginger serves as his secretary. He's trying to convince AD Frisk to come to work with him. Mama and the two boys moved to Tampa with Jim and Ginger, and they are all living in a big house near Tampa Bay.

Major Jennifer O'Shane: Jenny returned to her new job at MacDill Air Force Base. She and Lieutenant Colonel Gary Patten became engaged. She now leads the Army Security Detachment for the Commander of Central Command. In addition to a second Silver Star, Jenny received another special performance evaluation. The Chairman of the Joint Chiefs of Staff wrote this one. The Secretary of Defense endorsed the report. They recommended that Jenny be immediately promoted to lieutenant colonel. If that occurred she would be the youngest female officer ever promoted to Lieutenant Colonel. *...Fat chance...* she thought.

KNIGHT TIME

Chapter One

The Initial Gambit

Two teenage sisters found the uniform. Clara and Vicki Mendez were walking home from school. The uniform was next to a dumpster behind Motel Eight on the corner of Highway 41, and Martin Luther King Boulevard in Sarasota, Florida.

The name ‘Crystal’ was embroidered above the pocket of the blouse. The short skirt had a dark spot at the hemline. Panties and a bra were wrapped up in the blouse.

“This is retarded,” Clara said. “Who’d throw nice stuff like this away?”

“Hey, who cares,” Vicki answered. “Finders keepers. I want the skirt. Like, it’s way cool.” She pointed to a brown discoloration at the hemline and added, “Get that little spot off and we’d be stylin’.”

Holding the bra up to her, Clara giggled. “It’d take both of us to fill this thing out.”

“Yeah,” Vicki laughed at Clara’s antics. “But we might grow into it. You never know, girl. Let’s jus’ tak’em home, and put’em away. The blouse, too.” Picking up the panties with two fingers, she added, “Ewww. Nice as they are, it’d be skanky wearin’ someone else’s underpants.” She tossed them into the dumpster.

Still giggling, Clara stuffed the clothes into her school backpack and said, “Come on. Let’s get home. We’re late as it is. I don’t want to get grounded with the prom coming up.”

Two weeks later, Clara heard, “Girl, where the hell do you think you’re goin’ dressed like that?”

“Mom, all the girls wear short skirts now,” Clara whined. “It’s fine.”

“Maybe it’s fine for some girls,” Nita Mendez said. “But, not you. I can darn near see your underwear as you stand there. Now, get your butt upstairs and put on somethin’ decent. And, bring that thing back down here. You got some explainin’ to do. Hurry up now!”

Ten minutes later, Vicki and Clara were stammering out an explanation to an irate mom. “You found what? Where? Let me have that skirt. You don’t have the brains of two kittens.”

Nita was an emergency room nurse at Sarasota Memorial Hospital. She recognized the spot on the skirt.

“Are you nuts? Do you know that this is blood? And, did you even bother looking at this tag on the inside of the zipper? It says ‘Property of The Kar Hop’. Have you any idea of the diseases you can catch from other people’s unwashed clothes? You’re both way grounded!”

Chapter Two

Pawn Swap

After school on the afternoon that Nita Mendez discovered the skirt, Vicki and Clara made a tearful confession to the police.

"Shorty, thanks for coming over," Nita said to the Sarasota police sergeant. "These fools are…"

"Nita, let the girls talk." he interrupted. "You and I have been friends for what…? Twenty years? We'll sort it out. Relax."

The girl's story began an investigation that was short-lived. Detectives discovered that a young Hispanic woman who called herself Crystal Tavar was employed as a waitress at the Kar Hop restaurant located at 17th Street and U.S 301.

The restaurant owner informed the detectives that he had identified Crystal as an illegal immigrant, and had paid her accordingly – a small hourly wage and tips.

Detectives also found that the social security number the owner had on file was faked. The Kar Hop employee file contained no other information.

"She left work late one afternoon and never came back," the owner explained to the investigators. "It happens all the time. We can't keep up with these girls. They're a dime a dozen. Crystal was prettier than the usual. What can I say?"

"Let's see what the Health Department has to say," the lead detective answered, disgusted by the cavalier attitude.

"Oh, come on, guys…"

"You come on, Asshole," the detective said, as he and his partner walked out of the restaurant door.

The detectives soon found that Crystal's trail ran cold. The dumpster had long since been emptied. They had no picture, address or phone number. With no ID to work from, the case ended in the Jane Doe inactive file, and the fate of the missing woman was never officially known…

…No one recalled seeing Crystal Tavares during her last few hours in Sarasota as she made her way home from work on a drizzly evening. She felt conspicuous in her Kar Hop uniform, but she didn't want to get her street clothes wet. They were in a plastic bag that she was carrying.

Florida Highway 41 was well lit, and traffic was heavy, so she felt secure in her walk toward her efficiency unit at the Lantern Inn. Even though it had started raining harder, she was looking forward to the evening. Some boys she'd met at a local teen club had invited her to a party.

Approaching a drive that crossed the sidewalk, Crystal noticed a parked van blocking her path. The driver's window was down. She recognized one of her friends.

"Joe," she asked him. "What're you doin' out here? I thought we were partyin' tonight?"

"Hey, Crystal," he answered. "Yeah, we're gonna party. But, I saw you walkin' in the rain. Thought you'd 'preciate a ride?"

"I really would. Thanks. I'm gettin' soaked. My place is down the street about a mile yet. Is that OK?"

"No sweat. Hop in the back. Sam's up front with me." The van side door slid open.

Crystal stepped into the van. Hands grabbed her arms and legs. "What the…?" was all she got out.

Someone put tape over her mouth and a sack over her head. She felt a pinprick in her upper arm. Her body became paralyzed. She could feel the hard floor of the van on her back and her mind was clear, but she couldn't move or talk.

Hands began to undress her; all her clothes were removed. Someone stroked her breast. A hand moved high up her thigh, between her legs.

Her mind was racing *…Dear God…Please don't let this happen…Mommeee…help me…! I'm sorry I ran away…I promise to call…come get me now…Please…Daddeee…!* She was screaming in her head.

There was a thunk of something hitting meat. A voice sounded for the first time.

"I told you, Tom. No touching the merchandise. You're a fucking pervert!"

"Sorry, Joe," a voice whined. "She's just so gorgeous." A brief silence was followed by, "Hey! You made my nose bleed."

"I don't care. We're getting paid a lot a money. You know the rules. If a hair on her head is mussed, we get nothing.

"Now, put that shift over her, and get her ready to move to the boat. This is our last pickup. If you even look at her sidewise again, I swear I'll kill you. Throw her things in that dumpster over there and let's go."

Crystal heard a door open and felt the van shift as someone left, and then reentered the vehicle.

Unnoticed was that Tom only half-heartedly threw Crystal's plastic bag toward the dumpster. The bag made it over the side and into the bin, but several items fell onto the ground nearby. The van roared away into the night.

Chapter Three

Opening Move

Jenny hadn't slept since the assassination attempt twenty-eight hours earlier. She stifled a yawn of exhaustion. The M-16 in her hands felt like it weighed fifty pounds.

However, checking weapons was a habit – a mantra she must have heard a hundred times, "...if soldiers know the boss will check, they'll be ready."

PFC Jackson, a member of Jenny's elite guard force, was no exception. The rifle was clean, the safety was on, and a round was chambered. Jackson was fully alert.

Handing the rifle back to Jackson, Jenny asked, "Where's the rest of your team?"

"Ma'am, Specialist Leonard is on the other side of the aircraft and Corporal Jennings is at the front. Sergeant Godfrey just went to check on the first sniper team." Jenny nodded her head.

"Are your communications up?" she asked.

"Yes Ma'am. We just had a commo check five minutes ago."

Jenny smiled in spite of her fatigue. These were good people. "Great. Stay focused. We won't get a second chance."

They stood together for a few minutes in silence enjoying the quiet before the storm...they knew that things were going to be frenetic very soon.

Jackson then said, "Ma'am, I've got to say, you were incredible yesterday. I've never seen anyone..." He had been on the security detail the day before.

Jenny cut him off, saying, "Thanks Jackson, but let's stay centered on this part of the mission. OK?"

"Yes, Ma'am."

Jenny glanced at her watch and said, "I'm going to check the aircraft one more time."

As she started walking toward the stairs, she spoke into her earpiece radio. "Sergeant Godfrey, how do the sniper teams look?"

After a brief pause, she heard in her ear, "Ma'am, both teams are set. If anyone pays a call tonight it'll cost'em big time." Reassured, Jenny called her other team leader.

"Sergeant Bloom, give me a status report." There was a prompt response.

"Ma'am, we're standing by. There are no unauthorized people near the perimeter. There are Saudi guards every twenty feet along the fence, and my guys are in two roving vehicle patrols. We're covered here."

She thought, *...Well, the airfield is as secure as we can make it...*

She spoke into the radio one more time, "Convoy teams; standby." She heard in quick succession.

"Roger...Roger....Roger."

She climbed the aircraft steps for what seemed like the hundredth time that night. Walking the length of the specially modified Gulf Stream V, she verified again it was empty other than the crew.

Nodding to the steward in the galley she said, "Airman Stokes, better put the coffee on. Backpack's on his way..."

ORDER YOUR COPIES

OF THE KNIGHT SERIES

Contact Mangrove Press at www.MangrovePress.com

Select the icon for a synopsis or for ordering information.

You may also write Mangrove Press at:

4025 Cattlemen Rd.
PMB 142
Sarasota, Florida 34233.

Request Knight Moves, ISBN # 978-0-9790701-0-5

Request Knight Time. ISBN # 978-0-0790701-1-2